"You're gonna get naked!" the club owner shrieked.

Sam knew she was in trouble when the cheap velvet drapes separating the howling audience from the stage started to open. The music grew deafeningly loud. So did the roar of male anticipation out front.

Now that she'd gotten the information she came for, she had to get the hell out of the building. Her hand closed around the exit door handle and she started to shove it open when a big paw grabbed a hunk of her hair and pulled her back.

"I paid you to strip."

"How about you strip?" she yelled, applying pressure on the nerves at the base of his flabby bicep just above his elbow. He yelped in pain and released her. Sam waited for him to raise his left hand, but before she could act, a loaded longneck connected with the back of his skull and he collapsed.

Sam looked up into her husband's furious face, seeing his eyes sweep over her almost-naked body. "What the hell are you doing here?"

Dear Reader,

Ever since I discovered Robert Heinlein in grade school, I've been a sci-fi fan. After hearing my son and his friends describe some of the incredible sci-fi conventions they've attended, I started thinking how much fun it would be if my heroine Sam retrieved a "Spacer" who appeared "spacie" but may have witnessed a crime.

Elvis Scruggs amazed me as he insinuated his way into my plot. It was supposed to be about Farley, not Elvis, but what could I do when a guy this interesting showed up? I love it when characters surprise me. Matt's jealousy when Sam went undercover as a stripper was another twist I hadn't anticipated. As to Sam, well, she handles any aggravation the men give her, but in spite of her tough exterior she remains a softie at heart. Sometimes it's good when a character doesn't surprise me, too.

Have fun,

Shirl Henke

SNEAK AND RESCUE

Shirl Henke

Silhouette®

BOMBSHELL™

Published by Silhouette Books

America's Publisher of Contemporary Romance

For Matt Henke,
My pop culture and music maven,
besides being the world's best son

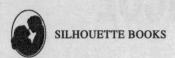 SILHOUETTE BOOKS

ISBN 0-373-51395-X

SNEAK AND RESCUE

Copyright © 2006 by Shirl Henke

www.SilhouetteBombshell.com

Printed in U.S.A.

Books by Shirl Henke

Silhouette Bombshell

Finders Keepers #61
Sneak and Rescue #81

*Samantha Ballanger adventures

SHIRL HENKE

received her B.A. and M.A. in history from the University of Missouri and then worked at many different jobs, including running the circulation desk on a small daily, writing and editing "house organ" newspapers, administering a federal information program for the elderly and finally as a university instructor, teaching in four different departments.

Ever since she was a child she read avidly, everything from Robert Heinlein's sci-fi adventures to the big historical sagas of the 1970s and 1980s. She always had ideas for stories and sold her first novel to Warner Books in 1986. Within two years, she was able to quit her day job. Now she can't imagine doing anything but writing for a living.

She and her husband, Jim, share their cedar house in the woods with an utterly spoiled and very geriatric tomcat. As with writing, life without cats would be unimaginable. For therapy when she's not at the computer, she cooks large dinners for their extended family, works in her garden and greenhouse and still reads avidly. When deadlines permit, she loves to travel. Visit Shirl on the Web at www.shirlhenke.com.

ACKNOWLEDGMENTS

Sam and Matt's second adventure was even more fun to write than the first and I could not have done it without the able assistance of many people and organizations. Any mistakes or excess of "literary license" are my own.

The setting for this caper is the beautiful Miami metro area. I owe thanks once more to Detective Juan DelCastillo and the Miami-Dade Police Department for information about how my fictional homicide sergeant, William Patowski, might have conducted his investigation.

For the fictionalized *Space Quest,* its fans and the wider universe where they boldly go, I received creative inspiration from my son, Matt Henke, and the Atlas Chapter of the real international organization.

I grew up listening to Elvis Presley's music and there is only one "King." But my Elvis Scruggs was pretty cool in his own way. I hope you think so, too. Who knows? He just might pop up in a future story. Let me know what you think: www.shirlhenke.com.

Chapter 1

"Quit hiding from me, you sneaky piece of junk!"

Sam dug through the stacks of receipts and file folders, frantic as a starving squirrel looking for its winter cache of nuts. One heavy binder slid off the chair in front of her and toppled dead center onto the neat piles of checks and bank statements spread out on the carpet. With horror, she watched an hour's worth of sorting flutter into its former chaos. Muttering a curse beneath her breath, she listened more carefully. The muffled chirp of the new cordless phone was coming from behind a tower of IRS pamphlets piled on the love seat next to the chair.

"It used to be so much easier—just start at the jack and pull the phone through the rubble," she muttered.

Crawling on hands and knees to the sofa, she tossed aside manuals with print so fine she couldn't read them with the magnification of the Hubble telescope. "Might've known it was the IRS's fault," she said, seizing the phone, which had been wedged behind a cushion.

Just before the final ring set off her answering machine— if she'd remembered to reactivate it—Sam answered, "Ballanger Retrievals," in her most professional voice. She pushed another stack of manuals onto the floor to create a narrow empty space where she could sit. The small sofa was so full of folders, pamphlets and papers that only the brown leather armrests were visible. Risking an avalanche that might bury her five-four frame if either side toppled, she gingerly leaned back, trying to catch her breath so she would not be huffing like an asthmatic marathon runner.

"Ms. Samantha Ballanger, please," a male voice with a clipped upper-class accent said, as if accustomed to instant acquiescence. She'd heard the type before.

"This is Sam Ballanger." If he expected her to have a private secretary to screen her calls, he was in for an unavoidable disappointment. After growing up poor in a big south Boston blue-collar family, Sam never wasted money on things she could do herself.

"My name is Upton Winchester IV, Ms. Ballanger. I understand you find and return runaways…discreetly."

"Who referred my service to you, Mr. Winchester?" She always wanted to know her clients were legit and not wasting her time. Lots of wacko husbands who used their wives and kids for punching bags wanted her to haul the victims back. No dice. She'd seen too much when she'd worked as a paramedic and then a police officer after moving to Miami.

There was a slight hesitation on the other end of the line. "I was referred by Jayson Page Layton. Jay and I golf together," he replied, expecting her to be impressed.

She was. Layton was a Bal Harbor real estate tycoon whose daughter had joined a religious cult and vanished into a commune in the Everglades a couple of years ago. Sam had literally wrestled an alligator while rescuing the poor kid from her nutcase captors, who'd been little more than child molesters and responsible for at least one dead cult member. That was Sergeant Will "Pat" Patowski's take on it. He was her mentor at the Miami-Dade Police Department, where she had spent seven years as a police officer. The Kingdom Come "prophet" and his "deacons" were presently serving ten to life in the state pen at Raiford.

"What seems to be the problem, Mr. Winchester?"

"I'd rather not discuss the matter over the phone, Ms. Ballanger. Please come to my office at the Seascape Building, say—" he paused as if consulting his day-planner "—four this afternoon. Winchester, Grayson & Kent Accounting is on the fifteenth floor."

She paused, as if consulting her own day-planner, which was a scratch pad and ballpoint buried somewhere in the income tax debris smothering her office. "Yeah, that'll work for me. Oh, my retainer's three hundred for consultation. If I take the case, I get three-fifty a day plus expenses," she said, figuring any guy with a Roman numeral in his name could afford a little extra.

"Very well. I'll expect you at four promptly."

She found herself holding a dead phone. "Jerk," she muttered. Obviously used to getting his way. But the address was in the Brickell high-rent district and he hadn't haggled over the price. She scanned the wreckage of the room, looking for the yellow pages, then spotted the volume on her desk next to the empty phone charger. Two feet of books and other papers were piled on top of it.

"Screw it," she said, getting up to dig for it. As she scooted out from between the piles of IRS manuals, they toppled, then slid with a loud series of thumps onto the mess on the floor.

She managed to extract the phone book without disturbing the "ordered chaos" on her desk. Sam thumbed through the accounting section until she reached the Ws, then whistled. A full-page ad, tastefully done in black and white—or black and yellow, more properly—proclaimed Winchester, Grayson & Kent had been in business for over fifty years. Corporate taxes were their specialty.

"Yeah, I did smell money. Must be a family business. Too bad I didn't up my fee even higher. Looks like Winchester could afford a lot more than three and a half bennies a day," she said regretfully.

Her mother, God rest her Irish Catholic soul, used to light candles and pray for Sam to abandon her avaricious ways. Avarice was one of the seven deadly sins, after all. But stretching a beer driver's income to feed six sons who ate as if each meal was going to be their last, Mary Elizabeth Ballanger never had an abundance of time to fret over her daughter's vices. Sam had elevated what she liked to think of as "fiscal prudence" to an art form.

Her ruminations about family back home were interrupted by a loud crash, followed by an oath as the front door slammed. "Dammit, Sam, I thought we agreed you'd call that cleaning service while I was gone," her husband yelled down the hall.

"Welcome home. I missed you, too, darling," she called back, walking down the hall into the living room of their condo.

Matt Granger sat like a disgruntled yoga student, rubbing the toes of his right foot while cursing inventively. "A man needs steel-toed construction boots to walk in this sty."

Returning from a weeklong assignment for the *Miami Herald,* he'd unlocked the door, juggling his suiter and laptop as he entered the dark room only to trip on one of an assortment of free weights Sam had forgotten to pick up. In a last-ditch save, he'd cradled his computer in both arms and pitched forward. He landed on an empty pizza carton.

"Let me guess. Double cheese and pepperoni, right?" He glowered at the orange stain on the knee of his best tropical wool worsted slacks. "You take these to the dry cleaners," he said, knowing it would provoke her, but not caring at the moment.

"No way. I have some cleaning solution here that will take that out in a jiff."

"Way. You're not touching my Natazzi slacks with some junk you bought in the discount store."

"Well, since they're Italian, they go with pizza," she said, stooping to pick up the carton and toss it in the general direction of an overflowing wastebasket. "You know, we could afford professional dry cleaning if you let me—"

"Let's not go there, Sam," he said, interrupting before she could restart the old argument. Why had he given her the opening? On the subject of money, his wife was as tenacious as a Boston bull terrier with teeth sunk into a letter carrier's leg. "I have a ton of work to do. Kiss and make up?" he suggested hopefully as he climbed to his feet.

She gave him a grudging peck that ripened into a long, languorous welcome. When they finally broke apart, she said, "I've been too busy working on income taxes to think of the mess. It is April, and besides, I have a business to run, too."

He looked around his once neat-as-a-pin bachelor pad. When had the hurricane hit? Everything from fast-food packaging to dirty laundry littered the room. He could only imagine what the kitchen looked like. No, on second thought, he didn't even want to imagine it. "You promised to get a maid."

"Do you know what they want an hour just to straighten up a little? I'll get around to it." She gestured vaguely.

"No, you won't. Like you said, you have a business to run and so do I. We're both gainfully employed, Sam."

"We don't make enough to afford a cleaning service...but we could if—"

"Don't start with Aunt Claudia again," he warned. "We can afford a damn maid—if any of them are brave enough to set foot in this landfill. And we don't need the Witherspoon millions to live quite comfortably."

Sam threw up her hands, cocking her head so she could look up at Matt. At six-six, he towered over her, but she never backed down. "You are nuts, you know that? First, after graduating from Yale, you turn your back on a trust fund Paris Hilton wouldn't sniff at." She ticked off number one on her finger, then moved to number two. "Whaddya do instead of living the high life in Boston? You enlist in the army!" Finger number three. "Now you bust your ass working the news beat at the *Herald* when we could have the deal of the century.

"Your aunt—your very, very wealthy aunt—has forgiven you for being nuts. Or maybe she's forgiven you because she knows *I'm* not nuts. She offered me—out of the goodness of her heart—a monthly stipend to stay married to you."

"Stipend," Matt snorted. "Try *bribe!*"

"Try allowance for the fodder and stabling of my jackass husband!"

Matt looked down into his wife's stubborn little face. "You know, you mercenary little runt, if I weren't kinda fond of you, I'd drop you off one of the causeways into the bay." There were days that it didn't seem like a half-bad idea. This was shaping up to be one of them.

"And if I weren't afraid of getting a hernia, I'd do the same to you, you Godzilla-sized jerk...wait a sec, if you were fish bait, I bet Aunt Claudia would settle a widow's jointure on me."

Matt couldn't help it. He burst out laughing in spite of the aggravation. "You've been reading those historical romances again. A jointure is something out of the last century."

"Yeah?" Sam poked her husband in the chest with a stiff finger. "Aunt Claudia is out of the last century. Hell, she's probably out of the nineteenth century!"

Matt grunted, rubbing his sore chest.

"Don't bother me. I'm thinking." Sam shushed him before he could interrupt. "With that money I could hire a maid…"

"And have our taxes done," Matt added.

"That maid would give me time to work on my own damn taxes. You know it's April and the vultures are circling."

"We should hire an accountant. You don't have to battle the IRS like the Lone Ranger—"

"Accountant! Damn, I'll be late. Gotta scoot, sweetie," she said, stretching up on tiptoe to plant another fulsome kiss on his mouth before she dashed down the hall.

As he watched her sleek little derriere disappear into their bedroom, Matt shook his head at her mercurial mood swing. He could never stay mad at her even when she drove him crazy. Their argument was over…but only for the moment. Matt knew she'd renew it. But he was damned if he wanted his eccentric millionaire aunt paying his wife to stay married to him!

Sam simply didn't understand how hard he'd struggled to break free of the smothering boardroom mentality of his rich family. Being born with a silver spoon in your mouth choked some kids. The Grangers and Witherspoons were a stuffy bunch of humorless old farts who only mingled with "the better sort." In other words, other Boston Brahmins. His great-aunt Claudia ought to know. She'd run away to Europe to escape. But since he was the last of the Granger men, she now felt it her duty to see that he fulfilled the very obligations she'd fled.

"Out of the goodness of her heart!" he parroted, kicking the offending pizza carton that had tumbled from the wastebasket. His aunt Claudia didn't have a heart—a spleen, sure, but a heart? Ha! If he gave in to her manipulations, she'd have him back in Boston, in charge of the family brokerage firm, attending high teas and charity auctions! He was an adrenaline junkie, addicted to the thrill of chasing after a hot story. He had acquired friends in low places and liked it that way.

"I'll never go back to that gilded cage—not even for Sammie. Damn, one week trying to be a society matron and she'd go crazy herself!" But he'd never been able to convince her that luring them back to Boston was Aunt Claudia's ultimate goal. His aunt and his wife had bonded the first time they met. Small wonder. Claudia had made Sam an offer a poor kid from the wrong side of the tracks couldn't refuse—a ton of money.

In spite of the differences in their backgrounds, they were sisters under the skin—ruthless schemers. He loved them both to distraction, but that was all the more reason to keep them separated. Claudia a thousand miles away was a good thing. The very thought of the two of them united and working together made him shudder.

Abandoning the ongoing argument that was giving him an ulcer, he trailed her into the walk-in closet where she was hastily stripping off a pair of shorts and a T-shirt. "I suppose it's too much to hope that you're taking our records to a tax accountant," he said, but could see she was too rushed to hear him.

Sam hated panty hose for a number of reasons besides the humid South Florida heat that fused them to her legs, but she grabbed a pair from an overflowing drawer. Shoving her way past Matt, she lay back on the bed and yanked them up her legs in one quick motion. "Gotta look like class to impress a guy with a 'fourth' tacked on the end of his name, after all," she muttered to herself.

She made a quick scan of her sadly depleted wardrobe, then seized the first suit that she found, a little black number with a fresh cleaners' bag over it, remembering gratefully that Matt actually took care of their dry cleaning. She started putting it on while she eyed the pile of shoes on the floor, praying she could find two size-six pumps, preferably the same color.

"An accountant won't allow you extra deductions for looking great," he commented as she pitched shoes right and left, trying to match up a pair of Via Spiga pumps.

After finding the second elusive shoe, she looked up at her husband. "Sorry, Matt. This tax man is a new case."

She thought he muttered something about her being the case as he turned around and stalked down the hall toward their Dumpster of a kitchen. God, she hoped there was some coffee and a couple of bagels left in the fridge—or that he wouldn't think to check until she was gone. Jamming her feet into the pumps, she ran a quick comb through curly brown hair and made her getaway.

Four in the afternoon in Miami was rush hour, but then the same could be said at four in the morning if you were driving on I-95. Convertibles with tops down and tanned halter-topped drivers with their hair whipping in the wind vied with leather-clad bikers racing up the wide highway. Both weaved in and out like demented triggerfish, changing lanes in front of semis who blasted them with deafening horns. Since her favorite uncle, Declan Ballanger, was an over-the-road trucker, Sam shared the semi-drivers' irritation. She'd made numerous cross-country runs with him while she was in high school and college. The money had helped her pay tuition.

She was late and far exceeding the speed limit in her—or rather, Matt's—sleek little Mustang. She had to admit the ride was pretty neat as she cut off a carload of college kids who should've been home studying and took the exit leading to Miami Avenue where she headed south, then angled east to Winchester's posh building.

She paid an obscene amount at the underground parking garage and searched for an open space. Just as she was about to give up and park illegally in a crosswalk, a car pulled out. The guy riding her fender since she'd entered the deck squealed his brakes to keep from hitting her as she waited for the SUV to back carefully out of the tight space. Sam resisted the urge to give the guy behind her the finger.

"Jerk, get your own space." She expected him to pass her and continue his search, but he just sat behind his darkly tinted windshield in a beat-up Olds that looked long overdue for the junkyard. When the soccer mom was gone, Sam executed a neat turn into the narrow space and jumped out of the car. The elevator was halfway to the other side of the deck.

"Should've worn flats," she groused to herself, hiking down the opposite side of the long aisle. She hadn't gone more than a dozen car lengths or so when she heard the sound of the Olds' tires' squeal as it came up behind her—fast. She whirled around and saw the crazy nut aiming directly for her! *Should've worn joggers!* Sam threw herself onto the hood of a shiny new Town Car and rolled over the side a second before the Lincoln's front fender crumpled like tinfoil when the Olds sideswiped it.

The Town Car lurched sideways, almost crushing her between it and the Chevy truck parked next to it. Sam jumped on top of the pickup bed and started a game of leapfrog from car to car, trying desperately to get to the elevator as the Olds backed up for another pass. If the heels hadn't been a splurge for her even though they were on sale, she wouldn't have bothered to stuff them in her handbag after pulling them off. But she'd be damned if she'd loose a pair of Via Spiga pumps just because some loony wanted to play dodgem cars!

Shoes in, .38 snub nose out. She always carried the small Smith & Wesson on retrievals. But since the job she'd met Matt on had run them both afoul of the local Russian mob, she carried it everywhere now. She felt the fillings in her teeth loosen when the Olds bashed against the little Miata she was balanced on. "A thirty-story office building. It's near quitting time, but does anybody walk out of the friggin' elevator or drive by?" she muttered, jumping onto the roof of a much more substantial Dodge Caravan. "Damned yuppies all work overtime!"

Sam flattened herself to aim at the attack vehicle when it again backed up for another pass. She grinned when the passenger window rolled down. "Come to mama," she crooned, drawing a bead on the big hairy fist holding a Glock out the window. Before he could fire, she did. A yelp of pain followed. As the Olds sped away, she only caught the first four figures of the letter-number combo on the plate. Even that was obscured by mud.

She drew a shaky breath when she heard the big engine's noise fade in the distance. "Bet he doesn't pay his parking fee." But she'd also bet even if the video camera got a clearer shot of the plate as it busted through the wooden crossbar, it would be bogus. Still it wouldn't hurt to check. She might get lucky.

Yeah, Ballanger. And you might win the lottery, too.

Sam slid off the dusty roof of the Caravan and started to limp toward the elevator. Suddenly she heard the sound of an engine coming up the ramp behind her. It couldn't be. No, thank God, it wasn't. A sweet little red Corvette driven by an elderly man barely tall enough to see over the wheel turned the corner and crawled past her. She leaned against the side of an old Buick and took a deep breath.

"Damn." She looked down at her clothes to inspect the damage. It could be worse. She could be dead, she reminded herself as she started to fish the shoes out of her handbag and replace the gun.

When another car whined down the incoming ramp, Sam jerked her head up, recognizing that particularly powerful old engine. "The chutzpah of some people," she muttered, diving behind the Buick as a shot grazed her thick mop of hair, then smacked into the wall behind her, dislodging a nasty chunk of concrete.

The Olds was back for a second try.

Chapter 2

This time the driver was doing the shooting. She could tell the shot had passed from the far left side through the passenger window. After she'd put his pal out of commission, he was apparently taking no chances, leaning toward the right of the Olds. If she stayed where she was hiding, he could smack into the car and crush her between it and the wall.

Glancing behind her, Sam could see a narrow pathway along the wall. The row of cars were parked far enough out to let her make a dash. The driver would have to back up or get out of his car to reach her. She spun and started to run while fishing frantically in her handbag for her cell. Damn piece of junk probably wouldn't work in the underground garage, but anything was worth a try.

The old car's brakes squealed in protest as her would-be killer tromped them, then fired several more shots. Sam was grateful he wasn't an aficionado of the target range as she ducked and dodged. Chunks of concrete exploded around her like land mines in Tora Bora. He slammed his Olds into reverse. She could hear the transmission groan in protest, but didn't take time to watch as its driver followed her. At least backing up in the confines of the dimly lit garage forced him to take his eyes off her.

She made it to the cover of a heavy concrete support beam surrounded by cars. "Let's see you ram this, sucker," she said, crouching down behind the steel-reinforced barrier. She pressed 911 on the phone. Useless. She might have known. Resisting the urge to throw the cell at her attacker, she took a deep breath and held her .38 Smith & Wesson Chief's Special with steady hands. She had only four shots left. Once those were gone, so was Sam.

Her buddy didn't disappoint. He pulled the Olds almost in line with the beam, then slipped out the driver's side. She could hear the door creak as it opened and see the changing pattern of light through the broken window. Using an old trick she'd learned as a beat cop in one of the city's less than secure neighborhoods, Sam knelt down and peered beneath the cars, watching for feet.

Nothing like a broken ankle or leg to slow a guy down. She caught a blur of movement, but this one was smart enough to use the rear wheel as cover before she could line up her shot at the awkward angle. She heard some moans and curses from inside the car and recognized it as the distinct local blend known as Spanglish. The one she'd hit was still alive but not happy.

"Looks as if we have what you might call a Cuban standoff, doesn't it, pally?" she asked. "Better get your partner to an E.R. before somebody calls the cops."

Her suggestion was ignored. Then he put one foot outside the wheel. Sam took careful aim and fired a single shot at the weathered denim pant leg. Another string of hybrid oaths in a Spanish-English combo.

"Bingo," she muttered as he hopped back to the car. From the quick leap he made, she knew she'd only nicked him, but that was good enough. The door slammed shut and the Olds took off like a rocket, careening around the corner and vanishing up the exit ramp, a lot faster than the old geezer in the 'Vette. She still only made out the first four digits on the dirty plate. Deliberately covered with mud? Probably.

Sam stood up and leaned against the cool concrete for a minute, collecting herself. Whoever had hired those gunsels meant business. Although she and Matt had made some nasty enemies in the local Russian Mafia, she doubted these two turkeys were connected. One or both of them might have .38 slugs in them—or at least a couple of real nasty gashes, maybe the first shooter a broken arm or hand. That meant they needed medical help of some kind.

She replaced the gun in her handbag and took out the Via Spiga pumps. Shoving the shoes over her mangled stockings, she sprinted toward the elevator to the first floor where her cell would work, then placed a call to Patowski to explain what had just transpired.

Pat was his usual gracious self. "Let me get this straight. You want me to run a check on *all* Miami E.R.s for a couple of Cubano shooters who you never even got a look at? Driving a rag wagon Olds, for which you only got a *partial* plate? These supposed Cubanos *may* have .38 bullet wounds? Hell, Sam, in the last hour you know how many shootings there've been in Little Havana alone? And how common .38s are? Talk about your needle in a haystack—why not ask me to pick fly crap out of black pepper?"

Sam sighed, glancing at her watch. "You're right, Pat. It's a long shot, but the one in the car I may have hit pretty solid. He wasn't shooting when the driver got out."

"What's this all about? More mob stuff?" he asked.

"I don't know. Just run the plate and see what you come up with, okay?"

After a martyred sigh, Patowski agreed. He owed her and they both knew it. She and Matt had helped him and his pals at the FBI break a case involving multiple homicides and stop a Russian mafia turf war extending from Miami to New York.

When she ended the call, she could see some of the well-dressed executive types in the exclusive office building giving her the eye. Sam could imagine what she must look like, but one glance at her watch and she also knew she didn't have time to repair the damage.

She brushed at the dust and oil on her formerly immaculate suit with an oath. For once in her miserable life, couldn't she look cool and professional? Muttering, "At least black doesn't show grease stains," she headed to the elevator and punched the up button.

A woman in a designer suit with a matching briefcase entered the elevator with her, practically stepping sideways through the wide door. She deliberately stood at the opposite side of the car as it began its ascent. "If you think I'm Typhoid Mary, you could've waited for the next car," Sam couldn't resist saying. Then she sneezed. Her fellow traveler quickly punched a second button and got off at the next floor. Sam rode to the fifteenth.

The elite offices of Winchester, Grayson & Kent were furnished in posh Danish modern, the redwood tones made more subtle by pale gray and mauve upholstery. Tall black urns filled with bamboo and those funny curlicues of decorative wood stood like sentinels flanking the massive reception desk. Abstract watercolors were strategically placed on the pearl-white walls, all of them by one artist, probably Scandinavian and most certainly expensive.

Several men in custom tailored suits occupied chairs that

overlooked a solid glass wall with a splendid view of the Intracoastal. One glanced up from his *Barron's* long enough to give her a sniff of distaste, then went back to the stock market reports. A woman with glossy blond hair sleeked into a severe French twist sat behind the reception desk. She obviously didn't like Sam's appearance, either.

"May I help you?" she said in a tone reserved for a vagrant who'd come to inquire if he could use the executive washroom.

"Sam Ballanger to see Mr. Winchester. I have an appointment."

Looking highly dubious, the blonde checked the computer screen at her side to confirm. "That was for 4:00 p.m. It's now—"

"Look, Blondie, I can tell time. I was unavoidably detained by a couple of bozos who tried to run me down, then shoot me in your parking deck. Next time that happens to you, let's see if that fancy 'do' of yours doesn't get a little messed up, okay?"

Ms. Chandler, as the nameplate on the desk indicated, glared disbelievingly before she caught herself and forced a smile as genuine as the mauve silk floral arrangement beside her computer. "I'll see if Mr. Winchester is still available. Please have a seat."

But only if I promise not to get grease on the upholstery. Sam walked over to the window and looked at the stunning vista, all blue skies, gold sand and green palm trees in the distance. Miami Beach with its Art Deco pastels beckoned from across the water, a faded diva ringed by garish new high-rise condos. Her kind of town. She'd known it since her first trip here when she was thirteen and stowed away in the sleeper of Uncle Dec's rig. He'd been mad enough to chew nails when he'd discovered her at a rest stop in North Carolina. Turned the air blue with his cussing, she recalled fondly. By that time it had been too far to turn back without sacrificing a big payload in Miami, so he'd called her frantic parents and reassured them he'd take good care of his favorite niece. She'd been grounded for the rest of her freshman year, but it had been worth it.

Her reminiscences were interrupted by Ms. Chandler. "Mr. Winchester will see you now," she said. "Please follow me."

The snotty receptionist looked as if she was trying to digest a bamboo stalk from one of those urns out front and walked as if another stalk was jammed where the Florida sun never shines. They moved down a long hall, footsteps muffled by two-inch-thick Karastan carpeting in a shade Sam would've described as Attica gray. Winchester's nameplate was inscribed in polished brass on the door of the corner office. Of course. He was the senior partner, after all.

Chandler knocked deferentially and was bidden to enter. She stood with her back pressed to the door, careful not to let Sam touch her when she walked inside. A tall silver-haired man with the narrow face and long, straight nose of a blue blood stood behind an immense walnut desk devoid of everything but a leather blotter and a set of Montblanc pens.

"Ms. Ballanger?" He did not smile.

"Mr. Winchester?" she shot back. "Pardon my appearance—and tardiness." She paused to glance back at the Chandler dame, who was slowly closing the door behind her. *Like to eavesdrop, don't you, honey?* When Sam heard the muffled sound of the latch click, she continued, "I was involved in an altercation in your parking deck. Can you think of any reason someone would try to stop me from taking your case?"

He blinked. "Certainly not. What do you mean by 'an altercation'?"

So much for well-bred manners. He still didn't offer her a seat. Even Chandler had done that much. She took one anyway, directly in front of him and he reluctantly lowered himself into the custom leather chair behind the desk. She gave him a quick rundown on the attack in the downstairs garage, studying his response. Hard to tell if he believed her, or even cared.

"It could've been related to another investigation, but I'd appreciate it if you'd have the building security check their video cams at the exits between three fifty-five and four-ten or so."

Winchester shook his head ever so slightly. "I'm afraid that's out of the question. If you report this...even to the authorities, I'll be dragged into something which has nothing to do with me. In fact—"

Sam put up her hand. "Okay, just a thought. The Olds is probably being fed into a compactor as we speak anyway." She decided to omit her little conversation with Patowski since she didn't want to lose what promised to be a lucrative job. She'd dealt with uptight types like Winchester before and knew how to handle them. As for a couple of dozen wrecked cars in the bowels of the building, well, let their insurance companies handle that.

"Who do you want me to retrieve and why?" she asked.

He hesitated, then replied, "Jay did recommend you highly." Although he still appeared skeptical, he continued, "My son, Farley, is missing. The boy probably thinks he's on a secret mission for the Confederation of Planets, but my guess is that he's still somewhere on Earth—with my stolen Jaguar and his friend Elvis."

"Elvis? Excuse me?" Sam couldn't help the incredulous expression on her face.

"Elvis P. Scruggs. And don't ask what the *P* stands for," he snapped. "My son is only seventeen and has been under the care of Dr. Reese Reicht for the past five years."

Sam waited for him to give her the rest of the story. He drummed a set of well-manicured fingers on the desk, as if debating. "Dr. Reicht?" she prompted.

"He's a psychiatrist. My son sees flying saucers, spaceships, even imagines he's part of some kind of intergalactic war." He pursed his thin lips in a tight line, then scoffed angrily. "A secret agent for the Confederation of Planets." At her blank look, he explained, "Farley is a...a *Space Quest* fanatic. Has been ever since he was a boy."

"You mean he's a movie buff—loves sci-fi films and television shows?" Weird, but not as weird as a pal named Elvis Presley Scruggs.

"I'm afraid Farley's situation isn't quite as simple as being an avid fan." Winchester grimaced. The drumming fingers stilled when he realized she noticed the agitated movement.

Sam bet if he had any papers on his desk they'd be aligned in perfectly straight rows. She'd lay a lot better than even money that everything on his computer was organized in perfectly ordered folders and every single item could be pulled up in an instant. And he had a double backup system.

"Farley has been known to use drugs—and I am not speaking of the medications Dr. Reicht prescribes."

"That could be serious. When did he disappear?"

Winchester gave a dismissive wave of his hand. "Sometime in the past two days. I've been out of town on business. I returned late yesterday. The housekeeper informed me Farley hadn't slept in his bed for the past two nights."

A real concerned parent here. Doesn't want the cops. No idea how long his kid's been missing. "Does his mother have any idea when he took off?"

"I regret to say his mother passed away five years ago."

The loss of a pet guppy would elicit more reaction from

most people so she didn't waste time offering condolences. "Any idea where he went? Is this Scruggs with him?"

"Yes. Farley's been spending time with that illiterate cracker for weeks, perhaps longer." The vagueness again irritated her as he continued, "Scruggs is from somewhere in the panhandle. Oh, I tried to put a stop to it, but my work requires me to be out of town frequently and my son has always been…difficult."

With a dad like you he oughta be impossible. "You think Scruggs is Farley's drug connection?"

"I don't know. I do know that he's a thief and I discovered quite recently that he may have spent some time in prison. In any case, Rogers, my chauffeur, informed me that Scruggs took my vintage Jaguar. Since Farley was in the passenger seat, he didn't question it. That was Monday afternoon. When I was going over my personal records this morning, I found twenty thousand dollars had been withdrawn from a savings account to which my son has access."

"You're sure Farley took it?"

"Yes, and I'm equally sure Scruggs encouraged him, but I won't press charges. I simply want you to recover my money, my car and my son. Quietly. No headlines. Do you think you can do that, Ms. Ballanger?" He glanced at his Rolex, indicating the interview was over.

"I'll do my best to bring back your son, Mr. Winchester. But I will need a few names and numbers—his doctor, your housekeeper and chauffeur, the registration info on the Jag."

He nodded, turning to the console at the side of his desk and pressing a button. "My personal assistant will be happy to furnish whatever you need."

Sam stood up. Winchester didn't bother. Neither did he offer to shake hands. "About my fee—"

"Ms. Ettinger will take care of that, as well. Send a bill." With that he swiveled his chair around and opened his computer.

She'd been dismissed like a chambermaid in an English melodrama! "Where do I find Ms. Ettinger?" Sam said to the back of his head.

He didn't turn around. "She'll be along."

As if on cue the door opened. A wraith-thin woman with gray hair pulled into a painfully tight knot on top of her head and the worst overbite Sam had ever seen, said, "Please follow me, Ms. Ballanger." She didn't smile, either.

The kid may be into Space Quest, *but his old man and this staff could play in zombie movies.*

Chapter 3

Ms. Ettinger furnished Sam with every name and address she requested, sniffing with obvious distaste when she came to Scruggs, whose last known domicile was in a trailer park in Liberty City. Sam had the distinct impression the old harridan imagined that *she* lived in a trailer, too...or under a rock.

Grinning cheerfully when she took the proffered fat retainer check from the older woman's bony fingers, Sam couldn't resist saying, "It's been fun, Ettie. Let's do lunch sometime."

"Ettie's" glasses slipped to the end of her thin nose when she jerked her head back at the moniker. Adjusting them, she peered over the tops with squinty eyes and said, "You may exit the premises that way," pointing to a narrow door at the end of the hallway.

I'll be lucky if it doesn't open on an elevator shaft with a fifteen-story drop. Sam turned the knob cautiously and saw the door led to a dimly lit hallway near the service elevators used by cleaning staff. Considering how scruffy she looked, Sam was not surprised Upton hadn't wanted her offending W, G & K's elite patrons again.

Maybe she should use the service elevator. That had been Ettie's clear intent. *No way.* She rounded the corner to the main hallway where the light was better and perused the directory. "Hmm, the shrink has an office a couple of floors up," she murmured to herself, wondering if he was available. Maybe she'd hit the ladies' room downstairs first and repair what she could before tackling a guy with an M.D. and Ph.D. behind his name. Half the alphabet, Roman numerals—did all rich guys have to be such pains in the ass?

Matt had come from money but he didn't want any part of it. And she'd fallen for him. But he was part of the club when it came to the pain part. All that lovely money just going to waste in Aunt Claudia's bank and he'd extracted a promise from Sam that she'd forgo the loot to become his wife. "He caught me in a weak moment," she reminded herself as she rode the elevator to the main level. A weak moment all right…in bed.

Just remembering that interlude brought a silly grin to her face. She quashed it and pushed open the door marked Ladies. Once she eased up to a mirror in the washroom and inspected the damage she knew why everyone was treating her like a leper. Her hair was standing up in clumps, her suit was grease stained and ripped, and one cheek was bleeding slightly from where sharp pieces of concrete had grazed her when that goon had shot at her and hit the wall.

She wet a bunch of paper towels and set to work cleaning herself up, then went into one of the classy marble stalls and stripped off the snagged panty hose, jamming her bare feet back into the Via Spiga pumps. One knee was skinned and a dandy bruise on her shin had already begun to discolor. Oh, well. She glanced at her watch. It was late, but if she was lucky, the doc would still be in his office treating patients. Shrinks didn't usually keep nine-to-five office hours.

Luck was with her. The receptionist, a plain middle-aged woman with a sweet smile, informed her that Dr. Reicht was with a patient at present, but would see her shortly. Upton Winchester must have called ahead. Reicht's suite was not as large as W, G & K's, but it still reeked of money. The smaller reception room was furnished with heavy oak chairs. To keep potentially violent patients from busting them up if they went off their meds?

The decor was all done in neutral tones of beige, tan and white as if a deliberate attempt had been made to offend no one. A wide array of magazines lay fanned across a massive coffee table. Ignoring the enticement of reading about the life-styles of the rich and famous, she checked over her meager notes on Farley Winchester.

Age seventeen. High IQ, low self-esteem and a probable drug habit, if his father was to be believed. She'd been provided with a photo, taken several months ago, according to the harridan. He looked like a geeky kid, the kind the jocks made fun of in high school. Tall, skinny, bad complexion, even horn-rimmed glasses, for Pete's sake! And he was dressed in some kind of weird getup with insignias on the shirt and a wide leather belt. It looked like cheap polyester fabric accessorized with plastic.

Not exactly a preppie, are you, kiddo?

Was it a "Spacer" uniform? Hopefully the good doc could give her more info before she set out to snatch the kid from Elvis's clutches. Her perusal of the photo was interrupted when a short, stocky man opened the inner door and said, "Ms. Ballanger?"

Reicht had a fringe of graying tan hair ringing his oversize head. Sam guessed that was a requirement to hold the brains for acquiring all those initials after his name. There were pouches the size of Pony Express saddlebags under his eyes and he possessed jowls that would be the envy of an English bulldog. Reicht's eyes were obscured by a hedge of eyebrows that flowed uninterrupted across his forehead. He wore a rumpled tweed jacket and even had a meerschaum pipe protruding from one pocket. Jeez, talk about a walking stereotype!

Sam stood up and offered her hand, which he shook heartily, grinning as he ushered her into his sanctum. "Please hold my calls, Heidi," he said to the secretary.

The office was as cluttered as its owner, with piles of folders and loose papers scattered everywhere. She could identify with the unholy mess, but there was something about him that gave her a hinky vibe. "I assume your friend Mr. Winchester told you why I'm here," Sam said as he offered her a seat.

"Indeed, he did. Most regrettable, most regrettable…" He seemed to lose his train of thought for a moment, then continued. "Farley requires close supervision and regular medication to keep in touch with reality."

"I don't think Mr. Winchester pays his housekeeper for babysitting while he's out of town."

"Mr. Winchester and I have agreed that Farley might do well in a private clinic, but such things take time to arrange. Of course, he's been hospitalized on several occasions in the past…." Again his voice trailed away.

"Didn't do any good?" she suggested.

"Well, you do understand about physician-patient confidentiality, Ms. Ballanger?"

"Yes, professional ethics and all. Like attorney-client, priest-confessor or P.I.-employer. Since his father's green-lighted me to find him, I need to know what I'm dealing with before I retrieve him."

The doctor sighed. "Farley has been delusional since childhood. Approaching his majority, he's shown no improvement. In fact, he's become worse."

"You mean the Spacie thing? How long's he been a *Space Quest* fan?" she asked.

"For as long as I've been treating him. Nearly…eight years. All he's ever wanted to discuss during our sessions is that show and its characters. It's his reality and the real world has ceased to exist for him…if it ever did."

"His father said he tripped on drugs."

Reicht nodded. "Cocaine, heroine, even methamphetamines."

"What—no Drano? I used to be a paramedic and we never like handling guys high on meth. Any idea who his dealer is?"

"Farley has made some…less than appropriate friends recently. I suspect one in particular."

"Elvis Scruggs?"

The giant caterpillar of an eyebrow crinkled when Reicht frowned. "Yes. When one is young, disturbed and wealthy, one can be victimized."

"Do you think Scruggs kidnapped him?"

The doctor shook his head. "Probably not. The boy would go along with any harebrained scheme Scruggs proposed, I'm certain. Farley's highly suggestible, particularly when he's high on illegal drugs."

"Suggestible to cleaning out one of his daddy's bank accounts?"

"If someone like this Elvis Scruggs urged him to do it, yes. You understand why you must bring him home. I'll see that he goes back on proper medication and provide supervision. In fact—" he began rooting around on his desk, pulling out a sheaf of papers with a grunt of satisfaction "—I have the forms here for Homeside. It's a fine facility. I'm on the staff," he added as if that guaranteed it.

"Will his father agree to commit him?" she asked.

"Of course. We've been discussing it for several weeks. Oh, we don't call it 'commitment' any longer. The term is too…pejorative. Homeside is just as the name implies—a home away from home for troubled individuals."

That might explain why the kid took off. It sounded to Sam as if his father's house and the loony bin would hold about equal appeal. Still, the poor kid couldn't be allowed to run around the country dressed like a sci-fi movie extra high on meth, with an ex-con chauffeuring him while he fleeced him.

Unlike Winchester after her interview, Reicht didn't dismiss her. She would've preferred that he had when he launched into a panegyric on Homeside and how happy poor Farley would be once he was tucked safely in the marvelous facility. When he got warmed up, the doc really loved to hear the sound of his own voice. Finally, she glanced down at her watch.

"Sorry, Dr. Reicht, but I have another appointment shortly. Gotta run."

"You will make Farley your first priority, I trust?" he asked intently.

"You bet I will. I'll call if I need any more info. Thanks."

As she rode down on the elevator, Sam considered the weirdness of the day—a pair of psychos tried to kill her, a snotty pencil pusher managed to snub her while enticing her with a hefty fee, the shrink played on her sympathy for a poor crazy kid. Did the thugs in the Olds have any connection to Farley's case? Doubtful, but Sam never assumed anything.

And something niggled at her about the shrink, too. He put on a nice-guy veneer, the complete opposite of Roman Numeral, as she'd dubbed Winchester. Still Reicht was a cipher. Of course, he was a psychiatrist and that might explain the creepy feeling he gave her. Some of them were as loosely packed as their patients. She made a mental note to have Matt check out Homeside while she was searching for Farley.

The last thing Sam Ballanger ever intended to do was to deliver a client into a worse situation than the one she snatched him from.

"Yeah, that's right, a 1980 Jaguar XJ6." Sam ticked off the license plate number to an old friend at Metro-Dade Police Headquarters. "Bright maroon. Oughta stand out like a black tux in a room full of brown shoes."

As she tapped a pencil against the edge of a front tooth, waiting impatiently for the cop to check the computer records, Matt watched his wife. Sam arched her back against the wreck of a swivel chair she insisted on keeping when she moved in. In spite of her small one-hundred-ten-pound body, the springs creaked precariously when she tipped it sharply backward. Her bare feet were propped up on the cluttered desk in her office and she was wearing a ratty old pink chenille bathrobe that he teasingly called her "Linus blanket."

He eyed the ugly bruise on her shin and the scrapes on her cheekbone, worried but knowing there was no way short of putting her in one of those custom straitjackets she used on retrievals that he could keep her safe. They argued about her dangerous job almost as much as they did about his aunt's money. Correction. She argued about the money. He argued about her safety.

Matt glided into the room and began massaging her shoulders while she leaned forward and jotted down information. What was a guy supposed to do with a bullheaded female like Sam? She wouldn't even take his name—unless he agreed to "really let me in the family by accepting Aunt Claudia's

offer." She'd signed Sam Ballanger on their marriage certif-
icate. The woman had the instincts of a first-rate black-
mailer—or a criminal defense attorney.

Sam hung up the phone and laid her head against his flat
abdomen. The man even had a sexy navel. "Mmm, that feels
good," she murmured as he bent over her for an upside-down
kiss. "Even better." She held his head in her hands and
returned the kiss for a moment before spinning her chair
around and considering the notes she'd scribbled on the page.

"Any leads on your lost boy?" he asked, then couldn't
resist adding, "Or on those two goons who tried to play crash-
test dummy with you?"

"Strike out on the Olds, but I figured it would be. Bogus
plates. I asked Pat to keep checking. Doubt he'll turn up much
on them, but he just might on Elvis Scruggs. I did come up
with where Farley and Elvis are heading. A vintage Jag stands
out almost as much as a flying saucer."

"And a guy named Elvis doesn't?"

"Depends on what part of the country you're in. Nobody
remembers him but thanks to my hacker pal, Ethan Frobisher,
we have a trace on cash flow to back up the runaways' desti-
nation. Seems Farley's been using several of Daddy's credit
cards. Hotels, meals, ATM withdrawals in Tallahassee, Nashville and Louisville. The last was in some hick burg in
southern Illinois. Then I used that info you so kindly dug up
for me on the Net."

She tossed him the printout of *Space Quest* conventions
he'd pulled off the Internet for her. One was circled. "Big one
in St. Louis. Starts tomorrow."

He shrugged. "Your crazy job's going to get you killed. I
don't know why I aid and abet you."

"'Cause you can't get enough of my bod," she said, grinning
as she stood up and wrapped her arms around his waist.

"You're the trained health professional, Ms. Paramedic. What do you think?" he asked, prodding her with an erection that always grew like Pinocchio's nose when she got within a dozen yards of him.

Sam rotated her pelvis against him and chuckled. "I think if I don't take care of this immediately, you could suffer a serious…backup."

"Speaking of backing up…" he said, turning her around while nibbling small kisses across her eyelids and down her nose to her throat. He backed her through the door and down the hall to their bedroom.

They were so engaged in the hot exchange neither saw the obstacle until their feet were tangled in it. They went tumbling across the threshold and landed on the carpet. Somehow Sam managed to come out on top. She always did. Matt looked down at what they'd tripped over—the ruins of her good black suit.

"As long as we're down here, might as well make the ride worthwhile," he said, rolling her onto her back.

Chapter 4

Sam let him pull off her old chenille bathrobe while she worked the snap on his jeans and carefully lowered the distressed zipper. By the time his tongue danced from one bared nipple to the other and back, she had worked the denim over his buns and he kicked the pants away. She arched into his delicate caresses as she buried her hands in his thick black hair, urging him on.

"Talk about steam-cleaning the carpet," she murmured. "I'm gonna have rug burns…again." She didn't sound particularly concerned.

"It serves you right," he growled as he felt her hands play along his back, down to curve around his butt. "Hussy."

"Hunk."

"Sammie, oh, Sammie," he murmured, gliding inside the sleek wetness of her body.

Was it always this good? Only with Matt. Always with Matt. Sam wrapped her legs around him as he moved in her, slowly, gently. She could feel the springy hair on his chest abrade her sensitized breasts, making her nipples tingle and draw into even harder little points. "I'll…give you…exactly one hour…to cut this out," she whispered breathlessly.

But when he started moving faster, she bit his ear and said, "An hour, remember? I can't last…if you don't…ahhh."

"Who says *you* have to last?" he asked with a wicked chuckle, feeling her body spasm around his. Matt concentrated on control. Dames did have the advantage when it came to coming. And his little Sammie had to be the world's champ.

When he renewed his sensual assault with slow precision, Sam took a moment for the world to stop spinning. Then she took control. She was little but she hadn't earned a black belt in judo without developing some serious moves of her own. With one heel and a lift of her hip, she rolled them over until she was on top, breathless, grinning triumphantly down at him.

"How…the hell…do you…do that?"

"In judo, it's called mat work." She chuckled, running her hands proprietarily across his hard pectoral muscles and tracing the narrowing pattern of black hair in its downward descent.

"We gotta…work out…more often." Now it was Matt's turn to be breathless. The view inspired it. He looked up at the most sensational pair of knockers he'd ever seen, standing high and firm above a slim waist and flared hips that perched neatly over him. Oh, my, yes…yes! Her sensational body, especially the breasts, had been the first thing he'd noticed about Sam Ballanger the day they met.

The day she kidnapped him at gunpoint.

But as she worked her magic on him, kissing and caressing, moving only the way she could move, memories of that incident faded. He felt the wild exhilaration building. When she tossed her head back and cried out his name, he let go with everything in him.

Sam lay prostrate over his much larger frame. When her heart returned to some semblance of a normal beat, she raised her head and looked over at the clock. "You're off, Granger. Only fifty-four minutes."

He came up from the carpet with her in his arms, growling, "Then I'll just have to practice more." With that he tossed her onto the bed and dived after her.

When they'd finally exhausted each other, they lay side by side on the pillows. Sam reached up and smoothed one devilish black curl away from his forehead. She always liked this time afterward. The quietness. Just pure relaxed enjoyment, being together with no words necessary. Raised in a big boisterous family, Sam was good at arguing, always had a quick comeback. She'd had to, as the only girl and the eldest of seven Ballanger children. But she'd never learned flowery talk. Didn't want to. And with Matt she didn't need to. If only he would come to his senses about Aunt Claudia's money, everything would be perfect....

Pushing that disturbing thought away, she said, "I should get back to Pat about Elvis. He may have something for me by now." She didn't move.

"Yeah, I guess you should." He didn't move, either, even though he had two deadlines tomorrow. Just because he'd been nominated for a Pulitzer for his exposé of Russian mafia activities in Miami didn't mean he could rest on his laurels. Besides, the Pulitzer Committee didn't meet to decide the winners for four months yet.

They lay quietly until the annoying beep of the bedside phone broke the spell. Matt reached one long arm behind him and groped for the accursed thing, then pressed Talk and grunted, "Granger here."

Sam recognized Patowski's cigarette-roughened voice on

the line but waited until Matt handed the phone to her. "Speak of the devil and up he pops," he whispered grumpily, climbing out of bed and grabbing his jeans. She admired the view of his bare buns while he slid worn denim up his long legs and stalked off toward his office.

"Whatcha got for me, Patty?"

"Don't call me Patty," Patowski groused, starting their usual ritual of ethnic insults. "I'm a Polack, you're the Mick," he added, beating her to the punch.

Sam rolled off the bed and walked into her office, seizing a notepad and pencil as he talked.

"Your pally Elvis P. Scruggs—by the way the *P* doesn't stand for Presley—it's Peter—he had an interesting childhood. A local bad boy from grade school on in some podunk township in the panhandle. Took a joyride in the sheriff's patrol unit, snuckered to the gills on moonshine."

"Guess that might tend to piss off the local constabulary," Sam said dryly.

"Especially since the sheriff was his father."

"Ouch."

"Yeah. Old man was a real hard-ass. Wanted to charge him with GTA but since he was still a minor, it didn't stick. Sealed court records. I had to do some pretty fancy footwork to come up with the bits and pieces I got."

"That your subtle way of saying I owe you, Pat?"

"You damn betcha you do."

Sam knew he was right in spite of the recent help she and Matt had given him breaking the Russian mafia murders. As an officer on the Miami-Dade PD, she had been blamed when a hot dog rookie on the force had been killed. Patowski had gone to bat for her, knowing it had been the kid's fault, not hers. Sam had still been cashiered, but by then she had been ready to move on anyway. Too many of her fellow officers had blamed her for the botched takedown. Besides, her retrieval business had proved to be far more lucrative.

"What's our boy Elvis been up to lately?" she asked Pat.

"He did some time in a pretty rough juvvie facility up there, then dropped off the radar screen. No record of him until he turned up here a few months ago."

"Usually that kind of bad actor rides the down bound train straight to hell, but Scruggs has no other records as an adult you could locate?" she asked.

"Maybe he went out of state. Out of the country. Or, maybe wrestling gators in that detention facility scared him onto the straight and narrow. Who the hell knows? Oh, one thing—you said he was twenty-one?"

"That's what I got from my client, who had him investigated. Not very well, it seems."

"He could pass for it, but the sucker's twenty-eight if the records from Tallahassee are accurate. Birth dates aren't something they usually screw up."

Sam hummed, doodling on the notepad, talking to herself. "Wonder what went on for those seven years?"

"Track him down and find out, I guess. That's what they pay you the big bucks for, isn't it?" Patowski asked sourly.

"Yeah, Patty, it sure is," she replied cheerfully. "Thanks. I owe you." Before he could curse at her again, she hung up. "Looks like I'm headed for St. Louis."

Standing in the doorway, Matt listened to her musing. "I'm going with you," he said.

"Nix on that. I have work for you here."

"I have an editor who sort of expects me to turn in stories by deadline. The *Herald* pays me for that."

"Then you obviously don't have time to drive to St. Louis with me."

She had that *gotcha* look in her eyes. "Look, Sam, are you

sure this kid's just a *Space Quest* fan run amok? I mean, he's not a psycho or anything, is he?" His wife was sometimes selective with what facts she provided him.

"Just a poor geek. Look at his picture, for crying in the night." She pulled the snapshot from the clutter on the desk and offered it to him.

"That's a Confederation Ensign's insignia," he murmured.

"You know about this *Space Quest* junk?" she asked, amazed.

"It isn't junk. It was a great series—still in syndication. And the films have made millions. Five spin-off shows since it premiered."

Sam burst out with a guffaw before she could stop herself. "You were a Spacie!" she exclaimed.

His look became at once thunderous and defensive. "The term is *Spacer* and yes, I was a big fan. Anything wrong with that?"

Sam was hard put to find a glib answer. "I never got the chance to find out. All we ever had on television at our house was baseball and boxing. Mostly, I worked part-time jobs growing up. Not much time for television." Now she was the one sounding defensive, so she shifted the subject. "But dressing up in those crazy regalias and going halfway across the country to conventions. Kinda weird, if you ask me."

"I don't see anything wrong with attending a Spacer Con. I always thought it would be fun."

"Then why didn't you go?" she asked, puzzled.

Matt cleared his throat, then looked her in the eye and confessed, "Aunt Claudia wouldn't let me. She didn't want me doing anything that'd make me more of a geek than I already was."

"You? A geek?" That was the very last thing she could imagine her six-six sexy husband ever being. "Get outta here!"

Matt could see the humor in the situation as he looked at her amazed expression. "My height was a bigger number than my weight in junior high. I wore braces and needed correctional glasses—though at least they weren't as ugly as these." He looked down at the askew horn-rims on Farley Winchester. "I can identify with the kid. Sometimes other galaxies can hold a real appeal."

"Maybe just being born with a silver spoon doesn't make up for other stuff," Sam said thoughtfully. "Your parents died when you were nine, right?" He nodded. "And Aunt Claudia popped in and out of your life like Auntie Mame?"

"Why do you think I went to private boarding schools all those years?"

She sighed. "I thought all Beacon Hill kids just did. Dumb, huh?" She walked over to him and laid her head against the steady beat of his heart. "I'm sorry, Matt." Before he could reply, her head shot up and she looked him straight in the eye. "But that doesn't mean I'm giving up on Aunt Claudia's offer. Ten K a month just to stay married isn't anything to sneeze at. Think of it as her penance."

His expression turned grim. "Episcopalians don't do penance. And even if they did, she wouldn't. Forget the money. We'll never agree about it."

"You're right about that, but don't think I'm gonna give it up," she said stubbornly. Feeling him tense in anger, she paused. "Okay, let's give that topic a rest for a while." She began tracing small circles on his bicep with her fingertips. "About doing some checking for me…"

"What do you need?" he asked, resigned. With her out of town, he'd be bouncing off the walls as soon as he finished his current assignments.

"This whole thing smells kinda funny. If Farley withdrew twenty large from one of his daddy's bank accounts, why are he and his pal Elvis using Winchester's credit cards instead of spending the cash? Even if the kid's spacey, er, a Spacer, a guy like Scruggs has to know how easy it'll be to trace them. Besides, according to the doc, the kid's crazy, not stupid."

"Good point." Matt rubbed his chin, considering. "You said something earlier about the shrink giving you bad vibes. Maybe I'll check him and your 'Roman Numeral' guy out while you're gone."

"You're the greatest—even if you were a geek before I met you," she said with a cheeky grin. "Oh, yeah, about being a geek, I wouldn't know a Reemulan from a rhinoceros. Fill me in a little about that stuff."

"Reemulans have pointed ears, not horns. I can explain what you need to know about the Confederation of Planets, their allies and their enemies." He began a lengthy discourse on the warlike Reemulans and their logical, peaceful cousins, the Vulcants. Both civilizations felt mere Earthlings were both technologically and ethically challenged. "Then there are the Klingoffs—"

"Are they anything like jackoffs?"

"Sort of, yes. Barbaric, living by a primitive warrior's code but highly advanced in technology. Everyone in the galaxy thinks they're animals."

"They the ones who look like they have turtle shells glued to their foreheads?"

"I see you've watched a smidgen of the shows."

"Went to a movie once—on a date. I didn't get to pick the show," she retorted. "Never went out with the guy again, either."

Matt regarded her with a smirk. "Ironically, it's Earth that first came to understand their culture and accept it. Come to think of it, you wouldn't make a bad Klingoff warrior woman." He pulled a volume from the shelf in his office and handed it to her.

"Thanks," she said sarcastically, flipping through the color photos and text about *Space Quest* in its various incarnations. "I can see why the kid's schizoid. This is weirdsville, but it'll give me enough background to fake it when I get to the convention. All I have to do is wait for a chance to snatch Farley."

"Be careful. If Scruggs did hard time, even as a kid, he won't want you taking away his meal ticket."

"I always come out on top, remember?" she purred, planting a quick kiss on his mouth.

Sam drove a specially equipped Ford Econoline van, an old model with an engine her uncle Dec had helped her soup up. It could go from zero to sixty in less time than most fancy European sports cars and had been remodeled to serve the nurse-transporting-a-patient cover she used on many retrievals. The paneled back was furnished with a unique set of restraints to hold her "patients" securely while she drove.

Going against Matt's advice, a frequent occurrence since they'd met, she headed out that night for St. Louis. It would be a long pull and the "Con" as he called it was set to begin the next day. Who knew where Farley and Elvis would head after that? Sam wanted the kid safely in her grasp while she could still reach him. Maybe they were saving the twenty K to skip to Mexico, for all she could figure.

Clutching a twenty-ounce paper cup filled with thick black coffee, heavy on the sugar, she headed up I-95 and hit the Florida Turnpike. Dawn was a faint glow on the horizon when she felt the blowout yank the steering wheel from her grasp. Cursing, she quickly corrected, grateful for her uncle's training, then pulled to the side of the road. Wonderful. A stretch so isolated she could dehydrate before Road Assistance found her.

With no time to waste, she climbed out of the van and opened the back doors. This was hardly the first flat she'd changed, but dammit, it was costing her time! Sam wondered why the hell the tire had blown. She'd checked them carefully, always did before she drove. "Probably some litterbug tossing a beer bottle out his window a few miles back," she snarled, placing the jack under the rear bumper.

Before she could start working the jack, headlights appeared on the horizon. Although she'd been careful to pull well off the highway, Sam had been drilled by her uncle Declan to always be wary of dozing motorists when the flat was on the left side of the vehicle. The inbred precaution saved her life. Still squatting, she glanced up to see the car veering directly toward her.

Sam dropped the jack and flung herself across the berm into the marshy weeds of the ditch.

Chapter 5

The car grazed her van, leaving faint dark smears on the white paint. Not a direct hit, but the speed of the encounter rocked the Ford's suspension. By the time she climbed from the muddy ditch, pulling briars and dry leaves from her clothes, the car had vanished into the distance. She couldn't even tell what make or model it had been. Too busy leaping for her life.

"What the hell is it about me and cars lately?" she muttered, thinking about the incident in the parking garage. Did someone want to stop her from retrieving Farley? She watched the horizon for lights as she walked to the front of the van and pulled out her cell. Dead zone. Big surprise considering she was smack in the middle of nowhere. May be best not to call Matt and worry him. And what could she tell Patowski or any of her cop buddies?

She hadn't a clue about the car, other than that it wasn't the Olds. That ancient rust bucket couldn't have moved that fast without the driver putting his foot through the floorboards and breaking a leg. And it had been an indistinct light color. The paint deposits on her van were dark.

"Damn, it'll cost a bundle to get this baby repainted." She would add the expense to Winchester's tab, but having a quality paint job done took time and aggravation. Just in case the jerk decided on another crack at her, she dug her snub nose .38 out of the glove compartment and shoved it into her belt before returning to the jack.

"Maybe I'm being paranoid. Just some drunk or dumb kid showing off for his buddies," she said. But all the while she fixed the flat, she kept an eye on the highway.

Sam caught a few hours sleep that night in a cheap roadside motel. By late afternoon the following day, she was past Atlanta, heading toward the Tennessee line. Scenery was great and traffic light. She hummed along with a Cole Porter tune on her CD player, watching a big Caddie coming up behind her. Fast.

"Who does that jerk think he is, Mario Andretti?" she muttered.

The highway wound its way through some very mountainous terrain with steep drop-offs and sharp turns. Definitely not the place for a big luxury sedan to be doing ninety. "Your funeral, buddy," she said as the Caddie pulled abreast of her. She slowed to let him pass as they approached a beaut of a curve.

But he didn't pass. Instead the black sedan started to crowd her, veering dangerously over the line into her lane. A quick glance at its right side showed scrapes and flecks of white paint. "Shit!" she gritted out, punching the accelerator.

All the wiggle room available to her right was a couple of feet of berm and then a flimsy guardrail. The drop-off below was a minimum of fifty feet. She could easily have outdistanced the heavy car on the uphill grade with her specially modified engine if not for the wicked curve coming up much too fast. But the Caddie driver's intent was clear, even though the tinted windows hid him from view. This bozo was out to finish the job he'd begun the preceding day.

"Uncle Dec, I hope you weren't exaggerating when you explained what this suspension can take," she said, along with a short prayer as she cut the wheel sharply and tromped the gas pedal again. Her speedometer approached triple digits. She'd left the Caddie behind but he was closing once more. If she dared to slow down to negotiate the curve, he could rear-end her and blast the van through the railing. Sam and the Econoline would fly over the edge like a Canaveral rocket.

But the landing would be a lot rougher.

She felt the van's two left wheels leave the ground as she entered the sharpest angle of the curve. Sam literally leaned to the left as she held the accelerator steady going into the final turn. When the wheels hit the pavement again and the van surged straight ahead up the road, she murmured, "Thank you Uncle Dec. Who'd a thought St. Jude was a mechanic?"

The Caddie was dropping back quickly when she checked her side-view mirror. Too far away to get a plate number, which would no doubt be as bogus as the one on the Olds. She felt the adrenaline rush begin to fade and took several deep breaths, calming her jangled nerves. It had been a lousy twenty-four hours.

At least she didn't have her usual scalding cup of joe between her legs, she considered philosophically. Now that would've been a really painful way to touch up her bikini line. She tried the cell as soon as she saw a tower on a nearby mountaintop. Dialing 911 she was patched through to the local highway patrol. Somehow Sam had a gut feeling that the black Caddie with its incriminating exchange of paint would be long gone before they could spot it.

On impulse, she dialed Matt. "Hi sweetie... Oh, no,

nothing much. I'm about halfway to St. Louis… Yeah, should get there tomorrow. Just wondering if you've had time to check out Winchester or Reicht yet… No, no particular reason… What do you mean, 'something's wrong'? Nothing's wrong," she replied, crossing her fingers on the steering wheel and the cell.

If Matt knew two more attempts had been made on her life, he'd go ballistic and protective all at once. Then he'd fly to St. Louis and mess up her retrieval. If she only knew what was going on, she could handle it. So she omitted a few pertinent details…okay, she lied to him.

Matt gave her the info he'd dug up. "Haven't had time to get beyond the society stuff, pure PR fluff on 'Roman Numeral.' He's on every civic board and committee from here to Tallahassee. Lots of political clout. Reicht's a different matter. Found some interesting dirt on him right off—but then you might not think so."

"Huh?" Sam responded to his voice on the other end of the line.

"Seems our boy's being investigated by your heroes, the IRS," he said with a sarcastic chuckle.

Sam pathologically hated the IRS. They had audited her twice in the past five years. It seemed some of her "retrieval expenses" didn't meet their criteria and she'd had to cough up a couple of small fines. To Sam, fines were like parking tickets. No such thing as a "small one." "Bloodsuckers. You're right, it could make me like the guy a little. What malfeasance is he supposed to have committed?"

"Can't get Ida Kleb to say but I'm working on her."

"Ida Kleb?" she echoed with an incredulous laugh. "Shouldn't that be Rosa Kleb?"

"You mean the KGB agent from the James Bond movies?" he asked. "Fits the little troll to a tee. All she needs is the poisoned knife sticking out from the toe of her shoe when she kicks you."

"Sounds charming. But I have complete faith in your way with the ladies. Find out what Reicht's up to. Maybe he's just a tad careless with his records. His office was a bigger mess than mine."

"Not possible. That stockpiled warehouse at the end of *Raiders of the Lost Ark* isn't a bigger mess than your office, Sam. And you have more stuff stashed inside."

"You're a funny man, Granger. Oughta go on Letterman." She cut the transmission, saying, "Call me if you turn up anything new."

If the good doctor was stiffing the Infernal Revenue, she could care less, but there could be more to it or to poor Farley's civic-minded father. But both men stood to gain if she quietly brought the kid back for treatment. That's what Winchester was paying her to do. A better bet was Scruggs. He and young Winchester were living large if the credit info she'd received was accurate. For certain she'd like to know where he'd spent those seven missing years and if he had any pals with an affinity for big cars and reckless driving.

The sun was a big gold ball centered just above the gleaming silver of the Gateway Arch when Sam crossed the Poplar Street Bridge over the Mississippi and entered downtown St. Louis. The traffic was horrendous and everyplace she looked, orange construction site barrels were either lined up or knocked aside as commuters made their headlong dash during rush hour. The place resembled a life-size pinball machine.

"Just like Miami, only fronting a river instead of an ocean," she muttered, dodging a barrel that a car in the oncoming lane had nudged in her direction. The van hit a pothole so deep she felt the jarring travel from her tailbone clear up to her front teeth.

Yep, just like Miami. Once on city streets, she glanced at her map, getting her bearings while stopped at a red light. The city's convention center was located a couple of blocks north.

She navigated up Washington and immediately figured parking might be an issue. But she was certainly in the right place. A huge neon marquee with bold red letters running across it proclaimed, WELCOME TO SPACECON XIV!! Farley and his dad had something in common—Roman numerals. How sweet. She found a parking lot and paid the extortionist at the booth, only willing to part with a sawbuck because it went on the expense account.

The price of admission nearly choked her, but Sam coughed up her credit card and accepted the three-day pass. It might take her that long to find her target in a crowd this big. The enormous hall was filled with several thousand Spacies. Oh, and were they ever! Maybe bringing Matt might not have been such a bad idea. He understood this aberrant behavior, liked it even. He'd assured her that physicians, attorneys, business executives and other successful professionals actually attended *Space Quest* Cons.

Looking at some of the middle-aged bodies and listening to educated accents, she was inclined to believe it must be true, but the costumes! Reemulans with pointed ears and superior scowls mingled with turtle-foreheaded Klingoffs carrying katliffs—dangerous curved blades with points on both ends. The damned things were big enough to slice and dice a mastodon.

One enormous lizardlike creature covered with glistening scales shambled along the aisles like a malevolent Barney, only green instead of purple. But the scariest of all were the junkyard rejects decked out with wires and pieces of glass protruding from bodies encased in metallic suits. She glanced around and found a relatively normal-looking kid dressed in an Eastley Masher Spacefleet ensign's uniform. He was selling Klingoff "blood milk" steins. "What are those guys?" she whispered.

He looked at her as if she'd asked what year it was, but then again, most of these people probably thought it was the twenty-third century, so who gave a flip? "Cybs. You know, Cyber organisms," he enunciated slowly. At her still-puzzled expression, he elaborated, "They're part human but integrated into the Cyber Collective. Enhanced cognitive abilities and superior strength."

Yeah. Pretty hard to tell who was on or off his meds in a joint like this. *Granger, I can't believe you were ever this much of a geek.* And to think he didn't understand baseball. Or car engines!

"I am one of the Folean Web. Would you care to link with me?" a short, stocky guy dressed like an oversize Pillsbury Doughboy asked, ogling her breasts.

"How'd you like me to tie your link in a big fat knot?" she muttered, shoving past him. At least a guy making a pass was normal behavior, even if he did it sci-fi style. Then again, maybe he hadn't asked what she thought he had. Who knew? These people were all nuts. Made Halloween on Lincoln Avenue in Miami Beach seem like a Republican convention.

She scanned the program issued at the entrance and tried to figure out where Farley Winchester might be. If he wore his Confederation uniform, he'd be a cinch to ID, but she'd have to walk her feet flat to locate him. The best course was to access registration information.

"Frobisher, help me, buddy." He could hack the info in seconds. She dialed her cell, leaving a message on his machine, explaining what she needed. Fro had had a crush on her since they attended St. Stanislaus in sixth grade. If he didn't come through, she'd have to wander the aisles of this menagerie for the next three days—maybe get carved up by a katliff or eaten by a Borne.

On that gloomy note, she doggedly set out again, cruising the next aisle where a white furry creature sporting long tentacles on his-its head conferred with a pair of pointy-eared Vulcants. Matt had explained the difference between Vulcants and Reemulans. She felt proud of herself for remembering.

Emboldened by her crash course, she smiled at the Vulcant and said conversationally, "Nice makeup job."

He stiffened and raised one eyebrow, inspecting her with disdain. "This is not 'makeup,' madam. The plastic surgeon charged me two thousand apiece to reshape my ears and a thousand for the rebrow work. I can assure you I am a true Vulcant," he said in a cultivated voice.

Sam nodded. "Whatever you say, mister." Oops, did one call Vulcants mister?

She scooted off fast, melting into the crowd but still feeling the Vulcant's icy stare following her. *I thought only Dobermans and boxers got their ears docked!* She wondered if the surgeon had shortened a tail on the guy while he was busy cutting. This scenario was starting to get to her, but a job was a job. She had to find Farley and get him out of here before someone grafted a tentacle to him—or worse.

"The only thing I can figure is that they registered under assumed names." Ethan Frobisher's voice came over the line sounding distinctly frustrated. He didn't like coming up empty when he hacked. "No one named Farley Winchester or Elvis Scruggs is registered for the con."

Sam tapped her toe on the cement floor, trying to think while a kaleidoscope of creatures paraded by. Some sort of laser show complete with fake explosions vibrated through the huge center. She held her free hand over her opposite ear and spoke into her cell. "Is there an official convention hotel? From what I could see, there are a dozen places around here."

"That's an easy one. The Holiday Inn Select and the Renaissance St. Louis Suites are both listed," Fro replied, almost panting his pleasure at being able to supply an answer.

If Sam had read the program closely, she could've found this out for herself, but she had to throw him a bone. "Say, Fro…you aren't…naw, never mind."

"A Spacer?" he replied, figuring that was her question. "Yes, I really dig the shows, especially the original episodes. The science is weak, of course. Worf drive could never work that way, but the philosophical issues they explore—"

"Uh, I know, Fro. Matt agrees with you." The minute she said it, Sam could've bitten her tongue. She knew how jealous of her husband Ethan Frobisher had become. She didn't need to rub salt.

But he surprised her. "Way cool! I'm happy for you, Samantha. Sounds as if you found an intelligent guy after all."

On some issues. But she wasn't about to discuss her and Matt's divergence of opinion about *Space Quest* or her quest for Aunt Claudia's money. She thanked him and signed off, then checked her program guide. The Holiday Inn was closer to the America's Center, but the Renaissance offered more luxurious accommodations. Farley and Elvis would go for the high end.

Loudspeakers were blaring that the con was closing for the night and lights were blinking the ten-minute warning. The crowd had thinned. Sam watched the swarms of what she'd loosely term humanity filing out of the big convention center. Other than the Confederation's Earth officers, no one was even vaguely recognizable, thanks to latex masks, complexions dyed every hue from maroon to bright green, padded costumes, even additional appendages in some cases.

"And let's not forget the ones with antennae or wires," she muttered. How the hell was she going to find Farley in the middle of the madness? She only had two more days.

Then an idea hit her. The lure of a big payday always brought out a real creative streak. Sam walked into the warm evening air and headed to the parking lot to retrieve her van before that pit-stop pirate charged her for another day. By the time she reached the Econoline, the place was so deserted she could have heard a pin drop.

But what she heard instead was the sound of footsteps dashing up behind her.

Chapter 6

She'd had to leave her .38 and the stun gun in the van because of metal detectors at the America's Center. Damn! Sam whirled around, crouching, prepared to use fists and feet to do some serious hurt to her attackers. At the last second she pulled her punch. They were midgets, under four feet tall, and looked like oversize balls of brown cotton candy.

"Sam, don't you recognize us?" the taller of the two piped up as the smaller one behind her started jumping up and down, clapping her hands and asking, "What are you doing here?"

Then Sam saw an adult figure puffing to catch up to them…as usual. "Jenny?" she asked incredulously, recognizing the voices of Jenny Baxter's two daughters, Tiffany and Melanie. A plump woman dressed in one of those uncomfortable spandex suits complete with high jackboots and a fake weapon strapped to her waist, nodded.

"Hi, Sam," she said, tugging on the inseam of the unflattering pants as she drew near.

Sam looked down at the taller kid swathed in what she could now see was brown fur. "Tiff?" Then turned to the littler one. "Mellie? What are you?"

"Oh, you silly, what are you doing at a *Space Quest* con if you don't know we're Dribbles?" Mellie asked.

"You know, the little furry animals that keep making more until Captain Turk's ship is filled with them?" Tiff supplied in the same tone of voice that a person might use to explain why woodpeckers don't like concrete posts.

"And I'm Harriett Mudd, the lovable but unscrupulous space merchant who brought them aboard," Jenny said brightly.

Sometimes Sam thought Jenny's voice was the only thing bright about her. "Uh, yeah, I get it. You're big Spacer fans, right?" She groaned inwardly. On the case where she'd met Matt, Jenny and her two dragon kids had been nothing but trouble, nearly getting Matt killed by the Russian mob. "I thought you and your sister were living in San Diego," she said.

"Oh, we are, but the girls begged to come to the con."

"Is it safe? I mean, you know…" Sam groped for words, not wanting to bring up the girls' father, who'd kidnapped them two years earlier.

"Oh, my ex got caught passing bad checks in Salt Lake. He's doing three to five in a Utah state pen," Jenny said blithely.

"Are you here to snatch somebody?" Mellie asked eagerly.

Great. All Sam needed were Larry, Curley and Mo bollixing up her retrieval as they had with Matt. "Nothing I can tell you about," she replied, trying to think up an excuse to keep them out of it. "But I am attending the con. Er, it's research for a case back in Miami."

"If you're going to snatch somebody at the con, you'd

better wear a costume or you'll never get close to whoever it is," Tiff said, not fooled for a minute by Sam's denial.

Sage wisdom from an eight-year-old. "I guess I could rent one," Sam replied uncertainly.

Jenny shook her head. "Every good costume in town's already been taken, but I have a great one for you. Why don't you come back to our suite at the Renaissance and we can fix you up? Oh, if I was you I'd leave your car parked here. During the day it's almost impossible to find a vacancy and the hotel's just up the street. We have plenty of room. My sister insisted on paying because she and her son had to cancel at the last minute."

What the hell? It was where she was headed anyway and there'd be no dodging their interference if they ran into her later and figured that she was after a guest. "Okay, I appreciate it," Sam said as they started walking. "Say, what kind of costume do you have? I sometimes have to move quick and those…" She paused, gesturing to the girls covered head to toe in fuzz. "Well, anything like that would stop me."

Jenny laughed but before she could explain, Mellie blurted out, "Mommy thought she looked fat in the outfit."

"Believe me, it won't keep you from kicking ass," Tiff said cheerfully.

"Young lady! I won't have such language," Jenny replied with a genuine bite in her voice. "You apologize to Mrs. Granger at once."

To Sam's surprise, the girl meekly bowed what looked to be the top end of her "dribble" and said contritely, "I apologize for using a bad word."

Now wasn't the time to explain that she hadn't changed her name when she married Matthew Granger. "Apology accepted," she said with a grin.

"Tiff's being good because Mommy says she won't take

us on the Questar battle simulation day after tomorrow if we don't behave," Mellie piped up.

That explained it, sort of. Whatever a Questar was.

Ida Kleb was a wiry little woman with a bulldog's face and gorilla-size hands that looked capable of snapping the neck of anyone who crossed her. She wore a perpetual scowl and her gray eyes cut like lasers. No one in the IRS messed with her. Matt wasn't about to break that rule. He stood in the door of her cramped little office, looking from Kleb to her austere surroundings. All the papers in the room were lined up with razor-edged neatness as if even inanimate objects understood her demands.

"You, again, Mr. Granger. I've already told you, our investigation of Dr. Reicht is confidential. Go find something else to write about for the *Herald*."

"I'm not here on a story. I thought maybe you and I could have an exchange of information about the good doc." Her eyes narrowed to tiny slits, seeming to move as if she were a Cylon Centurion from the original television series *Battlestar Gallactica*. Matt smiled inwardly. *Guess Sam was right. I'm still a geek.*

"Any information you possess about Dr. Reicht you are obligated to give the Internal Revenue Service." Kleb stared up at him as she walked around the desk. Despite the disparity in their heights, she was utterly undaunted.

He couldn't help looking down at the rounded toes of her sensible shoes, wondering about a poison dagger for an instant before he replied, "Whatever happened to First Amendment rights for the press?"

"Nowadays, it doesn't have any," she shot back, standing almost toe-to-toe with him.

He refused to back away, but he did raise his hands in mock

surrender. "Look, I just want to help. He's involved in a case my wife's working on and I'm looking out for her safety. I found out a few things that might help your investigation…if you help me, it might protect Sam."

"You go first," she said.

"You play chess?"

She turned and shuffled a stack of papers, straightening them even though they didn't need it. "I don't have time for hobbies, Mr. Granger." Then, crossing her arms, she placed her big hands around her elbows and waited him out.

"Could I at least sit down?" he asked, eyeing a battered chair in front of her desk. Ida nodded and returned to her own counterpart behind it. Matt was stalling, figuring the odds of getting anything useful out of this cagey dame. Might as well go for it. "I did a little digging through a source with ties to the drug scene." She might buy it since he'd done a big exposé on Russian and Colombian mobsters last year.

"Go on," she prompted, tapping a sharpened pencil impatiently on a blotter.

"The doc's been a naughty boy. He couldn't disclose all of his income the last couple of years because it's drug related. He's got a lot of very rich patients with expensive recreational habits—illegal recreational habits." He watched her for a reaction. The best she gave was one minute twitch of an eyebrow.

She tossed the pencil across the desk to cover it up. "We knew that, of course. You're wasting my time."

"I don't think you did."

"Give me the names of these patients."

"Tell me what tipped you to go after him first," he countered.

After sleeping poorly on the Hide-A-Bed in the sitting room of Jenny's suite, Sam had arisen with two kids jumping up and down, yelling at each other while their mother entered the room carrying the promised costume. Sam took the outfit and headed to the bathroom to change into it. When she walked out the door and looked into the full-length mirror across the room, she flinched. "I look like a hooker from South Beach," she said, then could've bitten her tongue.

"What's a hooker, Mrs. Granger?" Mellie asked.

"Sorry, you'd think I didn't grow up in a house with six younger kids," Sam said to Jenny, not about to admit that her street-tough south-Boston brothers knew a lot more than that when they were Mellie's age.

"A hooker is a bad lady," Tiff explained, although from her expression, her mother and Sam figured she really wasn't sure.

"But Lt. O'Hara isn't bad," Mellie said.

"I didn't mean it that way. It's just that this getup's uncomfortable." Sam tugged at the spandex miniskirt and tried to shift the plunging neckline of the uniform so it didn't reveal quite so much of her "best assets," as Matt liked to call them.

"You can see why I decided the costume wasn't for me," Jenny said with a blush. "The skirt fit me like a girdle. I don't know what I was thinking when that rental clerk talked me into it, but I still thought my sister was coming and Tess would look great in it—just like you do. Harriett Mudd's pants and shirt worked a lot better for me."

"Well, at least I can move in it," Sam conceded. The low boots that came with the outfit had small heels but not enough to bother her if she had to sprint after Farley. *I'll probably catch pneumonia in that air-conditioned hall.* But with any luck, she could locate young Winchester and be back in her nurse's scrubs, transporting her "patient" home by afternoon. All she had to do was give Jenny and her girls the slip.

"How about room service for breakfast?" Jenny asked. The girls immediately chorused agreement.

"Er, I don't do breakfast. I'll catch something later," Sam said.

"Breakfast is the most important meal of the day," Tiff parroted like the merit-badge-winning Girl Scout she was.

"You're right, kiddo, but if I'm gonna stay in this uniform, maybe I'd better skip it just this once. I'll see you on the floor, okay?"

She left as Tiff insisted she'd have waffles and Mellie demanded French toast. Their mother fecklessly insisted they have yogurt or eggs for protein. Sam knew Jenny'd lose. She always did.

The outrageous Lt. O'Hara costume worked to her advantage. When she slithered up and leaned over the registration counter, the young clerk's eyeballs bulged out of their sockets and his tongue practically lolled on his keyboard. After flashing Farley's photo, she had her "cousin's" suite number in a flash. But when she arrived at the room on the fourteenth floor, which was really the thirteenth, her luck ran in that direction. A maid was already busy making up the beds.

Farley and Elvis had departed for an early start at the con. "What were they dressed like? Could you describe their outfits?" she asked the smiling young woman with the fresh-scrubbed face of a kid working her way through college.

Cyndi, as her name tag identified her, rolled her eyes. "I loved *Alien* and *Lord of the Rings,* but these guys are way out there, if you know what I mean—oh, I didn't intend any offense," she hastily added, looking at Sam's skimpy "uniform." "Er, are they family?" she asked, dubious.

Sam grinned. "Not a chance in hell. One's a car thief, the other's a druggie."

That alarming news oddly seemed to reassure Cyndi. *Kid must really need this job bad.*

"Well, the shorter one had this icky bulging forehead and a long brown fright wig, big bushy eyebrows and thick, dark makeup. The taller one wore white fur but he didn't look like the Easter bunny, believe me. Had these antennae sprouting out of his forehead and extra arms—kinda like a big hairy white spider."

Sam paged through her memory and recalled the photo plates from the reference book she'd brought. "A Klingoff and a Pandorian. Great. Two of the most elaborate costumes. I'll never recognize them on the floor," she muttered. "Do they ever come back to the room to chill, have lunch, anything like that?" she asked.

"I don't know. I work the early shift so I can get to SLU for classes starting at ten. But you might ask Tilda. She's the floor super and keeps a pretty close eye on what happens with the guests."

Sam thanked Cyndi and went in search of Tilda, who was as crazed as most of the staff was coping with hordes of people in otherworldly costumes roaming the hallways. All she learned about Farley and Elvis was that they usually returned to their suite and ordered room service around midnight.

Since her odds of locating her target in full Klingoff regalia were less likely than winning the lottery, Sam decided to wait until he and his Pandorian pal returned to their room that night. In the meanwhile, she had escaped Jenny and her girls. They meant well, but this was business and she couldn't risk having a pair of out of control kids and their noodle-kneed mom get in the way of her earning Roman Numeral's hefty fee.

With any luck—and heaven knew she was overdue for some—she'd have Farley in custody and be all the way to the Tennessee border by dawn's early light. Making sure they were gone, Sam used the key they'd given her and slipped into the suite. Her first impulse was to leave the costume behind along with the hasty goodbye note she scrawled on hotel stationary, but she reconsidered.

What if she blew the snatch and had to go back on the floor? No need to stand out. She pulled a wad of cash from her wallet and carefully counted out what she thought was a generous rental deposit. Once she had Farley back in Miami, she'd figure a way to get a receipt from Jenny and add it to Roman Numeral's bill. Stuffing her personal belongings in her travel bag, she headed back to her van.

Just as she was stashing her gear, her cell rang. Recognizing Matt's number, she picked up. "Hi sweetie," she answered brightly.

"How's St. Louis?"

She looked at the cloudless sky. It was 10:00 a.m. and already the heat was starting to fuse spandex to her skin. At least there wouldn't be much of it to peel away. "Hot, hot, oh, and did I mention hot?"

"Got a little info on Reicht." He explained about the illegal prescriptions the doc was peddling. "He's a supplier for a lot of rich clients, according to my sources."

"Which we know are always impeccable. The IRS nail him for not reporting illegal income?" she asked. "God forbid they should care about his contacts with drug dealers."

"She was pretty closemouthed, but I don't think Kleb knew about the drug thing yet. They started investigating him after stumbling across some large money transfers out of country."

"He could be a drug dealer," Sam said, digesting the surprising news. She paused a moment; then a thought occurred to her. "Say, you don't think he might be blackmailing patients? All kinds of dirty little secrets the rich and crazy in Miami might be spilling to their shrink." But she reconsidered. "Nah, somehow, I don't think that fits. Oh, he probably does what your sources said, slipping padded scripts to his patients, but that wouldn't be enough money to blip the IRS radar."

"Ah, Samantha, great minds work along the same courses. Guess our meeting was fate."

"Only if Aunt Claudia is its agent. She paid me to put you on ice, Granger," she reminded him.

"It was a lot more complicated than that," he reminded her, then headed off another argument about his aunt's money by saying, "What's going on there? Any sightings yet?"

"You ever try to tell one Klingoff from another? They look as much alike as Mary-Kate and Ashley, only with turtle shells glued to their foreheads."

"That would be tough. An international con like this one must draw thousands. You might have to wait until its over and they're out of costume," he said.

"No way. I have their room number. Tonight I'll be on the road with Farley in the back of the van all safe and secure. But I won't turn him over to Reicht…or to his loving father right away. The old man doesn't want the kid anyway. I need a good shrink."

"I've told you that ever since we met, Sam."

"This from a guy who married his kidnapper. I'll ask Pat to find me a legit doc to take care of the kid."

Matt snorted. "I've met Patowski. He'll suggest a state asylum and a lobotomy."

"Yeah, you have a point," she admitted grudgingly. "Okay, you find Farley a doc. Deal?"

"Right. Oh, and Sam, don't do anything crazier than usual. Deal?"

Chapter 7

The day turned out about as bad as she imagined. Her feet ached after hours of walking on the hard concrete floors, dodging extraterrestrials and ignoring leering stares from males of various species. No matter if they were from Mars or the edge of the Milky Way, men were appallingly predictable. Sam had a near brush with Jenny and her girls later that afternoon and decided it would be safer to wait for Farley and Elvis at their room.

She changed out of her costume in the back of the van. Considering the temperature was only slightly lower in the Econoline than the sunny side of Mercury, pulling a thigh-hugging spandex skirt down her sweat-soaked legs was a better workout than an hour on a judo mat and a soak in a sauna.

Visions of a cool shower almost made her pop for a hotel room, but if she ended up not turning the kid over to his father, she might be out a sizable bundle. Grunting as she put on a fresh tee and shorts, she muttered, "Once I get back in the air-conditioning, I'll be all right." As for anybody who got too close to her, well, they were on their own.

Who would have thought St. Louis could be as hot as Miami? The long summer day finally dimmed into hazy twilight. Sam caught a quick bite at a greasy spoon a few blocks down from the convention center and then killed some time using the Internet at the public library. It was as if Elvis Peter Scruggs had simply dropped off the face of the earth, then reappeared seven years later. Alien abduction? Jeez, she was starting to think like these weirdos!

She put in a call to Frobisher to see if he'd discovered anything on Scruggs, then returned to her van and dug her stun gun out of the glove compartment. After dark, she could get away with hiding it if she switched from a white to a black T-shirt, not an option during the blistering day. "Well, Sam, blastoff time," she said, heading up the street toward the hotel.

If her information was on target, Farley and Elvis should be turning in pretty soon. There was a large potted plant directly across from their room. She intended to be hiding beside it when they got off the elevator.

When she hit the hotel a large sign done in tasteful purple and green glitter paint announced Twelfth Annual Middle American Bowling League Championship. The picture of a buxom female clad in substantially less than Lt. O'Hara was pasted on the sign, her finger pointing toward the bar at the right of the lobby.

"Just what I need. Spacies armed with bowling balls!"

She headed to the elevator and the pseudo fourteenth floor. A sharp wolf whistle emanated from inside the bar as she passed it. Sam didn't pause to see if it was a Spacer or a bowler. How could you tell a bowler, anyway? The one with the bigger balls? The hallway was empty when she arrived at eleven-thirty and took her station.

After more than three quarters of an hour, she was glad she'd opted for tennies with cushioned soles. Around midnight, when her Klingoff and Pandorian had failed to appear, she knocked on the door after swiping a room service tray just set out down the hall. No one stirred inside to check through the peephole. This would have to be the night they were going to be super late.

As all sorts of worst-case scenarios started to play through her head, she heard the fire exit at the end of the hall open with a sharp click. Sam crouched behind her cover and waited. A big man dressed in a cheap suit that looked as if he slept in it, turned around after closing the door soundlessly. His face needed pressing, too. It was one of those hangdog kissers that had more ruts than a washboard yet was ageless. From the way his stocky body moved, she judged him to be no more than forty.

And up to no good.

Her trained eye picked up the bulge in his jacket at once. He was carrying heat. The hairs on the back of her neck stood up and it had nothing to do with the sudden eruption of the air-conditioning vents up and down the corridor. She knew he was headed to Farley and Elvis's room. Yep. She debated going after him before he got inside but he was armed and her stunner had a distinctly shorter range. She couldn't make it twenty feet down the hall before he'd hear her.

Sam cursed her stupidity for not bringing the .38 after two attempts to stop her en route here. All she could do was wait and let this play out. Her best hope was that she could divert Farley and Elvis when they came up on the elevator.

She watched him pull a small narrow instrument resembling a dentist's tool from his pocket and insert it in the door lock. A pro. It opened in barely a flash and he slipped inside the darkened room. She knew damn well this bozo wasn't there to turn down the bedcovers and lay out chocolates. Then one of the elevators pinged. "Please let it be them!"

Before the prayer could pass her lips, a second and third elevator stopped. Was the whole floor of guests returning to their rooms at the same time? The first two elevators disgorged what looked like an entire bowling league, dressed in striped shirts and bowler hats. *No honkin' way.* Sam groaned. They were stone drunk, singing off-key as they swayed hither and yon down the hall, most of them coming in her direction. Several of them were armed with heavy leather cases containing their weapons of choice.

But that was not the worst part. The elevator farthest away from her carried only two guys. One was a head taller than the other and they were dressed in grotesque Klingoff and Pandorian gear. They remained well behind the rowdy crowd of drunks. The taller one kept a hand on the shoulder of the little fellow, whispering what Sam imagined was a grain of common sense in his ear so he slowed down rather than attract the attention of the Derby League Bowlers, as their hats and shirts proclaimed.

Sam debated whether to try slipping past them or remain in hiding until they filtered into their rooms. No way could she allow her unsuspecting pair to stumble into the goon waiting for them. Unfortunately, a hard core of the revelers decided to hold an impromptu songfest in the hallway between her and her targets.

More unfortunately, one of the stragglers caught sight of her through the greenery and staggered her way, clutching a bowling bag in one fat fist. "Hey, lookee, guys. Our own persh'nal bowlin' trophy." He whistled again.

Sam remembered the off-key sound. The jerk who'd spotted her from the bar. Before she could say "Mickey, transpond me up," he had her cornered by the potted plant and his companions were shambling around him to see what would happen next.

That was when the cagey Elvis made his move. He and Farley started to ease along the wall toward their room, which was closer to the elevators than to her. No one but she was paying the slightest attention to them. Sam tried shoving the drunk away but unless she really wanted to hurt him, she had a better chance of uprooting a sequoia.

"I'm not your trophy, pally, so back off," she snarled, hooking her foot behind his knee and buckling it. Unlucky for her, he tried to regain his balance by seizing hold of her T-shirt. She went down with him.

Sam quickly rolled to her feet, mad enough to give him a sharp kick in a place where he'd feel it the most, but she didn't need an assault charge lodged with the St. Louis PD, so checked the impulse. He lay spread-eagle, shaking his head as the hallway spun around him and his friends guffawed and cheered.

"Hey, lady, that was some move!"

"Way to go, beautiful!"

"Who'da though a girl could take Griff down like that?" a third said on a loud beer belch.

Sam didn't stay to enjoy their plaudits but started to move toward Farley and Elvis, who were now unlocking their door. But before she could get clear, her woozy lothario had miraculously gotten to his feet, no doubt with a little help from his friends. Once again he seized hold of her shirt. Dammit! What was this—the best two out of three?

With a particularly nasty oath she'd learned from Uncle Dec when his rig was held at a weigh station on the Pennsylvania Turnpike, Sam whirled around to face him. Her shirt ripped but she was so furious she didn't even notice. She just grabbed the bowling bag from the guy who'd run up beside him and hurled it at her attacker's foot with the dead aim only lifelong practice affords.

Under her uncle Dec's tutelage, Sam had bowled her first three hundred game when she was twelve years old.

Griff let out a howl and tried to raise the injured hoof and wrap his big hands around it. She knew she could have broken his bones but didn't particularly care. The goon in Farley's room might do far worse to her client. The Derby Bowler toppled backward into his buddies, who by now had figured out that this was no longer fun and games.

"Give it up, Griff," one said.

"We better get him ta 'is room...or the hosh'pital," a second one slurred.

Sam was clear of them and closing on the door where Farley and Elvis had entered only moments ago. She could hear sounds of a struggle and cursed again. Of course, the door had locked automatically when they'd entered. She pulled her own small tool from her fanny pack and had the lock open almost as quickly as the thug. Holding the stunner ready, she stepped inside, flattening the door against the wall to be certain no surprises would come from that direction as she swept the room.

One large table lamp cast a pale glow across a wide sitting room filled with upscale hotel furnishings and one furry Pandorian lying across the center of the floor with a red stain oozing through one of his antennae. "Farley?" she called out, looking down the hallway to the bedrooms and bath.

Elvis groaned and tried to sit up, holding his injured head in his hands. Then Sam saw the sliding door to the balcony was ajar. Warm sticky heat poured inside. Practically leaping over Elvis, she yanked the handle to the side and looked out. She could see the thug with Farley slung over his shoulder vanishing over the side of the balcony railing three units down.

Not only big and good with his hands, but fast, too. Narrow

metal rails divided each suite's share of balcony space. Sam took them like hurdles until she reached the end—a fire escape ladder. She looked down at the parking lot and some carefully landscaped shrubbery and trees designed to conceal it. The big guy carried the slight youth as if he weighed no more than a feather pillow. He was already halfway to the ground.

Sam debated. If she started after him, he might drop Farley to his death in order to escape. She held back until he was close enough to the pavement that the fall wouldn't be fatal, then climbed over the edge and started half climbing, half sliding down the rungs the way she'd been trained during her stint as a police-paramedic. She only hoped the darkness and her fast movements would keep the kidnapper from hitting her with the piece she knew he carried once he was on the ground.

She lucked out. He jumped the last rungs and landed, pivoting and making a run across the crowded lot without looking back at his pursuer. In the distance an engine revved to life and started wending down the narrow aisles toward the fleeing felon and his prize. Sam had to get to them before the getaway vehicle.

Dammit, I'm not the one carrying a hundred twenty pounds of dead weight! She jumped the ladder from six feet and hit the ground at a dead run. The trip down the ladder must have taken some of the wind out of the abductor's sails because he slowed and she gained some yardage. But all she had was the stunner—paralyzing at close range, but useless until she closed the gap.

She let out a blood-curdling screech and yelled Farley's name, then "Stop, police!" at the top of her lungs, holding the stunner up as if it were really a firearm. By this time, a dark-colored van had pulled alongside the goon, its back doors open. Still holding the kid on one broad shoulder with his left hand, the kidnapper pulled the gun from under his jacket and fired at Sam.

The bullet whizzed by her ear, a narrow miss owing only to Farley's regaining consciousness. The kid started wriggling like a Dribble, throwing off his captor's aim. Sam dived for cover, then darted from car to car as bullets pinged and ricocheted around the lot. The thug tried to toss the boy inside the vehicle but Farley delivered a groin kick and received a swift drop to the pavement as his reward.

Sam dived closer as the thug jumped in the back of the van and yelled to the driver, "Run over the little bastard, then get the hell out of here!"

He closed the doors as the driver put the engine in reverse and aimed for where Farley lay, too stunned by his injuries to move. Sam made one clean leap and yanked at his inert body, pulling it from beneath the wheels an instant before he became Klingoff roadkill. With the boy in a death grip, she rolled them both beneath a big SUV, praying the kidnappers would give up.

Lights and people filling the balconies around the parking area made the decision for them. The van screeched forward, burning rubber to escape. From her cover beneath the SUV Sam tried to catch plate numbers but couldn't make them out as the van turned left and flew out onto a one-way street. It was some dark color, an older model Plymouth or Dodge, but she couldn't be sure.

Sam debated calling 911 on her cell but thought better of it when Farley began to groan again. If the police took him and Elvis to the hospital and questioned them, the boy would certainly be turned over to his father, who would leave him to Reicht's tender mercies. And she'd be out her fee. No way was any of that happening.

"Come on, Farley, let's get you to the E.R. and see what needs fixing," she said as she pulled off the rubber mask covering the boy's head. No signs of blood on him. That was always good. "Time to wake up, Farley," she said, knowing there was no way she could flip him over one shoulder and lug him away like that gunsel had.

"What… Where am I?" he said, eyelashes fluttering as he stared into Sam's face. His dazed expression reminded her of a deer caught in headlights. He had big brown eyes and a scraggly attempt at a beard darkening his jawline unevenly.

"You're gonna be okay, but just to be sure—"

"Where's El? That guy hit him over the head."

"That guy tried to run over you with a van. Right now I'd say that's a bigger problem."

He muttered something Sam couldn't quite make out as she helped him to his feet. Then he looked around and seemed to get his bearings. "We're in the parking lot."

Good. No addled brain—at least any more addled than it had been before the abduction. "Yeah, we are. You remember anything about the guy who tried to snatch you?" she asked.

"Wow! Wait till I tell El! His disguise was really good. He looked human."

"Nah, those kind of thugs are really a lower life form. Closer to muscular amoebas," she replied soothingly, trying to lead him toward the other end of the lot where she'd parked her van earlier that afternoon. How far was the nearest E.R.? She had a map and guidebook in the glove compartment.

Then she noticed the kid had started to look as if he'd just had a fabulous adventure instead of a brush with death. He was actually grinning. "Hey, you could've ended up as flattened fauna," she reminded him.

"I know. He's on to me." Farley tried to pull something from his pants pocket as he babbled on. "I'm really a Confederation agent, but you must know that. You have to be one, too, or else you wouldn't have been sent to rescue me."

Talk about being a few screwdrivers short of a Mr. Good-wrench set, hoo boy. "I'm not—" Sam bit her tongue and stopped. No sense getting the kid worked up so he wouldn't go voluntarily with her. She had to have him checked out by a doc before she dared use any kind of force to subdue him. Better to play along. "Yeah, guess you have me pegged."

"Who the hell are you?" a hostile voice with a pronounced panhandle drawl asked.

Sam looked from Farley to Elvis P. Scruggs, who was standing directly in their path. He'd removed his antennaed headgear and his right temple was covered with dried blood. He did not look happy to see her.

Chapter 8

"El, this is…" Farley looked at Sam as if realizing he didn't know her name.

"I'm using the name Sam Ballanger," she said, wondering if Scruggs was armed. In spite of his hostile glare, he looked barely older than the kid. But bigger, a lot bigger, with long greasy black hair that partially obscured his face, framing it à la Mr. Presley in his prime. Thick eyebrows curved around small, crafty eyes that missed little. What looked like a collagen-enhanced lower lip and a straight jawline added to the "Presley persona."

By the time Sam had decided Scruggs wasn't armed, Farley had his ID pulled out of his wallet and was flashing it in front of her, talking a mile a minute about the Klingoff conspiracy against the Confederation. "I'm an ensign and Elvis is a lieutenant. What's your rank?"

Knowing she couldn't pass ID muster, Sam said, "You shouldn't be carrying that. What if those guys had stolen it?"

"You're right. That's probably how they nabbed Leila last week. They had stolen ID. Being a Spacefleet officer, she'd know a fake from the real thing, wouldn't she, El?"

Sam studied him to gauge his reaction to Farley's nonsense. He nodded slowly, as if considering the possibility.

"Sure could be. Farley saw Commander Satterwaite transponded to a Pandorian vessel last week," Scruggs replied with a straight face.

"That's why Elvis is in Pandorian disguise. He's been trying to find out what they've done with her. The Pandorians have made a secret alliance with the Klingoff Empire. They're trying to conquer the Confederation."

Yeah. Gotcha. Sam figured there was only one way a street-smart guy who'd served time in juvvie would go along with this fantasy, and it wasn't to save Earth. "Say, you both look like you could use some medical attention. My van's just over there." She pointed in the general direction where she'd parked. Once they were at the E.R., she could call Pat and see about having the local cops detain Scruggs for questioning while she slipped away with Farley.

Elvis touched his hand to his injured head and winced, starting the bleeding again. "That jack—er, Klingoff really nailed me square on the noggin. You don't look so hot yourself, Far. Maybe she's right. What did you say your name and rank were, again?" he drawled, looking at Sam.

"Sam Ballanger and I'm not giving out my rank to anyone. Now, let's see how bad you're hurt."

That seemed to settle the issue as both of them followed her to her van and climbed inside. She toyed with using the stunner on Elvis, but decided against it. With a bleeding head wound, he might be injured further. Somehow, she'd have to convince Farley to split with his "lieutenant" and trust her. Putting the juice to his buddy was definitely not the way to win the kid's heart and mind.

* * *

"You know, Farley, considering that your cover's blown here in St. Louis, I think it might be a good idea if you went back to Miami with me. I could protect you. That's my prime directive," she coaxed as they waited while a doctor in the St. Louis University Hospital complex was stitching up Elvis's head wound.

They had agreed, for "security reasons," not to say anything about the abduction attempt that might land them both in custody as material witnesses. Instead, much to her relief, both Farley and Elvis produced insurance cards at the check-in and Scruggs smoothly explained that they'd been in a bar fight precipitated by some drunk making fun of *Space Quest*.

While they were busy doing that, she'd made her call to Patowski. Why couldn't she ever get in a scrape during sensible working hours? The old cop had been nasty as a poked rattlesnake when she'd awakened him, asking him to talk with his friends in the St. Louis Police Department After lots of cursing, he'd said he'd see what he could do.

It turned out to be zip so far. No cops.

Farley shook his head at Sam's suggestion to return home. Elvis, who had quietly slipped up on her from the cubicle where he'd been treated, chimed in. "Far 'n me, we drove a long way to get to this here convention."

"You drove Mr. Winchester the fourth's Jag. He told me he wants it returned immediately," she said, wondering how Scruggs would handle that curveball.

Fielding perfectly, he shot back, "Mr. W. said he was cool with us borrowin' it."

"Far" nodded agreement, then grimaced. "He did, but it's just like him to change his mind and spoil everything," the kid said petulantly.

"We got bidness and we ain't leaving till it's finished.

Remember, Leila Satterwaite was our commander. How'd you know about Mr. W's Jag anyways?" Elvis asked, oh so casually.

"All part of my job as an agent," she replied blithely. "If you borrowed the Jag, did you borrow the money, too?"

Both of them looked blankly at her.

"What money?" Scruggs asked.

"Yes, what money?" young Winchester seconded.

"The twenty thousand dollars you withdrew from one of your dad's passbook accounts," she said to Farley.

"I only took out two hundred the day we left—my allowance for the past month. My father 'forgot' to arrange for me to get it. He's done that a lot lately. We wanted some cash in case of an emergency on the road."

"You wouldn't by any chance have a withdrawal slip to prove that, would you?" Sam asked.

"Maybe, back at the hotel," the kid replied vaguely.

"What bidness is it of yours about Mr. W's car or his money? I thought you were a Confederation agent?" Elvis said, his eyes moving from Sam to Farley and back.

"Confederation agents don't steal from respectable businessmen on my watch," Sam replied.

With a crafty smirk, Elvis replied, "Oh, we got no reason to steal, do we, Far? His daddy lets Far charge anything he wants on that there credit card of his."

Scruggs might look like a kid, but Sam recognized the hard glitter in his eyes. He was light-years ahead of his young friend when it came to life experience. And, coming from a background of poverty and jail time, he knew a sweet deal when he'd latched on to one. She would have to figure a way to separate the two and knew Elvis wouldn't make it easy for her.

The best thing was to play along with the whole charade until she figured something out. Patowski's St. Louis PD connection obviously hadn't worked out. It was almost as if her old mentor had found out something about Elvis that he wasn't willing to share with her. Well, that sure wouldn't be a first.

After they got Farley checked and pronounced little the worse for his ordeal, the trio strolled back to where she'd parked her van. "Highway robbery!" she said as the electronic screen at the parking gate flashed what she had to pay to get out of the lot. "We're in the land of Jesse James, but he was an honest man compared to this. At least he used a horse and a pistol." Still muttering to herself, she paid up and asked for a receipt. Looking at her as if she were some yokel from the sticks, the yawning clerk pulled it from the machine and barely stuck his arm out of the booth. She stretched her whole body out the van window to reach the damn thing.

As they drove east down Olive Street toward the downtown area, Farley and Elvis carried on an animated conversation about the great conspiracy to destroy Earth. "The Klingoff Empire's behind it," Elvis said as if he believed it. "They're workin' with them Pandorian skunks."

"That's why we're undercover trying to infiltrate their inner circle," Farley explained. "Did you know they've been here for over a hundred years?"

"No!" Sam took her eyes from the wheel for a moment and cast an amazed glance at Farley.

"Yes! Who do you think Hitler was? Who was behind Lee Harvey Oswald? More recently—"

"Let me guess," Sam interrupted. "Osama? 9/11?"

"Now you're startin' to get the big picture," Scruggs said.

Farley nodded silently.

Her head was ringing with intergalactic conspiracy theories by the time they reached the hotel. Damn, she was going to have to pop for a room...or spend another night with Harriett Mudd and her Dribbles. At the front desk she asked for the cheapest room they had. When the clerk told her the price, Sam opted for the Dribble sisters.

As she walked Farley and Elvis to their room, Sam cautioned, "I want you to double lock this door as soon as I leave." She inspected the bath and both bedrooms, down to the closets to make sure no surprise visitors had returned to lie in wait. Satisfied that they were alone, she closed the sliding-glass door and placed the floor lock securely behind the moving frame.

"Don't open this for anyone and keep these drawn tight," she said, pulling the drapes until not a crack of light showed through from outside. "And, especially, don't open the front door, even if it looks like room service. Speaking of which, don't order it. Too easy for someone to pose as staff and get inside. Call my room in the morning and I'll come get you," she instructed.

"What if we get hungry?" Farley asked.

Sam pointed to the minifridge, filled with obscenely overpriced snacks. "Your daddy's paying. Eat anything you want."

Farley grinned like a kid in a candy store. At times, he looked more like one of the "Lost Boys" than the schizoid druggie Reicht had described. If not for his belief in an alien invasion, she wouldn't have thought of him as mentally disturbed. And she'd seen no signs of illegal drugs. But then Farley took a prescription bottle from his pocket and popped a pill after filling a tumbler with water to chase it.

"What's that?" Sam asked innocently.

"Oh, just something my doc says I have to take. I get kinda nervous when I miss one," he confessed.

She could see that the label had Reicht's name on it, but couldn't make out the name of the drug before he replaced it in his pocket. Could some of his "spaciness" come from what the good doctor was feeding the boy? Worth investigating, especially considering what Matt had told her.

Elvis, who had wandered down the hall while she was talking with Farley, returned, waving a Glock 9 mm. Her first impulse was to flatten the kid and herself on the floor, but Scruggs grinned and reassured them. "Don't you worry none, ma'am. I'll take care of Far now that I know they're on to us."

Ooookay. "You mind if I check to see if the safety's on on that thing?" she asked, reaching slowly for the Glock. He offered it willingly and she carefully took it from his big hand. Dear God, it wasn't! Clicking it in place, she handed it back. "You ever take a firearms safety course, Elvis?" she asked, suspecting the answer.

"Nope," he replied with a big grin. "Us country boys jest naturally know how ta handle guns."

"Do me a big favor, please?"

Scruggs shrugged. "What?"

"Put that cannon away now and leave it in the room tomorrow. If you set off the metal detectors at the con, the cops—or even Klingoff agents posing as cops," she quickly improvised, "could arrest you."

If only it were that simple. She'd love to see him picked up at the America's Center, leaving Farley with her, but who knew if the idiot might not shoot someone's foot off—probably hers—before they even got out of the hotel lobby in the morning.

"Sam's right, El. They have metal detectors at every entrance," Farley chimed in.

She beamed at him, then looked at Scruggs. When he nodded, she added, "And if you hear anyone trying to break in during the night, call 911, then me. No trying to shoot it out with Klingoffs or their allies. Deal?"

"Deal," Elvis said grudgingly.

After tucking them in, Sam felt as if she'd been trapped in

some weird time warp. She considered the facts. Yes, Farley believed all this *Space Quest* hooey Scruggs was feeding him while living high on young Winchester's money. But the kid might be high on more than space conspiracies if the prescription from Reicht was inappropriate. Then, too, someone else didn't want her to get her hands on Farley and return him to daddy and the doc.

That was one hell of a knot on Elvis Scruggs's head. He hadn't faked the fight with the kidnapper. If someone wanted to snatch Farley and hold him for ransom, then why try to kill the kid? She had definitely overheard that big thug yell for the driver to back over Farley. She pulled out her cell and punched in Matt's number in Miami as she rode down to Jenny's suite.

When he picked up so quickly at 3:00 a.m. she should've known it meant trouble, but it was so good to hear his voice, she wasn't thinking straight. "Hi, sweetie. Sorry to wake you but I—"

"Sam, what the hell's going on? I've been trying to reach you for the past four hours or more." He sounded cranky, not groggy.

"Oh, I had to turn off my cell so it wouldn't go off when I went after that guy breaking into Farley's room…." She cursed silently. *How could I be so dumb?* A couple of hours with that wacky kid and his gun-toting pal could melt down a polar ice cap!

"All right, Sam, I knew you were in trouble last time we talked. You know I can tell by the sound of your voice when you're lying."

He could, the rat. Even her own mother couldn't, but Matt Granger could. It was scary how he'd insinuated himself into her work and mind. Her body, fine, excellent…wonderful, in fact. But when he interfered with her job, that was another matter. She sighed. "Okay, I had a little trouble tonight…."

She gave him an extremely sanitized version of the attempted kidnapping, but he wanted more. "When we talked yesterday, something had already happened—on the road."

Uncle Dec's colorful vocabulary sprang to her lips before she could tamp it down. Matt just waited her out until she explained about the flat tire and the Tennessee road chase. "So, someone doesn't want me to bring Farley back."

"And if whoever this is can't stop you, they'll kill the kid and you in the process. Am I getting this right?" Matt asked without a hint of levity in his voice. "Your buddy Patowski called earlier. Bitched to me about a call you made to him, trying to 'suck up to the St. Louis PD', I believe were his words."

Patty, you roach! What was this, some kind of male conspiracy to keep her out of work? "You knew about the shooting."

"And couldn't reach you after I double checked with the St. Louis cops. I was half-crazy, Samantha."

He only called her Samantha when he was being romantic…or was seriously pissed. He spent most of his time alternating between the two. "Hey, I'm sorry, Matt, but it's over and done with now. I'm safe, I have Farley buying my story about being a Confederation agent and I'm going to bring the kid back to Miami tomorrow. No sweat…except that I'm rooming with Jenny Baxter and her dragons."

When she explained about running into them in full costume, it elicited the first genuine laugh she'd heard from her husband since she left Miami.

"So my daddy was a real mean one. Got hisself elected sheriff but he broke more laws than any of them folks he arrested," Elvis said as they sat in a hole-in-the-wall café having breakfast.

"I thought I had it hard with my father, but all he does is ignore me. He never put me in jail," Farley said, but his expression gave away the fact that he knew turning him over to

Dr. Reicht would be tantamount to the same thing. In spite of that, she watched as he swallowed another of the doc's wonder drugs with his orange juice.

Poor kid. Sam knew she would have to figure some way to help him. She had no doubt he was to one degree or another living in an alternate universe. But was it Reicht or Scruggs who was contributing to it? Farley appeared to be naturally high on *Space Quest*. Maybe the drug story implicating Elvis was another deception to lay at Dr. Reicht's door.

"I don't want to be anything like Upton Salisbury Winchester IV," Farley said with wistful sadness that touched Sam deeply. She'd seen other rich kids neglected and psychologically abused by their parents.

"Yeah, big-time boring, man," Elvis agreed, stuffing a forkful of scrambled eggs into his mouth.

"That's why I chose Spacefleet as my career. I'd rather risk dying in a futon spread than live tallying spreadsheets. This assignment is dangerous, but we'll break up the Klingoff-Pandorian alliance. If only Leila hadn't been taken prisoner." Farley shoved his plate of blueberry pancakes aside and turned earnestly to Elvis. "We have to rescue her, El. She's our commanding officer."

"We will," Scruggs assured him, chugging his coffee and waving down a waitress for his fourth or fifth refill.

Sam thought he must have a bladder extending down to his toes. Her ruminations were interrupted by a shrill squeal of delight. Damn, she'd picked this joint to avoid running into them. Who knew what they'd say to blow her cover with Farley and Elvis?

Tiff and Mellie, already in Dribble gear, came bouncing over to meet the Klingoff and the Pandorian.

Just great. Lt. O'Hara braced herself for the worst.

Chapter 9

"I wanted to come as a Pandorian like you but Mom couldn't find a costume small enough to fit me," Tiff said to Elvis after Sam made introductions.

Sam had omitted Scruggs and Winchester's "alter identities" as Spacefleet officers, praying to keep the meeting simple and brief before one of the Baxters really messed things up.

"I always wanted to be a Dribble," Mellie said, making a purring chirp deep in her throat that creeped Sam out big-time.

Seeing Sam's startled reaction, Tiff said, "That's what Dribbles do. It's supposed to soothe humans."

"Don't you like us?" Mellie asked Sam.

"Maybe she's not human," Tiff said, with a smirk in her voice. "Remember the Pandorian who was surgically altered to infiltrate Captain Turk's ship?"

"Ouch!" Sam jumped when Mellie gave her bare thigh a hard pinch.

"No, she's human," the younger girl piped cheerfully as Sam rubbed the red mark on her leg.

"I dunno," Tiff replied, shaking her "head."

All this interchange and she couldn't even see their faces! Good grief. Sam looked over at Farley, who had not yet put on his Klingoff mask. He seemed suddenly nervous and grabbed the chair he'd just vacated to greet the Baxter women, placing it between him and her. "Now, look, Farley, you know I'm not a spy any more than these kids are really Dribbles. Ask their mom."

"Are, too!" Mellie piped up.

Sam looked at Jenny pleadingly, trying to make her understand the harm her kids could do. "Uh, oh, no, we're just in costume for the con," Jenny assured Farley.

He started to relax until Tiff said, "Say, Mrs. Granger, are you bringing these dorks in cause they're...you know?" She tilted her head to one side and stuck her hand out of her puffball costume, making a circle with one finger.

That kid is positively sadistic! Sam's mind raced for a way to salvage the situation.

Farley looked confused and more than a little uncertain as he turned to Elvis. It was plain to Sam who led and who followed, no matter whose daddy was the richest. Scruggs looked past the taller of the Dribbles directly at Sam. His eyes revealed about as much as a Vegas shill in a high-stakes poker game. She was dead meat if she couldn't snatch Farley soon.

Damn! "It's been fun talking, Jenny, girls, but we really have to get going," Sam said carefully. She leaned toward Farley and whispered, "Don't pay any attention to the kids. They might be working a scam for Harriett Mudd and you know how slick she is. You could blow our cover."

"I don't know..." Farley hesitated.

"Why don't we all go together? We're ready to leave and

so are you," Tiff suggested as the waitress started to bus their table.

"We haven't paid," Sam answered quickly.

"Aw, I can take care of that," Elvis said magnanimously, pulling a wad of bills from his wallet and peeling them off atop the check, winking at the cute girl picking up dishes.

As they approached the door, Sam sighed in silent resignation. Once they were inside the big hall, she would have to figure a way to give the Baxters the slip and hang on to Farley. The immediate problem was keeping the boy believing she was a Confederation spy and stopping the cagey Elvis from learning what she really did for a living. Could nothing be easy?

The street was crowded and traffic noises sufficient to keep conversation to a minimum as they walked the short distance to the America's Center. Once they were inside, Sam tried to steer the guys away from the direction the girls wanted to go.

"We ought to check out the Pandorian Embassy display," she said after Tiff announced they were going to the "blood milk" drinking contest.

But Elvis had other ideas. "I wouldn't mind seeing that myself. Say, Far, you bein' Klingoff 'n all, you oughta sign up for the competition."

That elicited shrieks of glee from both girls and the idea took hold of Farley's imagination, which by Sam's lights was way too fertile already. "I guess I could do it," he replied.

So Elvis kept them stuck like cheese on a pizza to the Dribbles while Farley signed up to drink "blood milk." Just thinking about the syrupy red liquid made Sam queasy. She could smell the sweet, nasty aroma from twenty feet away. Like mixing sugar and varnish. Farley managed to consume three heavy steins of it before giving up as much larger Klingoff contestants continued quaffing the horrid brew.

"Aw, are you quitting now?" Mellie asked, clearly disappointed.

"I think he's green under his mask," Tiff said.

"Now, Melanie, we wouldn't want Mr. Winchester to make himself sick. Remember how you felt after eating six boxes of caramel corn last Halloween?" Jenny reminded her younger daughter while bestowing a quelling look on the elder.

Drooping as if chastened, Tiff said, "Blood milk's pretty icky, isn't it?" to Farley.

Whispering conspiratorially to her, he replied, "I hate to admit I don't like my home world's favorite drink."

Sam restrained herself from rolling her eyes as they went down the aisle until Farley stopped in front of a vendor displaying what looked like some very lethal hardware. Besides obviously fake "Dazers" and other odd-looking plastic handguns, real steel swords and knives gleamed evilly.

"Whoa, some katliff, huh, Far?" Elvis said, pointing to the big curved blade, at least a yard long with double-edged ends.

The kid nodded, his eyes gleaming inside the Klingoff mask. As he examined the weapon, Scruggs asked the price.

"Do they let kids walk around armed like that?" Sam asked the vendor.

"Nah, Lieutenant. Unless the buyer is twenty-one, we gotta wrap 'em up when we sell them."

Jeez, did being twenty-one make the chopper any less dangerous? Sam wondered. Then she thought of the Bornes and several other creatures whose giant size might allow them to hide a chain saw inside their costumes. The thought did not comfort her. She'd noted that several of the metal detectors were malfunctioning when they'd come in that morning. How hard would it be for someone to slip a howitzer onto the floor?

I gotta get Farley out of here and head for Miami. Her thoughts were interrupted when Elvis laughed as he said,

"Hey, Far, 'member when we tried to take your katliff into yer old man's country club?"

"All I wanted was to take a swim in the pool," Farley replied.

"Thought that there feller at the front desk was gonna have a heart attack when you took a swing at him with it." Scruggs chuckled, looking at Sam to gauge her reaction.

Deadpan, she said, "Doesn't look like a flotation device to me."

Even Jenny looked a bit alarmed by this turn in the conversation. "Girls, look, it's almost time for the fight between the Reemulans and the Klingoffs. If we want good seats, we better take off."

"Thank heavens for small favors," Sam muttered beneath her breath as Jenny and her Dribbles waved goodbye and headed toward an auditorium entrance. Outside it, a poster had been set up, complete with flickering colored lighting effects. It looked like a film from a lunar landing.

"I don't feel so good," Farley said, doubling up suddenly.

"Too much blood milk." Sam gave Scruggs a hard glare.

"I'll jest take him to the men's room and evcrythin'll be fine, won't it, Far?"

Sam nodded. "I'll be around," she said vaguely, gesturing to the next aisle. Like hell was she trusting Elvis not to whisk Farley out a back door! She followed them at a discreet distance. They made it to the men's room in the nick of time, judging from the sounds emanating from inside.

She waited directly outside the door until a low voice said, "Well, looking for a little action, Lieutenant?" A guy with pointy Vulcant ears waggled his arched eyebrows at her and moved closer.

"Looking for me to rearrange your nose so it matches your ears?" she hissed.

He backed away, putting up his hands. "Jeez, sorry. What'd

you expect trolling the men's room?" He pushed open the door and fled inside.

Sam heard Elvis and Farley's voices drawing near. She quickly slipped around the corner and followed them, then pretended to run into them as they approached the mock battle between Reemulans and Klingoffs. "Oh, there you are. I was afraid something might have happened. After last night, we can't be too careful," she said to Farley. "Do you think the Klingoffs could've poisoned your blood milk?"

"Maybe," Farley said, smiling at her for giving him a face-saving excuse.

He'd taken off his mask and parts of his uniform were wet. Sam had overheard Elvis cleaning him up with paper towels at a sink. "Hey, let's enjoy the show," Scruggs suggested, pointing to the line of people filing into the auditorium. "We been waitin' to see this shoot-out ever since we read about it."

They found seats near the front, but just as they were sitting down, Sam saw Jenny and her girls walking toward them. Dammit, how could she shake them? The kids had unzipped their heads from their costumes and were juggling plates of something pink in their hands. Jenny got them seated but before she could grab a chair herself, Mellie whined, "You promised we could have Reemulan brandy if we were good."

She turned to Sam apologetically and asked, "Mind keeping an eye on them while I get the stuff—oh, it isn't really alcohol," she added.

Sam nodded and Jenny trudged toward the food court. What was the use?

"Hi, everybody," Tiff said, taking her seat and leaning forward, holding up a forkful of something that seemed to be wriggling. "Sagittarian Worm Groton," she explained, shoveling a mouthful of the glistening pasta in her mouth. It left slimy trails of pink running down her chin. "Do you want some?" she asked Sam.

By then Farley wasn't the only one looking green around the gills. *Damned if it doesn't look like worms.* Sam pasted a smile on her lips and managed, "No, thanks. I had a big breakfast."

She was saved from more importuning by the sadistic Tiff when the lights dimmed off stage and the show started. A pair of men dressed in full Klingoff regalia crouched behind a cluster of boulders, wielding lethal-looking weapons that Sam identified from the photos she'd studied as Dazers. Then a phalanx of Reemulans in full military gear marched onstage, seeming to be unaware of the ambush awaiting them.

She watched Farley lean forward in his seat, his earlier indisposition forgotten. The poor kid really believed in this stuff. She sensed Scruggs watching her. No sense challenging him. She looked at the action beginning to unfold onstage when out of nowhere two more Klingoffs dashed across the front row of chairs and started pitching small devices into the audience.

Sam instinctively knew this wasn't part of the show. She reached for Farley, but before she could get a secure hold of him, a series of loud explosions drowned out the action on the stage. Tiff and Mellie stood up and shrieked with delight, their "worm groton" pitched away in the excitement.

The force of the explosion caused Sam to lose her grip on Farley. He toppled out of his seat. Mini concussion grenades! And one had been aimed directly for the kid. Elvis, too, was on the floor on all fours, shaking his head. Sam kicked another of the grenades across the open area. It detonated against the side wall.

People jumped up all across the audience, overturning chairs as they panicked and ran in every direction. Sam seized Farley, yelling over the din, "Stick with me!" She helped him stand up but before she could move him toward an exit a red laser dot suddenly appeared, centered on his chest.

"Down!" She knocked him over just as the shot ripped by them.

"Laser tag!" Tiff yelled behind her. "Let's play, Mellie!"

"No, get down! This isn't a game," Sam yelled over the din. To no avail.

Both girls pulled small laser pointers from inside their costumes and started shooting beams at the goons in Klingoff disguise. When one of the gunmen saw a red dot on the forehead of his companion, he yelled, "Gus, somebody's got you targeted!"

Both of them hit the floor, using overturned chairs for cover as red laser beams crisscrossed the pandemonium. Still trying for a clear shot at Farley, the second one raised his weapon. Sam caught the movement out of the corner of her eye while trying to reach the girls who were ducking and dodging, yelling like banshees. She kicked an interlocking tangle of felled chairs toward the gunman. He missed his shot when the chain reaction of chairs knocked the wind out of him.

The frightened crowd and actors onstage continued fleeing the area but the special effect lights still flickered overhead, creating a surreal scene. Into the middle of the chaos, Jenny entered, climbing over toppled chairs and dodging fleeing people amid screams of panic. She continued calmly in the direction of her shrieking children, clutching two big containers of "Reemulan brandy." Apparently used to the wreckage surrounding her offspring, she yelled angrily, "How many times have I told you, no laser tag out in public!"

"Get down!" Sam yelled the same instant a shot ripped through one of the "brandies," splattering blue liquid every direction.

Jenny stamped her foot. "Now look what you've made me do!"

The girls ignored their mother just as she'd ignored Sam's warning. "Stay behind this chair and don't move," Sam whispered to Farley, then started crawling toward the children. Even little dragons didn't deserve to be cut down in a cross fire. But then she heard one of the gunmen yell to his companion, "Zipper, one of 'em's got your belly in his sights!"

The second guy dropped like a falling meteorite, then rolled toward an exit sign at the side of the stage. "Let's get the hell outta here. Nobody warned us about midgets packing heat!"

Chapter 10

Sam watched the two gunmen vanish through an exit door. She wasn't about to go charging after two armed men when all she had was a plastic "dazer" strapped to her waist. She could see the girls were unharmed as was their mother, who was advancing on Tiff with anger seething from every pore. Let Jenny handle her kids. Sam had one to babysit herself.

"You all right, Farley?" she asked the boy, who was still crouched behind a chair. Scruggs, interestingly enough, was directly behind him. Was he trying to shield the kid?

"Oh, I'm okay. Did the Klingoffs hurt anyone?" Farley asked. Although there was concern in his voice, there was also that creepy excitement glowing in his eyes. All of life was a game to him, fantasy and reality meshed hopelessly together.

"Naw. Nobody's been shot. Them there Klingoffs couldn't hit a barn with a shovel load of cow plop," Elvis said, helping his friend to his feet.

Jenny was busy lecturing Tiff and Mellie, but somehow her stern expression was undercut by the bright blue droplets oozing from her hair and dripping off the tip of her nose. Then two police officers entered the auditorium and started questioning stragglers who had not escaped before the shooters did. One cop engaged Jenny. Taking advantage of the opportunity, Sam murmured to Elvis, "We'd better get Farley out of here before the cops get to us."

Bingo. Magic words. If anything would work, she gambled that would. Scruggs nodded and took his young friend by his arm, whispering, "She's right. We don't know who we can trust. This here was a real close call."

They slipped out the opposite door before anyone noticed, melting into the crowd. "Now, you see what I mean about how dangerous this convention is?" Sam asked, steering them to the main entrance and out onto the street. "The Klingoffs and Pandorians know who you are. We should head back to Miami."

"Now don't go gettin' your mini in a twist, Lieutenant," Elvis drawled. Then before she could stop him, he reached over and picked a piece of glowing pink spaghetti off her thigh.

Sam looked down at herself with disgust. She was covered with Sagittarian Worm Groton. Cursing Jenny and her dragons, she started picking pieces of goo off her "uniform" and her legs. Her knees were Day-Glo pink! She must have crawled through the disgusting stuff. Farley seemed embarrassed but Elvis was enjoying the sight altogether too much. Sam abandoned the project as hopeless. The only way to get clean was to soak under a shower.

"Them girls is pure trouble, ain't they?" Elvis asked innocently.

You don't know the half of it. "Yeah," she said, wanting to divert his quick mind before he made Farley mistrust her even more. "But right now, Ensign Winchester's safety is what we have to consider. I can protect him better in Miami."

"We know the danger, but we got us a mission."

"Yes, Commander Satterwaite was captured by Pandorians and we have to find her," Farley chimed in as they crossed the street. His face was still flushed with excitement…or something else.

Sam watched the traffic, almost expecting a car to come skidding around the corner aimed straight at them, but none did. She only half listened to Farley and Elvis discuss the mysterious woman they seemed so concerned about. She was too busy wondering about the glaze in the boy's eyes. It looked to her like more than just an adrenaline rush. Farley was definitely "spaced out" on something.

"We got inside info they brought Leila here. Thought you knew that," Scruggs said, implying that she certainly should have.

Her uncle Dec always said when you don't have the straight skinny you have to bluff. "Nobody told me anything about a Commander Satterwhite," Sam replied with cool authority.

"It's Satter*waite,* not white," Elvis said. "Her cover in Miami was working as a stripper before she transponded to that Pandorian ship. Far seen the whole thing, didn't you, buddy?"

What had the kid seen, Sam wondered—Leila doing the bump and grind, or being "transponded"? She didn't have the least interest in some bimbo Scruggs was probably boffing when he wasn't chasing space aliens.

Farley nodded vaguely. "I…I was kind of messed up. You know, when she was taken prisoner or I could've helped her." The poor kid sounded guilty.

"What do you mean, 'messed up'?" she asked.

"All that stuff I'd been drugged with…"

"Drugged? Who drugged you?" she asked, watching Scruggs's body language out of the corner of her eye.

He never missed a step. "He was havin' some problems, but we 'bout got him straightened out," Elvis said quickly, calmly.

"El's trying to keep me from being court-martialed."

"Don't you say no more, Far," Scruggs instructed firmly as they entered the hotel lobby. Then he turned to Sam and looked her up and down. "Hey, 'pears to me you need to get yerself cleaned up. We could stand a change of clothes, too." Although they were only spattered with flecks of pink, the Worm Groton had obviously hit them, too.

"I'd like to lie down for a little bit—if that's okay?" Farley said tentatively.

"Sounds like a plan to me. You get some rest, Farley. How about I meet you at your room, say around five? We'll head for the evening show then," Sam suggested.

Farley, his faith in her seemingly restored, smiled eagerly and nodded. Elvis aimed his index finger at her, drawing back his thumb as if cocking a trigger. "See ya at five."

After getting out on the seventh floor, she ran up the next six flights of fire stairs to where Farley and Elvis stayed. She could hear them inside their room. Good. She waited until she was pretty sure they wouldn't try to sneak out. Maybe the attempts to kill them had spooked the crafty Scruggs enough so he'd let her stick around. She hoped so as she rode back down and walked out the rear entry to the parking lot.

Roman Numeral's Jag stood out like a beacon. She approached carefully, using other cars for cover just in case Elvis was watching from the sliding-glass doors above. Luckily, the trees around the lot provided cover for the Jag. The coast appeared clear. The drapes to their room were closed tightly and the attendant at the booth was reading a newspaper. It took her only a moment to pop the hood. Pulling an all-purpose file from her fanny pack, she unscrewed the distributor rotor and replaced the cap. God, you had to love those vintage cars before fuel injection. So easy to disable.

Whistling, she retrieved her small suitcase from the van and walked inside. After asking a few questions, she found a bellhop going off duty. "Want to earn an easy fifty?" she asked the kid, whose name tag identified him as Edward.

He looked to be around Farley's age with ebony skin and a serious expression on his long, narrow face. "What would I have to do?" he asked politely but uneasily, eyeing the wreck of her costume.

"Nothing illegal," she assured him. "I'm a private investigator on a case." She flipped out her Florida P.I.'s license. "All you have to do is watch room fourteen-forty for me. If the two guys inside leave, call me." She jotted down her cell number and offered it to him along with a twenty and a five. "I'll give you the other half when I get back."

"I guess that'd be all right, since I'm off duty now," he said. "I need tuition money for next semester."

Knowing he was working his way through college made her feel a little better about blowing fifty hard-earned bucks. "Thanks, Edward." Maybe she'd even get to collect her fee and expenses, who knew?

She headed for the front desk and paid for one night in an obscenely expensive room just down the hall from Farley and Elvis. Sam absolutely refused to spend another minute with Jenny and her dragons. With any luck, maybe the cops would arrest them for starting a riot. At least confiscate those damned laser pointers. The thought made her smile as she unlocked the door and let herself into the room.

Her legs were starting to itch from the pink stuff. Stripping off the ruined costume, she considered whether she ought to pay

Jenny for the outfit. No way was Worm Groton going to be dry
cleanable. But it was Tiff and Mellie's fault that it had been
ruined in the first place. The hell with it! Besides, Jenny's sister,
Tess, had come into a substantial hunk of her ex-husband's legit
money when he went to jail. Tess could afford to pick up the
tab.

Humming to herself, she turned on the water in the shower,
good and hot, then adjusted the thermostat in the bedroom to
keep it cool. She set her cell on the bathroom sink where she'd
hear it beep if Edward spotted Elvis trying to make off with
Farley. "Please don't let me have pink hair," she muttered as
she stepped into the steamy compartment.

Although she kept watch over the phone, she didn't hear
the door to her room being unlocked. She'd been too preoc-
cupied with getting her clothes off to remember to slip the
inside latch on the door. Her head was lathered up with
shampoo when the shower door opened, letting out a big
whoosh of steam.

Instinctively she crouched and assumed a fighting stance,
but the soap running into her eyes kept her from seeing her
attacker. She started to kick out anyway but his voice stopped
her at the last second.

"If you kick me there, you'll be as sorry as I'll be, Sam."

"Matt! You idiot! I could've made you sing soprano if I
hadn't stopped. Sometimes you have the brains of a starfish!"

"This from a woman alone in a hotel room who goes in
the shower and leaves the door guard unlatched? You think
you're Janet Leigh by any chance? Keep being that careless
and you'll end up like she did in *Psycho*."

"You're the psycho. What are you doing here? You're
supposed to be in Miami."

"After two attempts on your life en route here and then a
kidnapping that nearly turned you into road kill, you think I

was gonna stay home like a good little boy? And, I might mention that when I stopped at the convention center everyone was talking about a shoot-out in one of the theatres. Of course, you wouldn't know anything about that, would you?"

Ignoring the question to which she knew he knew the answer, she changed the subject. "You picked the lock. You know how to disable those door guards, too," she accused. "I taught you."

"Did not," he said, pulling her into his arms and digging one big hand into the suds covering her head, massaging her scalp.

"Did, too," she practically purred as she let her soap-slicked hands glide across his broad shoulders and down his chest. He'd stripped before entering the bath. Who cared how he got inside the room? She wanted him inside *her!*

Matt reached for the soap and started to do maddening things to her breasts, teasing the nipples into hard points, then letting his hands travel around her hips, cupping her buttocks as he pulled her against his erection. The pouring water rinsed the shampoo from her short hair when she tipped her head back and looked up into his face. She reached one hand up and wrapped it around his neck, pulling herself up to kiss his lips.

With the water raining down fiercely, they devoured each other's mouths like two starving people, angling their heads one way, then another, tasting, plunging, their tongues dancing madly together. He backed her against the smooth warm tiles as she held on to his shoulders. Using her arms for leverage, she hoisted her body up and wrapped her strong athletic legs tightly around his hips, opening herself for him. Their kisses grew rougher as he plunged deep inside of her.

Steam rose in pulsing clouds as they moved together, fast

and hard, then slow and languorous. He stepped back, holding one arm securely around her waist while she arched her upper body away from him. The water poured over them as she rolled her hips and let her nails dig into the thick muscles of his shoulders. He bent his head and took a nipple in his mouth, sucking fiercely, then moved to its twin.

"Aah, Matt," she groaned, tightening around him, feeling him fill her. "Do it, yes, yes…"

He loved it when her voice faded breathlessly away like that, as if she were helpless, but when it came to his wife, Matt Granger knew he was the one who was helpless. Damn, but he loved the woman! Couldn't get enough of her. When he felt her clench him so intimately, he followed her over the edge, barely able to keep his legs from buckling.

They remained motionless as the waves of bliss gradually subsided and the water started to grow cool. At last Sam slowly slid down his big body, her hands locked behind his neck as if she never wanted to let him go. "I should be mad with you," she said dreamily, "always interfering with my work."

"Occupational hazard. I'm a nosy newsman, remember?" he said in a low voice. He snatched a towel and started to dry her off.

Sam practically purred like a cat, too utterly content to think straight. "All I remember is… Say, we have a king-size bed."

"Yeah, I noticed," he replied with a wicked chuckle. "Voracious wench."

"Wench?" she echoed. "That sounds like something from one of those history books you read," she said, leading him toward the bed.

"More like from one of those historical romances *you* read."

The cell hadn't beeped forty minutes later.

Hoping Edward was earning his money and Farley was still

tucked safely inside the room down the hall, she explained recent events at the con. "Can you believe Jenny Baxter and her brood of vipers are here?"

"Dribbles?" A big grin lit his face as he digested the picture of Sam smeared with Worm Groton.

"Okay, let's forget that—it's a dead end. I couldn't ID the gunmen in that regalia, but I have Farley rounded up...almost. What I can't figure is Scruggs. One minute he's this hick, the next, he's a crafty ex-con. Any luck finding his missing seven years?"

"Afraid not, but I do have some more dirt on Reese Reicht, M.D., Ph.D."

"Yeah?" Sam was sitting yoga style on the big bed. She grabbed a notepad and pencil from the nightstand. "We have prescribing illegals and tax evasion. What else has our good doctor been up to?"

"Patowski was mum, but I have other sources on the force. Homicide's investigating his connection to a suspicious death. Cold case file that just heated up again."

"Damn, I knew Patty was holding out on me! What are they after?"

"Remember Susan Winchester?"

"Farley's mother. Died of a drug OD around five years ago. You mean maybe it wasn't just an overdose?"

Matt nodded. "She may have been involved with Reicht. He was her shrink before he treated Farley."

"You mean the good doc was giving her more physical than mental therapy?" She chewed on the pencil eraser. "Doesn't work for me. The man's a toad and from the pix I've seen of her, she was a looker."

He shrugged. "Who can figure the taste of women?"

"Yeah, I married you, didn't I?" she couldn't resist saying, laughing as she dodged the pillow he threw at her. "What else about her and Reicht?"

"If she went off the deep end, maybe threatened to tell her hubby, Reicht administered that OD. At least, that's what the cops are investigating."

"Yeah, he might have been giving her drugs. He seems to have Farley on something potent. But this is a cold case. What made the cops activate it now?"

"They got a tip from an anonymous source a couple of weeks ago. Complete with photos of Susan Winchester driving away from a hotel in Palm Springs with a guy who looked a lot like Reicht."

"What about the wronged husband? Anybody working on Roman Numeral? If his wife was having an affair, he'd have motive," she said, not really seeing Upton Winchester IV as a likely suspect.

"That's the other part of the equation I was about to get to," Matt replied. "The marriage had been in trouble for years. Lots of gossip about that. Susan apparently wasn't the type to suffer in silence."

"And Upton's the type to make anyone suffer," Sam agreed thoughtfully. "Still, I can't see him offing her with a drug OD. If she had a habit, he'd want to hush it up, not broadcast it. Bad for his image, that kind of thing."

"Also assuming he cared enough to bother. Her complaint was that he ignored her and their son. I doubt a quiet fling with her shrink would upset old Upton much as long as it didn't cause a scandal."

"That fits what I got out of interviewing him. Cold fish, prissy proper," Sam agreed. "If he wanted his wife dead, he'd find some more discreet, less scandalous way to have her killed. Say, a car crash or drowning. A tragedy without a hint of scandal."

"Yes, but how does a tight-assed CPA feel about having a Spacer kid who drives around Miami in full Spacefleet regalia? The boy was already in special schools and on medication for years."

"Elvis told me they got in a brawl at Upton's country club a few weeks ago. Tried to take a katliff inside when they were going for a swim."

Matt shook his head. "To fight off pool sharks, no doubt. For now, I see Winchester being a hell of a lot more upset about his son than his wife."

"But would he try to kill his own son? Maybe," Sam answered her own question, remembering his icy disdain. Anyone who didn't meet Roman Numeral's standards of perfection would be expendable. "Still, after losing his wife in a drug scandal, I figure he'd rather keep the boy sedated at some place like Homeside. Safer and easier and the kid's out of the picture as far as dear old daddy's concerned."

"But Winchester hasn't been able to keep the kid under wraps very effectively. Look at this escapade, stealing a car, the whole enchilada that brought you into the case," Matt argued.

"Yeah, if Winchester wanted to kill anyone, his logical choice would've been Scruggs. With him out of the picture, Roman Numeral could make the kid go away permanently."

"Did that goon the other night kidnap the wrong guy?" Matt asked. "Maybe he was sent to kill Elvis, not Farley."

"You haven't seen the two of them together. No way anyone could mistake one for the other. Think Yoda and Darth Vader."

Matt grinned at her. "Now who's the space geek?"

She waved that away. "Oh, everyone's seen at least one of those old movies." She sighed and started doodling on the notepad. "Reicht's already up to his ass in alligators with the IRS and Miami-Dade Homicide. Would he dare chance hiring goons to kill Farley or Scruggs? For sure Winchester wouldn't want his kid run over at a *Space Quest* con. Too messy. Not to mention those shooters this afternoon. And I'm still getting strange vibes from my good ole boy Elvis. Nothing adds up." She flipped the pencil across the bed in disgust.

Then her cell beeped.

Chapter 11

"Ballanger here," she answered. "Good work, Edward. I'll have your cash—with a bonus if you follow them to the parking lot… Yeah, that's where they're headed. If I'm wrong, give me a quick call back. I'll be right down."

"What's up?" Matt asked. Already brackets of worry began to form around his mouth.

"Looks like Scruggs is trying to slip off with his meal ticket. God only knows what line of extraterrestrial excrement he's fed the kid to get him to leave the con."

"If they get out of the parking lot, we'll never catch them."

She grinned and pulled a small plastic and metal disk from her fanny pack, holding it in the palm of her hand as she asked, "What's this 'we,' kemo sabe?"

"What's that gismo?" he asked, ignoring her objection to his horning in on her job.

Sam yanked on a pair of shorts and a tee as she replied,

"Distributor rotor." She looked up from tying her tennies, knowing he didn't have a clue. "I love it when a guy's dumb. Makes 'em sexy," she said, standing up to pat his cheek.

"It's something that stops a car from running," he grumbled as he reached for his shorts and a shirt.

"Only before fuel injection engines were developed. You see, back in—"

"Never mind, I don't need another lecture on automotive design."

"Couldn't agree more. What you need is to take a couple of years at a good vo-tech."

"Deal, if you sign up for cooking and household management," he said cheerfully. "I can get by not knowing how to repair my own car, but you don't even know how to make a bed."

"I can get by without making a bed," she shot back. "Why make a bed when you're only going to sleep in it again that same night?" That one was a no-brainer for Sam. She checked her stunner and the .38 and placed both in her fanny pack. When she looked over at him he was fully dressed and holding the door open. "You're not going with me," she said.

"Think again. No way am I leaving you alone with this Elvis character. He's a con artist who's served prison time. And you said he's a big bruiser."

She shook her head. "Being protective is a sweet quality in a husband—only not for this wife."

He stood in the doorway, daring her. "No way, Sam."

She didn't have time to argue. "Just let me handle this and do what I say, okay?"

He nodded, gesturing for her to go ahead of him. She dashed for the elevator with Matt beside her. "What if Scruggs decides to leave the Jag behind to ditch you?"

"Nah, he wouldn't give up that sweet little jewel. It's every man's wet dream," she said as they burst through the opening door and dashed toward the rear exit.

Her intuition was right. Elvis was bent over the engine while Farley stood helplessly by. She could hear Scruggs curse as she paid Edward his bonus. He thanked her and accepted the money, returning to the hotel as they walked toward the conspirators.

"You must've really pissed him off," Matt whispered.

Just then Farley saw Sam and called out sheepishly, "Oh, hi, Sam."

Elvis cracked his already injured head on the hood when he tried to straighten up. He let fly another string of oaths, wiping greasy hands on his jeans. He eyed her like a cat checking out a canary. "Now why is it, Lieutenant—oh, that's right, you never did give us your real rank, now didja? Why'd you take out the distributor rotor?"

"If you know what it is, then you have your answer, don'ja?" Sam replied, mimicking his drawl.

"The car won't start," Farley said, looking nervously from Sam to Elvis.

"Give that young man a cigar," Matt interjected, leaning against the Jag's door.

"Who the hell are you?" Scruggs said, eyeing the stranger who had a good two inches on him, and Elvis was well above average height.

Matt watched the other man puff up. "Lordy, you do look like Mr. Presley when you stick your chin out that way."

"You didn't answer my question." Scruggs's tone was menacing now, all the good old boy evaporating like gasoline fumes.

"Granger. Matt Granger." He waggled his eyebrows at the awful 007 parody.

"Relax, guys, he's with me," she said. "Why were you running away from me, Farley? I'm here to protect you."

"El said—"

"Don't say nothin', Far. Told you I checked with Space-fleet Command and she's not an officer."

"Of course not, you idiot," Matt said, flashing a badge he pulled from his pocket. It had some kind of fancy insignia on it that Sam had never seen before. "I'm not supposed to show this to anyone outside those we know we can trust in Space-fleet. I'm Commander Granger to you."

"Let me see that," Farley said, excitedly.

Matt showed him the badge. "We're a covert operation assigned to undermine the Klingoff-Pandorian alliance. My field agents aren't on record. Neither am I."

Sam took back every crack she'd ever made about his hokey acting. He halfway had her convinced he was some kind of super space spy. Judging from Farley's expression, she knew he'd bought it. Scruggs was another matter. "We're sitting ducks in this open area. Someone tried to run me down a couple of times already. My van's over there." She pointed to the Econoline. "We can talk inside it, then decide what to do next."

"I don't think so," Elvis said.

"You want to expose us all to the Klingoffs?" Matt asked, seeming to be genuinely angry. "If you two slime worms piss me off, your next duty station will be a garbage scow circling Tantalus Seven."

"He's the ranking officer on-site, El. We can at least listen to what they have to say," Farley said, looking up at all the open balcony doors surrounding them. He was obviously re-membering his brush with death in that very place as he pulled his prescription bottle from his shirt pocket and popped a pill with shaky hands.

"What do you know about Commander Leila Satterwaite's disappearance?" Scruggs asked Matt suspiciously.

"The Pandorians have her," Sam said, knowing Matt had no idea who she was.

"Yes, now will you come with us?" Matt added impatiently.

Scruggs wasn't happy about it, but he went along, keeping more of an eye on Matt than on Sam. That was exactly the way she wanted. Sometimes having Matt around was okay… well, it was always okay when they were in bed…or the shower…or, hell, on a garbage scow circling Tantalus Seven…. *Dammit, focus, Ballanger!*

She unlocked the van and Matt climbed inside first, taking the front passenger seat. She motioned for Elvis and Farley to get in the back. The boy climbed in without protest. Sam was pleased. Matt knew so well how her mind worked that it sometimes scared her. Warily, Scruggs followed, keeping an eye on Matt while Farley slid across the backseat. Between watching out for his companion and his nemesis, Elvis forgot about Sam.

Big mistake. Cosmic mistake, she thought as she pulled out the stunner and gave him a good jolt right between the shoulder blades. He dropped silently onto the parking lot, flopping around like a banked carp.

"Hey, what did you do to El?" Farley said, trying to get out of the back of the van before Sam could climb in, but Matt placed a restraining hand on the boy's bony shoulder, saying, "He's a traitor who sold out to the Pandorians."

By that time Sam was inside the van with a nasal inhalator hidden in the palm of her hand. She waited to see how Farley was going to react to Matt's spiel before she risked drugging the kid.

"We have inside information about Elvis Scruggs," Matt began. "You know he grew up poor. Well, the Pandorians offered him one of the moons of Orion Four. You know how rich they are in trilythium crystals. He thinks he'll be a billionaire."

Farley shook his head. "I don't believe you. El wouldn't do that. He's my friend…my only friend. I don't know you…" His voice faded away and he blinked back tears, then made a sudden lunge, trying to knock Sam away from the door.

Damn, she had been afraid of this. Sam ducked just enough so that Farley overbalanced when he attempted to push her out of his way. Then she grabbed him by the collar of his shirt and yanked him back into the van. Before he could regain his footing, she clamped a hand over his mouth and shoved the inhalator into one nostril just as he gasped for air.

Matt knew the effect of the drug was almost instantaneous. She'd used it on him the first time they met and he'd gone down in barely a minute. The kid weighed less than half what he did. He didn't even have to help her as she got Farley to take a second sniff in his other nostril. Then he went to sleep.

"Help me move him to the back," she said to Matt.

"Finally, she asks for my help." He threw up his hands in exasperation, then picked the kid up and lifted him over the seat to the padded floor space in the rear of the van where Sam had installed specially designed straps for her "patients." "What were you planning to do without me? Drag the poor kid around to the back of the van and hope nobody noticed?"

"I would've thought of something, but speaking of unconscious bodies, Scruggs won't be down for long." She quickly placed the restraints around Farley.

"What, no straitjacket? You used one on me."

"You were dangerous. The kid's harmless and I don't want to freak him out any more than I have to. He's pretty rocky as it is." She finished her job, then climbed over the back and front seats, taking her place behind the wheel as Matt closed the passenger door. "Oh, by the way, you did good with the spacie stuff back there. Thanks, sweetie."

"You're welcome, I think," he groused as she pulled the van away from Elvis Scruggs who had stopped flopping and was struggling to sit up.

"Where did you get that badge thingee that Farley thought was the real deal?"

"Had it since I was fifteen. Sent for it through the mail."

"And you kept it all these years?" she asked incredulously.

"This from a woman who's never cleaned out a closet in her life!"

"But my stuff's good stuff! Guns, fishing gear—"

"Engine parts, bowling balls."

"Like I said, good stuff," she replied as she approached the parking attendant's booth.

"You never know when something like that badge might come in handy," Matt argued, climbing into the front seat. Then he glanced at the side-view mirror. "Uh-oh, our boy's on his feet."

Sam grinned. "He can't chase us in the Jag and I don't think he'll call the cops."

"Neither do I," Matt said dryly.

She handed the ticket to the attendant and didn't even complain about how expensive the rates were. But she did ask for a receipt.

Farley woke up several hours down Illinois Route 3 headed for a cutoff to link them to I-24. Sam had decided on an alternate way back to Miami, just in case whoever had sent those goons in the Caddie had hired more players for a repeat performance. They were in the wilds of southern Illinois when Farley started thrashing against the bands holding him down.

Sam quickly pulled the van to the side of the road, concealing it beneath the low hanging branches of a weeping willow on the wide berm. "Let's see if we can talk some sense into the kid."

"Fat chance," Matt said.

Sam opened the back of the van with a water bottle in her hand. "Here, Farley, I'm going to give you a drink. I know how thirsty you must be. Now, when I loosen the restraints, I want you to sit up, not try to fight us, okay?" she asked in her most soothing professional tone.

Matt had heard it before. All it had done was infuriate him, but then she'd taken him away from a hot story, and he had all his marbles, something this poor kid obviously didn't.

"You're a Klingoff agent. I'm not drinking anything you give me. El said they'd been drugging me."

"Pure water," Sam said, taking a long pull on the water bottle and swallowing. It was a hot afternoon. She offered the water to him again.

Stubbornly, he shook his head, then started to tremble. "I…I n-need my medicine." He tried to reach his shirt pocket where a pill bottle was visible.

"That the stuff Dr. Reicht's been giving you?" Sam asked.

"Y-yes. How did you know about him?" Now Farley looked less like an outraged kidnap victim, more as if he was acutely embarrassed because he had been under the care of a psychiatrist. "I never told you. I…I never told…"

He was shaking like a dog passing peach pits. Damn, why hadn't Roman Numeral warned her about the boy's condition? Probably because he had no idea about it and didn't care. But Reicht had to know if the meds he'd given the boy caused withdrawal problems and he hadn't told her, either.

"Okay, here's the deal, Farley. Your father hired me to bring you back to Miami. I know you were under Dr. Reicht's care. In fact, I talked with him about you before I came to St. Louis to get you. That's my job. I'm a retrieval specialist. I bring people home."

Her words rang hollow to her as she gave the same talk

she'd given dozens of times before. Sam watched the kid's eyes glaze over, as if he hadn't heard a word she'd said. He obviously wasn't firing on all cylinders. Farley's mother had been a socialite druggie and his father cared more for his accounting ledgers than he did for his only child. Where was "home" for this boy?

"We aren't taking you back to Dr. Reicht, Farley," Matt said gently.

"Or to your father," she added.

The boy was shaking hard now, struggling to get free of his bonds. "I don't believe you! You're K-klingoff agents— or P-pandorians…in disguise. I know. El will come get me…and you'll b-be sorry. You'll be sorry."

"Help hold him. We have to hydrate him," Sam said, genuinely frightened now. She'd had enough paramedic training to know when someone was in trouble. Matt immobilized him while she tightened the restraints again. Then she forced his jaws open and held his nose closed. "Pour the water a little at a time. He'll swallow." *Please, Farley. Please, God!*

At first the kid tried to resist but thirst won out and he drank a slow steady stream of water, until Sam knew he'd had enough for now. Matt fished out the pill bottle and looked at the script. "You have any idea what this stuff is?" he asked her.

Sam read the label. "New psychotropic drugs come on the market fast as confetti tossed on New Year's Eve. Never heard of it, and we can't dare give it to him without knowing. Especially considering that Reicht prescribed it."

"What if he didn't?" Matt asked.

"You mean, Farley—or Elvis—pulled a ringer. Another drug in a legit script bottle." She cursed and combed her fingers through her hair.

"I'd suggest we head for the nearest town with a pharmacy and find out what this is."

"Just my thought," she said, looking down at Farley, who lay with his eyes closed, mumbling incoherently. Thank heaven the shakes had stopped. His breathing was almost regular. She took his pulse and it was okay, too. He'd probably had a hysterical reaction to the kidnapping, not completely dissimilar to an asthmatic attack. Sam knew how dangerous that could be and again cursed the boy's father and his doctor. Winchester had hired her knowing she was going to have to subdue the boy and place him in restraints to bring him back to Miami. So did Reese Reicht, M.D., Ph.D.

"'First do no harm,' my dying ass," she snarled.

Chapter 12

"It's a variant on Clozaril," Gene Warton said, explaining, "One possible symptom is recurrence of psychotic episodes, especially when the patient isn't properly supervised. For example, if the patient consumes caffeine products, that will interfere with the medication. It could simulate withdrawal symptoms similar to those of a heroin addict."

"You mean like soft drinks?" Sam asked, remembering all the sweet and doubtless caffeinated junk Farley had consumed at the con.

The elderly pharmacist nodded his shiny, bald head. They'd reached a small town just off the interstate and she'd caught him as he was locking up his shop for the evening, sweet talking him into checking our her "cousin's" prescription.

"This drug isn't prescribed much anymore in such heavy dosages, especially outside of mental facilities. Too many contraindications."

"Such as dependency and acute physical withdrawal," Sam said with a sigh.

"I'd say you'd be wise to get your cousin to a doctor," Warton advised. "In fact, I can recommend one right here in Ganntown, Dr.—"

"Er, no thanks. We're headed straight to Nashville. Our family has a psychiatrist there who'll be able to help him," Sam interjected before the helpful old man could reach for the phone and call in a local physician. "I just wanted to know what he'd been taking. When we started for home he had a bad reaction and kinda scared us, but his doctor in Nashville will know what to do," she said. She'd told the pharmacist that Farley had run away to Florida and she'd been sent to fetch him.

"I just don't understand how a responsible psychiatrist would prescribe this kind of drug for outpatient use…even in Miami," he added.

"Well, that's why we want to take Farley home," Sam replied.

"You don't sound like you're from Tennessee," Warton said, his watery blue eyes becoming suspicious.

"Oh, I'm from New York—upstate New York," Sam hurriedly added. No sense making the guy even more likely to call the cops on her. "I'd better get Cousin Farley home. Thanks again for your help."

She went toward the door, smiling all the while and grateful she'd parked the van on the next block where Warton couldn't see it. As soon as she hit the all-American main street and turned the corner, she yanked open the van door and said to Matt, "I think it's time we did the burn patient routine, just in case we're stopped. With me in a nurse's uniform and a medical facility logo on the sides of the Econoline, I'll be less likely to raise any flags."

"What happened?" Matt asked. He knew it was risky but they'd had to find out what the kid was on. "Have any scrubs that'll fit me?"

"Nope, only pj's and house slippers," she replied, with a smile.

"In your dreams. You're never getting me into another straitjacket, Sammie."

"I might just make you eat those words…when we have time," she said. "How's our patient?"

"Farley's still peacefully sleeping, thanks to your special knockout nasal spray," he replied. "Potent stuff." How well he remembered.

"At least I had the med vetted by a reliable doctor in Miami before I used it on anyone. I hate to admit it, but I think I blew it with that old fart of a pharmacist. He probably dialed the local cops or the Illinois Highway Patrol the minute I walked out of the joint." She muttered an oath.

"What made him suspicious of you?"

"Oh, I dunno…maybe bringing in a script from a Miami shrink and asking what such a potent narcotic's side effects would be on my poor 'Cousin Farley'—and not having a Southern accent. I'm probably lucky if he doesn't call the DEA, too."

"I'll drive and you hide with the kid," he said.

Sam cursed again, then sighed. "I hate it when you're right. Just don't strip the gears on my baby."

"Yes, Ms. Andretti," he said.

As they drove through western Kentucky, Sam explained about the dangerous narcotic Farley was taking. "So, Scruggs didn't put a ringer in the pill bottle then," Matt said.

"No, but Reicht did prescribe a med that should never be used unless the patient is under 24-7 care. The soft drinks at the con made his condition worse."

"Keeping the kid doped and locked up is exactly what he intended to do when he got the kid to that Homeside joint," Matt said.

She nodded. "But he started Farley onto the junk weeks ago."

"To make him—pardon the bad pun—spacie?" Matt asked.

"Yeah, I bet so. And, I wonder if he might not have been behind the kid acting psychotic for some time. Maybe ever since he started treating him? The more Farley hallucinates and acts weird, the easier it is to get him committed…and to make people doubt anything he might say."

"Like what? And why? Remember, Reicht had excellent credentials until the IRS came on the scene."

Sam shrugged. "I don't know. But somebody's going to a hell of a lot of trouble to shut the kid up permanently."

"Scruggs?" he suggested.

She looked dubious. "He's had plenty of chances to off the boy. I think he just wants his meal ticket punched—and speaking of punches, you should've seen the lump on his head when those goons tried to snatch Farley. No, someone else is after the kid."

"I still don't trust Elvis Scruggs," Matt said doggedly.

She bussed him on his cheek. "You're sweet when you're protective—a royal pain, but a sweet one."

They got as far as Tennessee when someone driving a tan Mustang passed them going fast enough for liftoff from the highway asphalt. "Crazy kids," Matt muttered to himself.

From the backseat where she'd been keeping an eye on Farley, Sam said, "I don't think so. Slow down and pull over—quick!"

"What the hell—" He didn't have a chance to say more before the muscle car cut directly in front of them and a MP5 submachine gun materialized from the passenger window. Matt swerved to the wide berm and hit the brakes at the same time. He could hear Sam climbing over the seat to reach the glove compartment where her .38 snub nose was concealed. "Stay down, dammit!" he yelled, not taking his eyes off the road as the first burst of fire whistled past the driver's window. The Mustang fishtailed as the driver put on the brakes.

If Matt hadn't slowed and pulled over, the automatic weapon fire could've taken him out and crashed the van, killing all three of them. Sam had the glove compartment open, crouched down as she rooted for her gun.

She lowered her window and hissed at him, "Now you get down. You're a much bigger target. Just be ready to get us out of here when I say the word."

"I don't like this, Sam."

"What? You think I do?" she replied, glaring at him until he complied. The attack vehicle started to back up. She knew he wanted to do something to protect her, but she was a better shot. And she needed a driver if they were going to have any hope of escaping this alive. She waited until the Mustang was only about twenty yards in front of them. The driver did just what she hoped he'd do. The MP5 poked out of the passenger window again.

"I need a distraction," she said to Matt. "Open your door but don't raise your head above the dash and for crying out loud, don't stick your foot on the ground and get it shot off."

"Think of all the dough we could save if I bought shoes one at a time, you tightwad," he muttered, doing as she said. The minute he shoved the door open, the shooter blasted away, but to do it, the gunman had to lean partially out of the car.

Sam took careful aim, using the van's large side-view mirror as cover for her hand. She fired and the automatic flew from the attacker's hands. It landed on the ground a few feet away. She could hear his curses and grinned grimly. "Bet that hurt like a bitch," she said, hoping she'd hit his fingers as well as the weapon. She fired again, this time at the car's right rear tire. When it went down with a soft whump, she turned to Matt. "Now, peel out before he recovers that cannon."

Matt gunned the powerful engine and took off, spraying gravel and dirt behind them. He swerved the van into the passing lane and sped by the disabled Mustang. Another single shot fired by the driver hit the side of the van but did far less damage than the automatic had done to his door, which looked kind of like a chunk of metallic Swiss cheese. At least the lock held as they sped away. A short burst of automatic fire echoed after them, but by the time the shooter had recovered his weapon from the ground, they were out of range.

"Who the hell are these guys?" he asked.

"Don't know but I got the plates this time," she replied, rooting for a scrap of paper and a pen. "Not local talent. Florida plates."

"You think they followed us all the way from St. Louis?"

"No way could they know what route we'd take," she said, shaking her head. "And after all this time, I'd have spotted a tail…unless…"

"You thinking what I'm thinking?" he asked.

"Let's put some distance between us and those charming fellows, then check the van for tracers."

They drove for another half hour at speeds Spacefleet would have envied. By the time they pulled into a large truck plaza and hid the van behind a cluster of Dumpsters in the back, it was dusk. Matt kept a lookout for their pals in the Mustang while Sam searched her Econoline.

"Bingo." She held up the small honing device. "Pretty high-tech," she said, looking around the plaza's parking lot. "Give me a minute."

Matt watched her sprint across to where a truck was starting to pull out of its space, gears grinding industriously. She pushed the magnetic device onto the rear door and stepped back, being careful to keep the driver from seeing her in his side view mirror. Damn, the woman was a wonder. He'd been hearing stories about her driving one of those behemoths cross-country from her uncle ever since they met at the wedding in Boston. At first he'd found it hard to credit. How could a small woman do it? He grinned idiotically.

Sam could. Of course.

She rejoined him, watching the direction the truck was heading. "Southbound on I-24," she said with a thumbs-up. "Perfect."

"But that's the way we were going," Matt said. "Don't tell me. We're taking the scenic route again." It wasn't a question.

She ignored him. "Think it might be better if I drove for a while. Although," she added, giving him a quick kiss, "you did really well during the getaway. For an amateur."

"Amateur! I've seen *The French Connection* twelve times," he groused, watching her open the rear doors of the van.

"How're you doing, Farley?" she asked the boy, whose eyelids were fluttering. He looked pale but his breathing was steady. She perched on the edge of the floor and took his pulse. Some irregularity, but not bad. "No use playing possum. I know you're awake. I didn't give you much and we've just had quite an adventure. Too bad you missed this one." Actually she was very glad he'd been unconscious during the shoot-out. She didn't need him going into another attack while they were in the wilds of the Smoky Mountains.

"El will come after you. You're not Starfleet," he said in a hoarse voice.

"I doubt he'll be able to find us. Look, Farley, I'm gonna explain this to you again. Somehow I don't think you quite caught it all the first time." As she spoke, Sam loosened the restraints and helped him into a sitting position. "You were right about me not being Spacefleet." She could see Matt ready to interrupt but she waved him off. "Commander Granger is, but I'm really a P.I."

"A private investigator?" he echoed, shaking his head as if trying to recall something she'd said before.

"Your father hired me to bring you back to Miami—"

"I don't want to go back to him," he said sullenly, his body stiffening with anger—or was it fear? "All he'll do is turn me over to that doctor and then I'll get sick again…"

"Right," Matt interjected. "We don't intend to take you back to either one of them, do we, Sam?"

She shook her head. "Someone's trying to kill you and until we figure out who it is, we'll keep you under wraps where they can't find you, but to get to the bottom of this we have to go back to Miami," she said in her best patient-medical professional tone of voice. Sometimes it worked.

This time it didn't. "No! I never want to go back there again! I want El. He's the only one who believes me. He knows about the conspiracy…the Pandorians…" His voice faded away. "I-I think I n-need my p-pills."

"Those pills Dr. Reicht prescribed for you? Why would you trust him? The stuff's bad news, Farley," she said.

"I g-gotta have 'em, p-please," he begged.

She exchanged a glance with Matt, who shrugged and said, "If what that pharmacist told you was right, he can't just quit cold turkey."

"How long since he took the last one?" she muttered to herself, checking her watch. She'd seen him pop one as they reached the Jag in the parking lot, around three. It was nearly eight-thirty now and they'd confiscated the junk the minute they had gotten him away from Scruggs. "I guess a half of one wouldn't hurt." She removed the cap from the bottle and snapped one of the tablets in half, offering it to Farley with more water.

He swallowed it and drank greedily, then looked up at her, then Matt. "Are you really Spacefleet?"

"Word of honor," Matt said, raising his hand. The poor kid had to have some familiar talisman to keep him calm until they could figure this out.

Farley seemed to weigh that, then nodded. "Okay, I guess if you vouch for her," he said, looking suspiciously at Sam, "then I'll trust you."

Matt gave Sam a wink and whispered softly as the boy tipped his head back and drank again from the water bottle, "Sometimes my way's better."

She mouthed a faintly obscene expression at him with a forced smile.

"But we gotta find Leila," Farley said, wiping his hand over the back of his mouth.

"We will, son. That's why Command sent me here. We'll stop whoever wants to hurt you, too," Matt reassured him.

Against Sam's best judgment, she let the two guys talk her into allowing Farley to sit in the backseat while she drove. Matt kept a close eye on him and he behaved for the next several hours, dozing off to sleep by the time they reached central Kentucky via back roads that Sam navigated in the dark with more verve than her husband would have preferred.

"I think we should stop for the night. We all need some rest, especially you after all this driving," he argued.

"Quit worrying. I'm used to long hauls and the sooner we get home, the sooner we get to the bottom of this whole mess," she said, stifling a yawn.

"That cuts it," he said. "You're not going to drive us off the edge of a cliff because you have to be the baddest trucker on the road. Pull over there." He pointed to a flashing neon sign ahead at the approaching exit.

"Ah, the Bates Motel. Good thinking, Normie. What a creepy-looking joint," she said, but she did as he demanded, too tired to argue.

"Considering the kind of places you locked me up in, this is the Ritz," he replied as the van eased up to the Lazy Boy Motel's registration door. "Hold the fort while I get us a room."

"We gotta have at least two beds," she called after him.

He stopped and looked over his shoulder. "You wanna cuddle with Farley watching?"

"No show-and-tell, Commander. Just a reminder that we have to secure the kid. Best thing would be to get two rooms. I'll stay in one with him and you take the other. That way we'll both get a good night's sleep."

He could see the smug look on her face. "I think Farley and I'll bunk together. That'll spare your modesty since you like to sleep mother naked."

She snorted. "Only because this sex fiend I know keeps ripping my clothes off every time we get near a bed."

"But not tonight. We're professionals, remember? You'll just have to restrain your baser urges, Sammie." He waggled his eyebrows and walked inside to register.

The room they chose for him and Farley was typical cheap motel with a rustic touch. The generously stained orange shag carpet and striped avocado drapes were yellowed with old cigarette smoke, but a deer head with a twelve-point rack welcomed them with liquid brown eyes from its mount on one phony wood-paneled wall. A thick layer of dust covered the television screen.

"Probably hasn't been turned on in so long the connection's rotted," Matt said, not really caring since he was too tired to press a remote button—assuming the ancient equipment even had one.

Sam checked the bathroom window and the front door lock, then opened the door adjoining to her room, a clone of the first one, except for the wall trophy. "Good. I couldn't sleep with her staring down at me," she said, pointing to the deer on the wall in the other room.

"Him. It's a buck, Sam. Antlers, you know? Sort of a symbol of other things they can't mount on the walls."

"Around here I wouldn't count on it," she shot back. "Let's catch a few Zs, then hit the road. I'll set the alarm for six."

Several hours later, Sam and Matt slept soundly. Neither was aware of the Jaguar XJ6 that pulled into the parking lot, its powerful engine a low, even purr as Elvis Scruggs cut the ignition. He wore a big grin as he slipped quietly out of the vintage car and reached under his jacket with one big hand. He withdrew a large shiny knife concealed in a sheath.

After studying the dark, silent motel to be certain no one was stirring, he moved soundlessly toward the white van, parked directly in front of the room where Sam slept.

Chapter 13

The sound was enough to raise the dead. Loud, earsplitting and ugly. Sam bolted upright in the middle of the rumpled grayish sheets, disoriented, her eyes gritty from hours spent negotiating twisty back roads in impenetrable darkness. "What the hell—" She rubbed her temples, certain her head would split apart like a ripe melon if that noise didn't stop.

Then from the other room Matt's voice called out, "Shut off the damned alarm, will you! Shit, I've heard less horrible sounds coming from a slaughterhouse!"

She groped across the lumpy mattress and found the culprit, practically smashing it as she punched every button and dial on it until the buzzing stopped. "Thank you, all the saints, I'm not naming any favorites these days," she muttered, scooting to the edge of the bed where she dangled her legs.

Faint streaks of pale light filtered in from a crack where the drapes separated, hanging unevenly on their rod. Six in the morning. Time to hit the road again. She'd been doing retrievals for how long now? "Too damn long," she said to the empty room. Behind the wall she could hear the shower being turned on. The rusty plumbing protested with a vibrating screech that reminded her of a dentist's drill.

Great way to start the day. She climbed out of bed and dug through the small overnight bag, pulling out her robe. Before she showered herself, she'd have to check on Farley, then let Matt take over that chore. The kid was too weak to hurt a fly. No sense having him stink up her van by depriving him of bathing privileges.

She walked into the adjoining room and looked over at his thin body stretched across the mattress, one arm cuffed to the bed frame. That was a precaution she always took with retrievals. Remembering Matt's reaction the first time she'd cuffed him, she suppressed a grin. "Good morning, Farley. Sleep okay?" she asked as he blinked at her.

That glazed look was still in his eyes. Not much food in his system to counteract the drug. She sat down beside him. "Let me take a look at you, see if you're all right," she said.

"I'm fine, honest," he said, trying to scoot away as if embarrassed to have a woman see him up close wearing only pajamas. The cuffs stopped him.

She reached down and unlocked them, then took his hand in hers and measured his pulse. Fast but even. "How about I get us some breakfast?" she asked.

"I'm so starved I could eat that poor creature on the wall, antlers and all," Matt said from the bathroom door. "I'll go for breakfast while Farley showers. I saw some vending machines in the registration area last night."

Within ten minutes Farley was showered and Matt had set out big paper cups of coffee—decaf for the boy—packages of cake doughnuts white with powdered sugar and chocolate cupcakes. "The filling tastes like sweetened shaving cream," she said over a mouthful.

"Sorry. All the chef had to offer—the automated chef, that is," he replied cheerfully, chowing down.

After being certain they weren't intent on poisoning him, Farley ate a doughnut and drank some decaf. "C-can I have a pill now?" he asked, not for the first time since the alarm had awakened them.

Sam dispensed another half of one. Within thirty minutes they were back on the road. They made it about a dozen miles on the twisting mountain road when the van gave a sudden lurch and the power died. Sam fought to hold the wheel on a sharp curve, steering the Econoline to the berm. The drop-off directly to her right was a good fifty feet over a steep rocky incline sprinkled with scrubby evergreens.

Matt looked out the passenger window and shuddered. "Damn, I hate heights."

"I though you were a Spacefleet Commander," Farley said. "How can you be afraid of a little mountain?"

Matt gave Farley a stern look as he replied, "Obviously, you've never been aboard ship, Ensign. In space there is no sense of height. And for planetary exploration, we use Centarian Crawlers—not clunkers like this." He turned to her. "Any idea what happened?"

"Let me check the engine, sir," she snarled, getting out of her beloved Econoline.

He could hear her curse as she stomped to the side door and opened it, yanking her tool chest out from where she kept it behind her seat. "Can you fix it?" he asked.

"Timing belt's busted. I don't usually keep those in stock," she snapped, still angry at the insult to her van. "Hand me the first aid kit from under the dash."

"You gonna give the van CPR or something?"

"Funny, Commander, but then you spacers don't know jack about internal combustion engines that run earth *clunkers,* do you? Don't teach that at Spacefleet Academy, do they?" She slammed the door.

He got out of the car with the first-aid materials she always carried and watched, mystified as she used a screwdriver and wrench to remove a rubber belt from the engine. She held it up for his inspection. "What am I looking at— wait a minute, that's been cut partway through," he said with an absurd burst of pride. But his grin immediately faded. "Sabotage."

Sam had already pulled her .38 out of her fanny pack and was eyeing the road. "You know how to use this. Watch out while I jerry-rig the engine."

He took the gun and stood guard. Not a sound broke the silence on the deserted highway for a minute or so. Then one junker truck filled with watermelons wheezed past them. "So much for down-home Samaritans," he muttered as the ancient tub disappeared around the bend.

By then Sam pulled a roll of narrow elastic athletic bandaging from the kit and measured it against the belt, allowing for flex. "Not gonna last long, but if the map's right, we're only a couple of miles from the next burg."

In spite of their predicament, Matt had to laugh as he watched her. "You're using an Ace bandage in place of a running belt?"

"Timing belt. Yeah. It should hold until we can get to what passes as civilization around here." She had the thing rigged in a couple of minutes.

Matt held his breath as she started the car. The engine sputtered, then caught, but just as he was ready to let out a whoop of elation, a big maroon Jag pulled into sight, headed directly toward them.

"It's El! I knew he'd come for me!" Farley exclaimed, unfastening his seat belt, prepared to jump from the speeding van.

Matt seized the boy by his shirt collar, yelling to Sam over the noise of the engine, "Can you lock his door so he can't open it?"

"Done," she replied. "Just watch him so he doesn't hurt himself."

"Him!" he echoed in outrage as the boy's puny fist connected with his nose. Not much strength, but damn, it still hurt, reminding him of why he'd quit boxing in the army. He couldn't stand getting his proboscis punched. Matt leaned over the seat and subdued Farley, who was wriggling like an eel. Finally the kid started panting in exhaustion, too drug weakened to struggle further.

Matt suddenly realized they were in a desperate race and neither he nor Farley had on their seat belts. Bad. He used his long arms to strap the boy in, saying, "Don't do anything stupid or you could get us all killed, you copy that?" When Farley nodded and turned around to watch the Jag gaining on them, Matt decided the kid was willing to take his chances on being rescued by his hero instead of battling his own way to freedom.

He turned around and fastened his belt as Sam took a curve on two wheels. "Jeez, look at that drop-off," he said, shuddering. "Should I try to hit his tire?" he asked her.

"He's not shooting at us," she replied, her forehead creased in a frown of concentration as she caught up to the watermelon truck.

"He doesn't want to hurt his meal ticket," Matt replied.

"True, but I think I have a better idea," she said, swerving around the old junker just as they leveled out on a stretch with a scenic turnoff space on the opposite side of the road, offering respite from the steep drop-off. She honked at the truck, then hit her brakes when she was only a dozen yards or so in front of him, all the while watching her side views to judge the distance between the two vehicles. *Now, don't let anyone come from the opposite direction…just yet.*

The truck slammed on its brakes with a loud screech and started to swerve across the road toward the lookout turnoff rather than crash into her or the rock wall of the mountain. When the driver hit the gravel, his truck fishtailed in a circle as he cut the wheel to regain control. The flimsy tailgate's rusted hinges gave way and a torrent of big ripe melons started flying over the highway, airborne until they smashed like bright crimson cluster bombs on the road.

Seeing the Technicolor catastrophe unfolding in front of him like Fourth of July fireworks, Elvis hit the brakes of his Jag. Sam sped onward, heading downhill toward another switchback in the road. The last thing she saw in her mirrors was the Jag skidding on the slick mush of mashed melons, twisting and turning onto the wide gravel ledge where it came to rest against the guardrail.

"Roman Numeral's really gonna be pissed," she sighed.

"You ever think there might be more money in drag racing than retrievals?" Matt asked her.

"Too dangerous," she replied. "Now, how do we give him the slip?"

"You just did, and the slide, too." Matt looked at the map. "Cornersburg is about a mile down the road."

"Too far. He'll be on us in a minute and I can't keep up this speed or the jerry-rigged 'belt' will go out again."

"Whoa," Matt said, spotting an unmarked turnoff about fifty feet ahead. It quickly vanished into dense vegetation. "Turn there."

Sam took the van onto what barely passed as a gravel road that twisted down the steep mountainside, leading to God knew where. Out of the back window, Farley, with a start-lingly renewed burst of energy, started yelling at the top of his lungs, "El! El, I'm here, down here! Turn here!"

His high-pitched shrieking could've carried over the sounds of a jumbo jet during takeoff. Matt cursed and snapped off his seat belt, twisting around so he could grab Farley and clamp his hand over the kid's mouth. Farley bit him. Matt withdrew his bloodied fingers with an oath. "Sit back and shut up or I swear on my great-aunt Claudia's Cross of Lorraine, I'll choke the shit out of you."

"You're no Spacefleet Commander," Farley accused, sitting back with his arms crossed defensively over his skinny chest. "You're a Klingoff agent."

"And you're a bratty kid. Crap, I'll probably need a tetanus shot," Matt groused.

"Will both of you just chill out until I can figure out where the hell we are?" Sam snapped after the van hit a big rut in the road and she bumped her head against the roof.

Being much taller and without a seat belt, Matt hit his head a lot harder. "Damn, watch it, will you? I'd like to walk away from this wreck with my brains still in my skull, not on the roof."

"You're in no danger since you haven't got any to start with," she said, pounding the steering wheel in frustration as they hit another pothole. "First those turkeys turn the door into a lunar landscape, then the timing belt gets cut and now the suspension's shot. I'll be lucky if I can sell my baby for salvage if this keeps up."

They pulled out of the shadows of post oaks and kudzu, bouncing from the steep decline into a small clearing in the narrow valley. Only one building stood beneath a canopy of sugar pines. Perhaps *stood* was saying too much. It really sort of leaned together as if each warped, gray board was dependent on the kindness of its neighbor to hold it upright. The entire shack was just waiting for one swirl of wind or the removal of a single slat before the whole place went down like a row of dominoes.

"You think there's a still inside?" Matt asked with a chuckle.

"Wouldn't bet against it," Sam replied. "I only hope whoever owns the place doesn't take us for revenuers."

Matt snorted now. "I bet no one's inhabited that shack for a couple of decades."

"You lose," she replied as an old woman appeared in the door, which hung ajar at an off-kilter angle.

She walked the same way, leaning on a cane for support. It would have been difficult to guess her age—anywhere from seventy to a hundred. Wrinkles covered her sun-weathered face like the hide on an elephant's rump. She had no teeth. Her hair was gray and frizzy, pulled haphazardly back in a braided bun. She might have resembled an older variation of the female figure in *American Gothic* if it weren't for the pipe clenched firmly between her gums.

"Don't get many visitors," she said as Sam pulled up.

"I can't imagine why," Matt muttered beneath his breath. Ignoring his aching head and hand, he gave her his best Tom Selleck grin and climbed out of the van. "Howdy, ma'am. I'm Matt Granger and this is my wife, Samantha, and our—"

"Our patient," Sam said, jumping out from the shot-up door.

"They're Klingoffs in human disguise. Don't let them fool you," Farley said as he climbed out of the damaged vehicle. "It's all a plot to take over Earth—"

The old woman looked at the boy's flushed face, then back to Matt and Sam. "He—you know?" she asked, making a circling movement around her ear with one gnarled hand.

"Yeah, he thinks we're all characters from *Space Quest*," Sam replied.

"That one of them TV shows?" she asked with a frown. "I don't hold with watchin' that junk. Rots the brain. Why'd you come here? Not much of anybody does, 'cept for my boys."

"Your boys?" Sam asked nervously, half expecting to see a bunch of hulking knuckle-draggers in bib overalls carrying double-barreled shotguns materialize from the underbrush.

"Got two sons. Grown now. Had a husband, too, but he's gone to his reward." They way she said it indicated the direction he'd gone.

"Your sons live around here?" Sam asked.

"Nope. Would you if you didn't have ta?" She fussed with the pipe and relit it with a wooden match. Then she fixed them with shrewd dark eyes of an indeterminate color. "Like I said, I don't get many visitors, specially ones driving shot up trucks."

Sam almost corrected her and said it was a van, but decided Matt's charm would work better. She let him handle this.

"We had an accident," he said. "Someone wants to keep us from bringing Farley back to his family for medical treatment."

"They want ta stop you bad enough to open up with one of them newfangled IMI or H & K assault weapons? Nasty things. Don't hit what they aim for. Give me a good ole Mossberg .410 full choke any day. Knock a squirrel out a hickory tree at forty yards."

"To be honest, I'm kinda happy they didn't have one of those," Matt said with a disarming grin. "How'd you come to know so much about modern weaponry?"

"Just cause I talk slow don't mean I'm stupid," she drawled. "I read Tom Clancy, 'n some other stuff."

"We didn't mean to sound patronizing, Mrs.—?" Sam waited for a name.

"Flowers. Daisy Flowers. Ain't that a good one. Usta be

Daisy Grover till I met up with a slick-talking moonshiner named Bobby Ray Flowers. I never got to finish my school-in'," she said with genuine regret.

"But I bet your sons did," Matt ventured.

She nodded. "I seen to it. They're good to me." She appeared to take his measure, then turned to Sam. "Missus, you 'n your man 'n that boy look in a bad way. Come on inside and set a spell. It ain't much, but I got fresh, cool well water, 'n a bite to eat." With that she turned and hobbled up the single step into the shack.

Matt and Sam exchanged glances and shrugged. If Elvis had seen the cutoff, he'd have found them by this time. "Come on, Farley, we wouldn't want to turn down Southern hospitality," she said.

"El will turn you over to Spacefleet Intelligence for a mindmeld."

"Ouch, that sounds bad," Sam said. "What's it mean?"

Matt sighed. "Didn't you read any of the books I gave you? Earth's Vulcant allies use the technique for probing inside an interrogation subject's head."

"You better watch it, buster, or I'll check you into the same hospital with the kid," she whispered. Farley ignored them, walking inside as if entering an alien spacecraft.

The cabin was a surprise to all three of them. Composed of two rooms, it was as neat and clean on the inside as it was ramshackle on the outside. The maple table and chairs in the center of the room and the hutch against the far wall appeared new. Fresh curtains in a sunny yellow print hung over the side windows. A small but comfortable sofa sat in front of a wall filled with bookcases. Its shelves contained everything from Charles Dickens to Tom Clancy.

"No sci-fi," Farley said, perusing the titles.

"You don't read much, do ya, sonny?" she asked, hobbling over to one shelf and pulling down a volume of H.G. Wells. "Now this here's the real thing. None of that Hollywood claptrap."

"Hey, he wrote *War of the Worlds*," the boy exclaimed, his earlier anger dissipated. "I saw the movie."

Daisy shook her head. "Read the book. It's better."

"Your place is nice," Sam said.

"Kinda fools folks from the outside. Coy, he wanted to have it painted, run in electricity, all that stuff, but I told him no." She poured cool water into three tumblers with floral designs on the outsides. "Too hot to cook during the day," she said, indicating an unbelievably shiny iron stove with the firebox banked. It, too, appeared new. "But I got a ham in the smokehouse and some bread I baked last evening."

"We don't want to put you to any trouble, although we sure do appreciate the water," Matt said.

"And, we have to get out of here before those guys who were shooting at us show up. Wouldn't want to cause you any trouble," Sam added.

"My boys been pesterin' me to move to the city for years, but I like my feet planted 'neath my own table. I'm safe here, but mebbe you ain't," she said shrewdly.

"We need to get to the Georgia border," Sam replied honestly.

"Without any more shooters who might hurt Farley," Matt added, looking over to where the boy was sitting cross-legged on a small sofa, flipping through the book Daisy had given him.

The old woman laughed and the creases in her face deepened. In spite of adversity, she'd done a lot of laughing during her lifetime. "I might cud help. This here valley runs south for near fifty miles 'n there's a road—well, sorta—all the way."

Sam digested this. "I might be able to nurse the van that far if our Ace bandage supply holds out. There aren't any towns along the way, by chance?"

Daisy shook her head. "Jest lots a trees 'n kudzu. Oh, 'n did I mention skeeters? Here, I kin draw a map." She scuttled over to the hutch and pulled a stubby pencil and a notepad from a drawer, then sat down at the table and started to outline the twists and turns of the unpaved road, alerting them to avoid where it forked off to dead ends.

"You're one of them, too. I can tell," Farley said suddenly. "Real aliens aren't weak little green men," he scoffed, pointing at the book. "They're Klingoff warriors or sneaky Pandorians or—"

"Maybe it's time for a little more medication," Sam murmured to Matt.

"Boy looks doped up 'nough already. I got some good herbal remedies pounded up with balsam plant. Don't taste too good, but it'll clear his head, if anythin' will." She shoved the map at Matt and started to get up.

"We appreciate the offer but I'm a paramedic and I don't think it would be safe to give him any new medication—he might be allergic," Sam explained.

"I'm not taking anything that Pandorian spy gives me," Farley said, flattening himself against the wall.

Matt smiled at the old woman. "We better get going, Mrs. Flowers, but we do thank you for your kindness to strangers."

"You 'nother one of them folks that's always been dependent on the kindness o' strangers?" she asked him with a sly grin.

Damn, the old hill woman had read *A Streetcar Named Desire!* The expression on his face must have given away his surprise because she laughed.

"With a name like Tennessee Williams, how'd you expect me to pass that up?" she asked.

As Matt and Daisy talked, Sam chewed her lip and worried

about nursing her sabotaged van across the wilderness. It wasn't exactly a Conestoga wagon. And how the hell had Scruggs find them? They'd ditched the tracking device. "I'm gonna check my van and see if the jerry-rig's holding," she said.

Matt had been considering how Scruggs had found them, too. "Too bad we can't buy a used car or at least change the color of the van," he said as he folded the map and placed it carefully in his pocket. He allowed Daisy to precede him out the door and grabbed Farley by one arm, gently raising the boy. "Time to go," he said.

Farley clutched the book as if it were a talisman to ward off aliens, even if he didn't concur with Wells's idea about what they looked like. "Let 'em keep it. Mebee if he reads more, he'll watch TV less," the old woman said.

They watched as Sam checked her handiwork, pronouncing it good to go. She walked over to Daisy and gave her a hug. "You know, in some ways, you remind me of my gram back in Boston."

"Why, thanks, honey, even if she is a Yankee, that's a nice thing ta say." Daisy paused, then looked at the white van. "Can't help you with 'nother car, but mebbe we cud fix this 'un so's nobody'd recognize it."

"How?" both Sam and Matt asked in unison.

Farley said in awe, "She's got a Reemulan cloaking device!"

Chapter 14

"A still!" Matt said as he looked at the dust-coated apparatus, something out of a Rube Goldberg nightmare. Almost totally covered in kudzu, it was tucked away in a tiny shed down a twisting path. He ripped away more vines so he could follow the surprisingly spry old woman inside.

"It was Bobby Ray's. I ain't been down here since he died, but I know he left a couple o' gallons o' shine over there." She pointed to a cluster of stone jugs in one corner of the small room.

When they returned a few minutes later, Sam blinked in amazement. "Is that what I think it is?" she asked.

"Yep, it is," Matt replied cheerfully, tugging the cork from one of the heavy jugs.

"Now, you be real careful. Oh, 'n roll up the winders afore you start," Daisy cautioned. "Don't want it to touch the upholstery. Kindy eats it up."

"What?" Sam was beginning to feel as if she'd missed

something, as out of it as Farley, who sat on the doorstep of the cabin, clutching his book.

Matt rolled up the window on the shot-up driver's door and then hefted the jug. "I'm stripping the paint off the van," he replied, hefting the open container and splashing a generous amount against the side.

Almost immediately, the white paint started to bubble like something in a witch's cauldron. Wide-eyed with horror, Sam watched as he doused the whole side of her baby.

"My Bobby Ray weren't much o' a shine maker toward the end. A couple a fellers from down the road apiece went blind from drinkin' his stuff 'n word spread. Bidness kindy fell off after that…."

"I can imagine," was all Sam could manage.

Undaunted, Daisy explained, "This here last batch's been a sittin' fer nigh onto a dozen years. I use it to clean them fancy copper pans Ray—he's my other son—give me last Christmas. Figgered it'd work on car paint."

It was like watching the Wicked Witch of the West dissolve in *The Wizard of Oz*. Sam stood speechless, appalled. The dull gray primer and bare metal started to show through as the white paint slid off the vehicle. A snake shedding its skin was all she could think to compare it with. Matt was having a blast, damn his eyes! He knew how much she loved that van.

"Uncle Dec will kill me when he sees this—no, he'll kill you!"

Matt, who by now had gone around the whole car and was working on the roof, said cheerfully, "We'll have it repainted and the door replaced before he ever knows."

"You're enjoying this," she accused, eyes narrowed dangerously, but afraid to come anywhere near the toxic splashing.

"There are times when I think you love this old van more than me."

"There are times when I'm sure of it," she snapped. "Like right now."

"Yeah? Try to get it to take a shower with you," he said with a glint in his eyes.

In a little over an hour they were bumping and bouncing their way down the valley toward the Georgia border in their now-gray van. As soon as they reached the state line and drove onto a county road, they searched out the first auto store they could find in a sleepy town. Matt and Farley munched on lunch, watching as Sam removed the makeshift replacement and installed a new timing belt on the van.

Daisy had sent them off with a bag of ham sandwiches, a jug of cold well water and her best wishes for a safe trip. "You should take a break and eat," Matt said around a mouthful of salty ham and crusty bread. "It's really good."

"When I'm done," she replied, wiping sweat from her forehead and leaving a smear of motor oil on her face. As she completed the task and stepped back to admire her handiwork, he took a handkerchief from his pocket and held her chin in his hand while he rubbed the stain away.

Then he kissed the spot. "You're cute even when you're greasy. Wish I could've been more help."

She grinned at him and used his formerly snow-white handkerchief to clean her hands. "I'm starving." She seized a half sandwich and took a big bite. "Daisy cured this herself and baked the bread. You know, Granger, you guys could take a lesson from free-spirited women."

"I have. I grew up with one and married another," he replied with a martyred sigh. He'd promised to write Daisy when they had things sorted out for Farley. Her final advice had been, "Throw away that TV and set that boy down in a good library. Do him more good than all the doctors in Florida."

Watching the boy as he sat in the backseat, engrossed in the slim volume the old woman had given him, Matt was inclined to agree. Farley hadn't asked about any meds since they set out. Sam said something, and he turned to her. "Sorry, I didn't hear you?"

"You seemed a million miles away. Still gloating about the paint job on my van?"

"No paint job. A strip job." He couldn't resist a little smirk, knew he'd pay for it. "No one will recognize this van once we get the door replaced."

"Yeah, that's got me thinking," she said, taking a long pull from the water jug.

"Always dangerous, Sam."

Ignoring his smart remark, she replied, "We know how those goons tracked us, but how did Scruggs find us? I double-checked for more honing devices. We're clean."

"It's an ion signature registration. Spacefleet uses it all the time," Farley said, turning a page of the Wells book without looking up.

"Right," Sam said, not bothering to ask Matt for the explanation, which they both knew had to be irrelevant.

Matt shook his head. "No ideas, but we should be okay once we hit I-75 and pass Atlanta. If we're real lucky, he may get lost in the Smokies and eaten by kudzu."

"Or 'skeeters.' I feel like a pincushion with scabies," she said, scratching her bare arm.

"El will find me," Farley said again, putting down his book. "We have to find Leila."

"Tell me more about this Leila," Matt said, wanting to keep the kid happy and avoid using restraints on him again. Of course, considering how Farley had reacted the last time they encountered "El", maybe he should rethink that idea. His fingers were still bruised and abraded from that bite.

As they climbed back into the van and resumed their journey, the boy answered. "Leila's beautiful and smart, too."

Teenage crush on a slick momma, Sam thought as Farley described the blond stripper. She made a mental note to check out the woman when they reached Miami. Somehow, Leila Satterwaite must fit into this puzzle. Sam had spent a fortune driving to St. Louis and renting that hotel room. She didn't even want to think about what it was going to set her back to have the Econoline restored. Damn, how was she going to get paid if Farley's father had changed his mind and wanted the boy dead now?

Atlanta had moved urban sprawl from a social problem to an art form. Sam negotiated the outer belt during rush hour, a 24-7 madhouse that rivaled her own Miami. After she drove through the last of the southern suburbs and they hit the south-bound interstate, Matt took over the wheel, allowing her to catch a few hours of sleep. They'd agreed it would be best to drive straight through. Taking turns at the wheel was the safest course.

Once on the open road, he started to make up lost time. After about an hour on the flat highway, he caught a car in the side-view mirror, moving up on them fast. "Uh-oh," he muttered, tromping the accelerator the way he'd seen Sam do it. The van responded. So did the maroon Jag.

Sam jerked awake and immediately saw Winchester's vintage car approaching. "How the hell did he find us again!" She dug into the glove compartment and came out with her .38. Cursing, she started to roll down the window, but from the back Farley released his seat belt and jumped at her, wrestling to get the gun away from her.

As they bounced around the front of the van, Matt struggled to keep it on the road when they smashed into his right shoulder. "Who the hell put him on steroids?" he asked, while Sam fought to immobilize the kid without hurting him.

By now the Jag was beside them, cutting closer, the passenger window rolled down. Scruggs's nasty-looking Glock pointed directly at Matt's head. Matt might have considered making a run for it with Sam's souped up engine but with her and Farley thrashing around the front seat, he didn't dare risk wrecking the van. If he was shot and lost control, she and the kid would go crashing through the front windshield.

"He has a gun on us, Sam. I'm stopping," he said over the grunts and curses. By the time he'd cut the wheel and slowed, taking the van onto the wide stretch of red dirt at the side of the highway, Sam had Farley pinned to the seat. The Jag pulled off the highway directly in front of them.

She looked over and hissed breathlessly, "Why the hell did you do tha—oh," she corrected herself, seeing the cannon Scruggs pointed at Matt while he walked toward them.

"I...told you," Farley choked out, "El'd rescue m-me." He started to hyperventilate again.

Sam cursed, removing her knee from Farley's thin chest. "The strength of Hercules one minute, a kicked puppy the next. Cover me," she hissed at Matt, reaching down to the floor where she'd dropped her snub nose during the battle with Farley.

Matt started to get out of the van, hands in the air. "Hey, El, how're you doing, good buddy?"

Scruggs looked decidedly out of sorts, eyes narrowed on Granger as he called out to Sam, "I wouldn't try anything stupid with a gun, Sam, or I'll have to put a slug in the big guy, here."

"Okay, okay, let's talk this over," she said, climbing off Farley. "Your pal's in bad shape. Needs a doctor. We have to—" Before she could say more, Scruggs suddenly turned and bolted toward the Jag. He jumped in and pulled away. "What the hell happened?" she asked Matt as she jumped out of the van.

He tipped his head at the approaching Georgia Highway

Patrol car cutting off the road behind them. "I think that officer might've just saved our bacon. You'd better get your signed release for transporting Farley out. I have a hunch you may need it."

"The kid needs a doc more," she said to Matt. She walked toward the highway patrolman, who had just opened his door.

"We have a medical emergency," she said in her most calm, professional voice.

"I believe you just might—if that fellow waving a gun at you had decided to use it," the gray-haired man replied. His face was harsh and weathered as the dry countryside around him. "I called in his plates. He won't get far. You folks all right?" he asked. Then, noting the condition of the driver's door, he said, "I'll need to see some ID."

"I'm Sam Ballanger," she said, pulling her driver's license from her fanny pack while Matt dug for his wallet. "That boy is having a reaction to some medication he's been taking."

Farley lay back against the seat, not moving, but not acting particularly stricken, either. Probably calmed down after she got out of the van. The highway patrol officer glanced inside at the boy, then back to Matt. "It looks to me, the way you were weaving all over the road before the guy in the Jag pulled you over, that you're the ones on something," he drawled, glancing at their licenses.

"I had to subdue my patient when he became violent. That's what caused Matt to lose control of the wheel. The man who forced us off the road was trying to kidnap the boy." As she pulled out the legal paper for the retrieval that Upton Winchester had signed, she waited for Farley to accuse her of being the kidnapper and Elvis Scruggs his savior. But the boy remained eerily quiet, just watching them with glazed brown eyes.

The officer went to his car, radioing their ID and info on the document allowing her to return Farley to his father. That killed the better part of an hour while they roasted on the scorching roadside. Sweat rolled down her face and neck, pooling between her breasts and soaking her T-shirt to her body.

"Remind me never to complain about the heat in Miami again. At least we have the ocean to move the air," she said, running her fingers through her wet hair.

"I think we'd better give up on driving directly home and get a motel again. Now that the fuzz will snag Elvis, we'll be in the clear."

"Don't speak too soon. They may get Scruggs, but I'm not sure the cop bought my story about those goons who blasted the door with automatic weapons."

Matt shrugged. "Then he'll ask us to stay in the nearest burg until they can verify it. Either way, we could use some sleep. So could the kid."

Sam looked over at Farley, who leaned back, arms crossed stubbornly over his chest, staring at nothing. "He put some new bruises on me. Damned hard to subdue him without hurting him."

"Too bad you never learned the Vulcant nerve pinch," he said with a straight face.

She ignored him as the officer got out of his car and approached them. "Checks out. You're free to go, but take care with that boy so you don't have a wreck."

"Any word on Scruggs?" Matt asked.

A frown creased the man's already battered face. "That's no longer my jurisdiction," was all he would reply.

"No comment," Matt said as they climbed back inside the van.

"Yeah, kinda like there's something going on and he was told not to let us in on it."

"You think Scruggs gave them the slip?" Matt asked, dubious.

"Pretty hard to believe in a car that easy to spot. No place to hide around here," she replied, scanning the flat horizon that stretched to the south. "Let's roll. We'll check on Scruggs once we get back to Miami. Somehow I have a gut feeling we haven't heard the last of good ole El."

"Funny thing. So do I," Matt said.

After a lengthy heart-to-heart, Sam moved Farley to the backseat and sat beside him, ready to restrain him if he tried anything crazy again. They ate supper in a roadside diner, then stopped for the night in Macon and got a motel. This time Sam paid extra for a lighted parking lot with a security guard. "I don't want to come out at dawn and find my tires slashed or any other alterations to the engine," she said.

Matt only grinned, knowing how it killed her to pay for decent lodging. They had the same sleeping arrangements as before with adjoining rooms. After allowing Farley to shower and change into pj's, Sam cuffed him to his bed. "You get some sleep while we decide what to do when we get to Miami," Matt told the boy.

"You can't let Dr. Reicht have me. He's one of them—the Pandorians. I know he is," Farley said, shaking his head, as if trying to clear it.

"What about your father?" Matt asked, curious to see what the boy would say.

"N-no! He's one of them, too. They're in it together. Hc's bad." Then he stopped suddenly.

"Don't worry, Farley," Sam assured him, wanting to stop another panic attack. "We aren't going to give you to either your father or the doctor."

"Then what are you going to do with me?" the kid asked, sounding frightened.

"Good question. I have some contacts. We'll find a safe place for you until we figure out this mess," she replied.

"I know where he can stay," Matt said.

Both Farley and Sam looked at him.

"A real Spacefleet officer's house," he replied with a smile.

Chapter 15

"Okay, so who's this Spacefleet officer? Anyone I know?" she asked.

"As a matter of fact, it is. His name's Bill Montoya." He couldn't resist a grin when she blinked in astonishment.

"As in Captain Montoya, Miami-Dade Tac-Ops? No way."

"Way. He's been a Spacer since he was in college. I interviewed him after one of the section's dogs found that lost toddler a couple of years ago. While we were talking, I happened to notice an autographed photo of Captain Turk on the wall in his office and we got to talking about it. He's the president of the Miami chapter."

"It's an international organization with local chapters in ninety-three countries around the world," Farley said. "I belong to the Miami Chapter. Captain Montoya's our regional commander, but I've never had the chance to meet him." He sounded excited about the prospect.

Funny how the kid could be so clear on some things, so fuzzy on others, Sam thought. "Are you a member, too?" she asked Matt.

"No. When I started working for the *Herald,* I didn't have time. Maybe I'll have to re-up to get Bill to give us a hand."

"You think he'll go for it?" She was dubious.

"If we explained the situation to him, yes, I think he will. The Montoyas have three teens around Farley's age and his wife's parents live with them, so there'd be plenty of supervision. They're good people, Sam—even if Bill and his kids are Spacers."

She threw up her hands. "Hey, you're the one volunteering for them, not me. If they agree, go for it."

"What say, Farley?" Matt asked. "Will an honest-to-God Spacefleet captain be okay with you?" He had no idea what he'd do if the kid said no.

Farley brightened at the idea. "Yes. Maybe he'll know about what's happened to Leila. He might be able to help with our mission."

"Right now your mission is to stay safe and out of the hands of those goons who tried to run over you and blast you with automatic weapons," Sam said. "Let us look for your friend Leila."

"You sent the police after El," Farley accused her.

"I didn't have to. If you recall, he was pointing a very large gun at Matt's head. Highway patrolmen happen to take a real dim view of stuff like that."

"He wouldn't have shot you. Only stunned you," Farley said to Matt.

Right. "Glocks don't come equipped with stun settings, Far," Sam said. "It wasn't a dazer."

"I—I d-don't k-know. I didn't s-see the gun, but El's my friend." The boy sounded utterly miserable and was tensing up again.

"We're your friends, too," she said earnestly, praying he wouldn't have another withdrawal attack. He'd made it through the day without any more pills and she wanted to keep him off the stuff, if possible, until they got a full medical evaluation in Miami.

"We'll see if the authorities in Georgia have released Elvis as soon as we get you safely back to Miami," Matt said. "I promise."

"How about we all get some sleep?" Sam suggested.

Taking her cue, Matt yawned loudly. "I'm hitting the hay," he said, turning off the bedside light in their room.

Farley dropped back onto his bed and closed his eyes. Sam gave Matt a quick buss on his whiskery cheek, then walked to her room and flicked out the lights. She lay down on the bed, which seemed lonely without Matt's big body. Trying not to think about that, she considered Farley.

Whether he trusted them even a little was still impossible to gauge. The only thing she was certain about was that the kid knew more than he was telling them. But about what? Maybe when they had him safely stashed in Miami and could start digging on Roman Numeral and the smarmy shrink, they'd find out. She hoped so. The kid had been given a raw deal in life.

First thing in the morning the trio ate a hearty breakfast in the motel's restaurant. Then while Sam lingered over her third cup of coffee, Matt excused himself to make a call to Montoya. He returned smiling as if he'd just won the lottery. Apparently the kid had gotten to him same as her, Sam thought.

"Bill will be happy to have Farley stay with him until we can clear this mess up. He even recommended a doctor at the Cedars Med Center."

"I don't need a psychiatrist!" Farley protested. Several people around them stopped eating and stared at him.

In a low voice, Sam said, "Dr. Reicht gave you some bad medicine, Farley. We have to find out what's in it and what it's done to you. You have to see a doctor so they can run some tests. We won't let them lock you away. I promise."

Farley turned from her to Matt. "Will Captain Montoya be there?"

"If you want, I'll ask him to meet us there, but first we have a long hard drive ahead of us. Okay?"

"Okay," Farley agreed. He looked suspiciously around the crowded restaurant filled with tourists and people eating before heading to work, as if trying to figure out who the Klingoffs in disguise were.

Sam said a silent prayer to St. Jude, promising the impossible. *Just let us get the kid safely to Miami and I'll go back to church. Honest.*

Captain William Montoya was a tall man in his late forties with curly dark hair just going salt-and-pepper. He wore a pencil-thin mustache and had movie star teeth. Though handsome enough to play a starship captain, he was a consummate professional police officer, extremely well thought of by the men and women who worked in the Tactical Operations Section he commanded.

He met them in the waiting room at the Cedars Medical Center where the psychiatrist he'd recommended was evaluating Farley. The cool pale green walls were offset by a brilliant morning sunrise pouring liquid gold through the windows. The room was deserted except for one elderly couple who sat at the opposite end, engrossed in a morning news show.

After they exchanged hellos, Matt explained, "Dr. Bester's

still waiting for blood analyses and other test results. We owe you big-time for helping with this, Bill."

"Glad to do it. Any time we get a kid off drugs and under good medical care, it makes our work easier." He looked at the dark circles ringing their eyes and their rumpled clothing. "You look as if neither of you've slept in a week."

"It's been pretty hairy getting the Winchester boy back in one piece," Sam said.

"Matt told me about the attempts to kidnap, then kill the boy—and you in the process. I understand his family's choice in shrinks leaves something to be desired. I asked my friends over in Narcotics to run a check on this Reicht guy. Sounds as if he might be involved in the…ah, illegal pharmacy business."

"Yeah, I talked to Patowski about him a couple of days ago. Lots of nasty rumors floating around but nothing anybody can nail him with…yet."

Montoya knew she'd left Homicide under a cloud but didn't indicate it as he nodded, stroking his mustache while he listened to what they'd learned so far about Reicht. When Sam mentioned Farley's fixation on Leila Satterwaite, he immediately interrupted her. "You haven't heard any local TV news since you've been on the road, have you?"

"No. Too beat last night to even flip on the remote. Why?" Sam asked.

"This Satterwaite woman, was she a tall blonde, flashy dresser—a stripper?"

"That's her 'cover' according to Farley," Sam said. "What do you know about her?"

"She's wearing a toe tag in the morgue. Homicide fished her out of the Intracoastal below Rickenbacker yesterday. She'd been beaten and then strangled. Would've washed out to sea if not for a lucky fluke. A fishing trawler's nets got fouled up and guess what they found?"

"Gruesome. Farley will take this pretty hard," Matt said. "Might be best not to tell him yet." The captain nodded.

"When did she die?" Sam asked.

"M.E. says the injuries were about a week old. Being in the water makes it harder to calculate. She was in pretty rough shape, but their best guess, she was killed no more than forty-eight hours ago."

"Any idea who did it?" Sam asked.

"Not my bailiwick, but I don't think Homicide has any leads so far."

"I'll find out if Patty's working the case," she said.

Just then the door to the medical facility swung open and a small man with straight black hair and a worried expression approached them. He wore a white coat identifying him as Dr. Bester. "Your young friend is fortunate to be as coherent as he is, all things considered," he said to Sam and Matt, looking questioningly at Montoya, who showed the psychiatrist his badge while Matt made introductions.

"Captain Montoya's going to be taking care of Farley for now," Sam said.

"Well, somebody needs to. He's been on enough contra-indicated medication to produce more violent personalities than a stadium of hockey fans."

"You mean besides the Clozaril prescribed for him?" Matt asked.

"Although not at all well-advised, that was the least of it. He's been given injections. I'd hazard to say for at least a month or more. A nasty hallucinogenic combo showed up in his blood work. Enough to cause the rapid shifts in reality perception you described, as well as the panic attacks and dreamy vagueness. I'd recommend he remain under observation for several days."

"Is there still enough of this stuff in his blood to make him a danger to himself?" Sam asked.

"That's difficult to say, but any deviation in routine or sudden upset could trigger another episode such as the ones he's experienced over the past several days."

If they could get him home with Montoya, Sam doubted Winchester would dare to send Reicht to whisk him off for more swell drug cocktails. "So, if we kept him quiet, someplace safe and hired a psych nurse to take care of him, he'd be all right?" she persisted. If they left him here the doctor would be obligated to contact his legal guardian.

Bester looked down at the his reports and considered. "That would be satisfactory, but I would like to monitor his progress. You never did explain about his family."

"What did he say?" she asked.

"He refused to discuss it."

Good for Farley. "He has a great-aunt back in Boston, the one who hired us to find him, but that's about it. She's too frail to travel, but we'll keep her posted about his condition." Sam knew Matt was watching her ad-lib his family background, except that Claudia Witherspoon was about as frail as an M60 tank.

Dr. Bester gave them detailed instructions for how to handle Farley, emphasizing the importance of keeping him hydrated and off any kind of meds, even aspirin. Then he showed them to the room where the boy was being held. "He's still anxious, insisting that we're Pandorians, whatever that is." His expression became faintly puzzled.

Sam looked from Matt to Bill Montoya and suppressed a grin but said nothing as the physician went on, " I'm afraid the orderly had to strap him down before the tech could take blood samples. He was that agitated, but I spent some time showing him that we merely withdrew blood, didn't inject him with anything. He said someone he called 'L' insisted that he not let anyone give him any further injections."

"Elvis," Matt corrected, but Sam gave him a sign to say no more.

"Elvis? Does he think the King's still alive? That's so common I'd hardly call it delusional," Bester said dryly.

"Hey, can I go now?" the boy asked when he saw Matt and Sam. "I don't like hospitals. I told you."

"Yeah, you're sprung. This is Captain Montoya from Spacefleet," Sam replied, watching Farley's expression turn from hostility to awe as he stood up and saluted, obviously recognizing his hero.

Montoya returned the salute with all seriousness. "At ease, Ensign. Are you ready to ship out?"

"Yes, sir!"

The doctor exchanged a puzzled shrug with Sam as Matt grinned. In an hour, they'd completed the paperwork and Farley headed home with the captain. Before they left, Montoya explained to the physician that under no circumstances was he or any of his staff to tell anyone that Farley had been treated there. Most especially, no one was to know that he would be staying at the captain's home. If anyone made inquiries, Bester agreed to contact Montoya immediately.

"Once he's had time to calm down, I want to talk to Farley about Leila," Sam said to Matt as they drove home. "He keeps saying he saw her 'transponded' to a Pandorian ship." She chewed her lip, mulling over what that might imply.

"You think he witnessed her death?"

"Or maybe her kidnapping. Let's see what Patty will give me on the case." She pulled out her cell.

Matt listened to the one-sided conversation. Although she insisted she didn't miss the force, he sometimes wondered if deep inside she was kidding herself. Oh, the money was a lot better in the retrieval business, but he understood Sam well enough to know that she would have preferred to leave of her own free will. She had been forced to resign because of a screwup that had not been her fault, even though a handful of her former colleagues still blamed her for a rookie's death.

Matt had a sneaking hunch she blamed herself, too. When she ended the call, he said, "I take it he's on the case."

"Yeah. Wouldn't give me much, though, and I didn't want to say we'd gotten the word from Bill Montoya. Anyway, the M.E. says Leila Satterwaite was worked over pretty thoroughly before she was killed."

"Someone wanted to extract information from her. Wonder if they got it?" he mused.

"She worked at a joint called the Pink Pussycat." Sam looked over at him. He knew every strip joint along the Intracoastal after writing an exposé on the mob connections to prostitution and drugs in Miami nightlife.

"Yes, it's in South Beach, but no, I've never been there. As far as I know it's clean—or as clean as that kind of place can be."

"Guess I'll have to find out," she said.

"I don't like the sound of that, Sam."

"You make nice with your pal Ida Kleb and see what the IRS has on Reicht. Let me worry about Leila."

"You are not going to get a job as a stripper," he said, knowing even as he formed the words that she would do just that.

She pulled into their private parking spot in the garage under their condo and turned off the ignition. "What? You think I don't have the right equipment?" she asked, daring him.

Matt sighed. "If ever a man was asked a question with no right answer, this is it." Once in their condo, he watched her root through her closet until she came up with a skimpy miniskirt, halter top and spike heels. "An outfit I never saw before," he said, raising one eyebrow.

"A gal in my business has to dress for the occasion. This isn't the first time I've worked undercover, you know."

"I'm more concerned about what's *un*covered," he said, watching her shed her shorts and tee. "But as long as you're gonna get nekked..." He consulted his wristwatch. "It's only 10:00 a.m. No self-respecting strip club opens before noon."

"You mean I have a couple of hours to get my beauty rest before I make a job application? I could use some time in bed."

"Yeah, funny thing...so could I," he murmured, pulling her into his arms.

Chapter 16

Sam still had a smile on her face when she reached the club precisely three hours later. The Pink Pussycat wasn't quite as tacky as the name suggested. Then again, what could be, she thought as she strolled toward the low pink stucco building in the heart of the Art Deco district of south Miami Beach. Actually, she could have walked from their condo if not for her wretchedly uncomfortable four-inch heels.

Inside, she blinked to adjust her sight to the dim lighting, a fuzzy pink neon effect that made the cigarette haze around the bar seem somehow less carcinogenic. Loud music, de rigeur for all strip joints, assaulted her ears, some Madonna masterpiece perfectly suited for the woman doing her writhing bump and grind on a big metal pole stage center.

Lousy sense of rhythm. Sam brightened. Her chances of employment just took a big leap forward when she looked around at the strippers working the bar area. A pretty skanky crowd. She caught the bartender's eye almost immediately. A huge, balding guy with a ridiculous pink bow tie half hidden by folds of blubber at his neck, he leered at her scanty outfit and the equipment it displayed.

"You lookin' for somebody special, baby?" His tongue could have polished his shoes and he wouldn't even have to lean over to do it.

"Yeah, the boss," Sam replied, pretty sure he wasn't it.

A look of disappointment crossed his face before he yelled over the blasting music, "Hey, Louie, some floozy here to see ya."

A little man who resembled Danny DeVito wearing a cheap rug shambled out of a door at the end of the bar with a bunch of papers in one meaty fist. He gave her the once-over and motioned with a tip of his head for her to follow him into his lair. Sam sashayed behind him, swinging a beaded bag by its drawstrings. She'd taken the precaution of weighting it with a plastic sack of quarters. There was nowhere on her outfit to hide her gun except a purse and in a pinch she knew there wasn't usually enough time for a woman to reach for it anyway.

"So, you want a job? Got any references?" he asked, taking a seat behind a cluttered old desk.

Sam pushed out her chest and cocked one hip. "You're lookin' at 'em, Louie."

He laughed, revealing surprisingly even white teeth. *Must have a good dental plan.*

"Uh, my name's not really Louie. It's Ralph," he said. "Everybody just calls me that because they say I look like some dago actor." He shrugged. "Whatda they call you?"

She almost said Rhea Pearlman, but stifled the impulse. "Jinx. Jinx Cavanaugh," which was an alias she'd used on various jobs, but she'd never worked a strip joint before.

"Can you dance?"

"Better than whoever was on when I walked in the joint."

"Okay, you're hired, Jinx. Start tonight. Pay's fifty a day in cash, plus tips. If you're any good, you'll make a bundle."

So much for the dental plan. Sam nodded. "Do I have to supply my own costumes?" she asked, knowing that had been an issue for several strippers when Matt had interviewed them for his story.

Louie-Ralph waved his hand. "Nah, we got plenty. Root through the dressing room in back and find something that fits."

Since there wasn't more than a good-size handkerchief to anything she'd seen on the girls out front, Sam figured finding something that fit wouldn't be a big issue. "What time do I start?"

"You're on at eleven. Play your cards right and you can headline for me. I just lost my best girl last week. She really blew 'em away."

Until someone blew her away. "Cash up front every night?" Sam reiterated. When he nodded, she sauntered to the door.

His parting question gave her a chill. "Say, Jinx, you wouldn't mind wearing a long blond wig, wouldja?"

Sam had the rest of the day to kill before she reported to "work." Maybe she could put the time to good use. Captain Montoya and his family had spent the day settling Farley in to his new surroundings. If the kid was halfway coherent, maybe she could get more information about Leila's "transpondence" or whatever the hell it was. Poor Leila. Replaceable with a blond wig.

She punched in the number jotted on the back of the business card Montoya had given her and spoke to his wife Josefina. Yes, Farley was doing well and they would be pleased to have her pay a visit. Sam stopped at the condo to change into more conventional clothes. Matt wasn't home. Probably at the newspaper. He did have a day job, she reminded herself. But damn, she was sure happy he'd been willing to spend the morning playing hooky before he headed out.

Feeling refreshed after shedding her smoke-enshrouded costume, showering and changing, she drove to a quiet residential neighborhood in south Coral Gables. The Montoya family had a large white stucco house trimmed with light green shutters. It looked homey and inviting. She walked past a kid's bicycle lying beside the flagstone walk and rang the doorbell.

A gray-haired woman with a megawatt smile answered. She was short and plump. Sam judged her to be in her late sixties, probably the captain's mother-in-law. "You must be Ms. Ballanger. Please come in," she said with a gracious wave of her hand, holding the heavy door wide. "I'm Rosario Velasquez, Jo's mother, but please call me Rose."

"A pleasure, Rose. I'm Sam. We really appreciate your family taking Farley in this way."

"*De nada,*" the older woman said, leading her down the terracotta tile hallway to the back of the house where a large sunroom revealed an oversize backyard filled with a profusion of tropical shrubbery. "My husband's the one with the green thumb in the family. Me, I couldn't keep weeds alive."

"It's beautiful." Sam looked outside to where an old man was showing Farley how to wield a small shovel. They were planting a crimson rosebush.

"How's he doing?" Sam asked.

"It's strange. One minute he's normal, just like my grandchildren. He and Billy—the oldest—really made friends this morning. Billy loves *Space Quest*, so they had a lot to talk about. But then, Farley would start talking loco stuff, you know? As if a television show was real and aliens were trying to take over the world. My son-in-law said he'd been given some terrible drugs. I can't imagine a doctor doing such a thing to a boy!"

"We can't be sure the doctor gave him the injections," Sam replied, thinking of Scruggs. "But the doc did prescribe the other medication, which wasn't good, either."

"Wait here while I ask him to come inside. You timed it just right. Billy and Steve won't be home from baseball practice for an hour and Sara's at her piano lesson."

Sam did as her hostess invited and took a seat in the sunroom, watching as the patient elderly couple talked with Farley, who then walked to the house to see his visitor.

"Hi, Sam," he said, but didn't smile. He flopped into an overstuffed lounge chair, his slight frame dwarfed by the floral print upholstery.

"Hi, yourself." An iced pitcher of what looked like fresh lemonade and several glasses were arranged on the coffee table in front of them. Sam suddenly realized she was thirsty. "Want a drink? You've been working in the sun."

"I guess," he answered, staring out to where Rose, who couldn't grow flowers, was helping her husband, who could.

Sam poured two tall glasses and handed him one. He still had that fuzzy vagueness drawn around him like a fog—or a protective shield? She wondered if the drugs could be incidental to some deeper trauma. Farley had scarcely had a happy childhood by anyone's definition.

After he'd taken a couple of swallows, she said, "I'd like to talk about your friend Leila. You said you saw her transponding up to a Pandorian ship. How do you know it was the Pandorians?"

He shrugged and wiggled around in the big seat nervously. "It had to be. The glass…the glass…" His voice faded away as he stared at the drinking glass in his hand, then quickly set it on the table.

"What about the glass? Was it a glass ship?" *This is nuts, Ballanger.* Think. "Where was it? I mean, where did you see her disappear?"

"You don't believe me. She's in trouble."

Not anymore. "I know, Farley. That's why I need for you to tell me everything you saw so we can find the guys who took her." When he didn't answer, just stared out the window, she persisted. "Was it a man or another woman? Who was with her the last time you saw her?"

Still no answer.

"This is really important, Farley," she said gently, reaching across to where his thin hand dangled over the edge of the chair arm. Hard to believe such a scrawny kid could turn into a wildcat that even she and Matt had difficulty restraining. "When was the last time you saw Leila?"

"I—I don't remember d-days, you know? T-time gets sort of messed up in my head. I think El was right. They're using fotowaves on my brain."

"Just make a guess," she coaxed, ignoring the mention of Scruggs and fotowaves, whatever the hell they were. "A week ago? Two weeks?"

"M-maybe a week, I guess, or a little more."

Good start. "Where were you when you saw her?"

His eyes narrowed and he combed his fingers through his hair, leaning forward and resting his head in his hands. "The S-seascape B-building," he mumbled.

She couldn't see his face, but knew that had to trigger unpleasant thoughts. His father's office was in the building. So was Dr. Reicht's. Then an idea came to her. "Farley, describe how a transponder works, will you?"

He looked up. "Boy, you sure aren't Spacefleet, are you."

"Nope, but I want to help you. How did you know Leila was being transponded?"

He gave her one of the looks teenagers reserve for not-very-bright adults, which means just about everyone over twenty-two. "She was going up in a transponder beam."

"What does a beam look like? Is it glass?" All of a sudden an image was coming clear in her mind.

He shook his head as if trying to clear it, too. "Yes, glass. All around her glass. They were moving fast. I watched until they disappeared at the roof."

"The roof of the Seascape—you mean the top floor where the elevator stops?" The atrium elevator in the posh building was one of those glass tube jobbers that gave everyone with a fear of heights the equal opportunity of tossing their cookies while looking down on the plant-filled atrium below.

He nodded. "It m-might've been."

"You said 'they.' Who was with Leila in the elevator, Farley?" She wasn't leading the witness, your honor. No mention of Roman Numeral or the shrink. She waited until she was almost certain the boy would not or could not answer.

Then his eyes seemed to clear and he whispered, "I—I t-think it was D-Dr. R-Reicht."

Chapter 17

"It all fits, Matt. The time frame, the location, that damned all-glass tube elevator that whooshes you into the stratosphere. And now Reicht ID'd with Satterwaite," Sam said, talking on her cell as she drove from Coral Gables back to Miami Beach.

On the other end of the line, Matt talked over the noise in the newsroom. "I have a much better chance of winning a Pulitzer than Farley does of convincing Patowski he can ID Reicht. Who'd believe him?"

"You mean because he's a spacie?" she asked, unable to resist the cheap shot. "Well, I believe him. I checked with the servants at the Winchester family manse and they verified that he'd been driven to a 5:00 p.m. session with Reicht on the seventeenth."

"I thought when you interviewed the housekeeper right after Winchester hired you, she practically slammed the door in your face."

"She did, but Rogers, he's the chauffeur, was friendlier." In fact he was an old letch, but sometimes that helped. "I called him and he backs up Farley's story. He dropped the kid in front of the Seascape, then headed to the nearest bar. He said the kid was late coming back. He was ticked he had to wait until nearly seven for Farley to show."

"And he never considered parking the damned car and going inside to look for the kid?" Matt asked.

"He did call Reicht's office. When the secretary told him Farley's appointment had to be rescheduled because the doc had an emergency—" she paused for emphasis "—old Rogers finally got worried and asked the concierge to check the building. Discreetly, you understand."

"He didn't want to 'fess up to the kid's daddy he'd lost his charge, huh?" Matt surmised.

"That's what I figure. All came out just swell for Rogers, though. His pal on the desk found Farley hiding behind a potted plant in the back of the lobby."

"Okay, that's pretty good, Sammie," he conceded.

"It gets better. I stopped at the Seascape and verified the story with Joe Waltman, Rogers's friend."

"Did he see Satterwaite and Reicht?"

"Don't I wish. If you stand out in the center of the atrium you can watch the elevator go all the way to the top, but not from where his desk is located. However, he remembers how upset the kid was when he found him, mumbling about Pandorians and transponders. He thinks Farley's bonkers. But apparently the kid had just gone through something really traumatic. When I questioned Farley, I asked if Reicht and Leila struggled on the 'transponder.'"

"And?"

Sam sighed. "He wasn't sure but he thinks so. I bet it scared him so much he blocked it. As soon as he saw them, all he does remember is popping another one of those swell pills Reicht prescribed. Then the next morning he had another session with Reicht to make up for the one the doc canceled. Farley insisted he couldn't remember what they talked about, but Rogers told me when he picked up the kid, he was rubbing his arm."

"The shots."

"Yeah. I think we have enough nails to seal the coffin—if we can find a credible witness to Leila's abduction."

"Not to mention Reicht's motive for killing a Spacer moonlighting as a stripper."

"I'm working on that angle tonight."

"Sam," he growled.

"I'll be fine. All I need is a little time backstage with the other women working there, see what they know about Leila's life."

"You got a job as a stripper, didn't you?"

"You knew I could pass the physical," she purred into the phone. "Besides, you gave me the idea."

"I gave you the idea! That's absurd, even for you."

"You wrote that series of articles on strip clubs and how the women in them bond, tell each other their darkest secrets, all that jazz, so see? You have nobody to blame but yourself."

With that she hung up and switched off the phone. Then a thought occurred to her. She switched it back on and punched in his number again. Before he could get out any more than, "Granger here," she said, "And if you show up at the Pussycat, the next time I catch you sleeping I'll shoot some of my nighty-night spray up your nose and shave you bald, got it?"

Sam drove to her first—and she hoped her last—night at the Pink Pussycat, humming tunelessly, thinking about how she was going to approach "the girls." The back parking lot fit the current condition of her van. At least stripped of paint and bullet-pocked as it was, no sane car thief would consider stealing it. Stepping around puddles of afternoon rain that filled the canyon-size potholes in the asphalt, she walked to the stage door.

Not so much as a guard to keep any drunk or stalker from shoving his way in and messing with the women who worked here. She felt the weight of her drawstring bag filled with quarters and drew a deep breath, trying to assure herself she'd been in far worse places than this, which was true. But she'd never had to strip, even during her brief stint working stroll. In spite of wearing a skimpy hooker's outfit, it had been satisfying busting johns as an undercover cop.

Confidence restored, she walked down a dimly lit hall littered with everything from glitter and sequins to chewing gum wrappers and ground-out cigarette butts. The music from out front wasn't quite as loud back here but the miasma of smoke and sweat filtered back like scum from an oil slick. Sam could hear female voices from the door directly ahead. She opened it.

A long counter made of Formica ran the length of one wall in the narrow room. Its chipped surface was Pepto-Bismol pink as were the cushions on the chairs bleeding their gray-brown stuffing through rips. Three women perched on various seats were peering into the bulb-lined individual mirrors on the wall at their dressing stations. No one seemed to notice her at first. One was busy gluing on false eyelashes that resembled tarantulas climbing down her cheeks, another applying foundation as if it were spar varnish while a third was attaching tasseled pasties to her nipples.

"So I says to him, Herbie, you gotta get a life, you know? Peddling knockoff Rolex watches on Flagler Boulevard's got no future. Get a real job," the big redhead said, giving her surgically enhanced breasts a heft to check the balance of the tassels.

"He ain't gonna change, Shel," the spider woman said,

batting her lashes into the mirror. "Dump the jerk. You've gone his bail how many times now?"

"Hey, we got company," the third woman said, looking up at Sam. Her pancake makeup crinkled as she squinted against the harsh lights. "You takin' Leila's place?"

"Yeah, I guess. Louie—Ralph, whatever his name, hired me this afternoon. I just got to town. Long bus ride from Boston."

The redhead grinned. "Yeah, everybody wants to live in sunny Florida, get away from the cold. My name's Shelly," she said, walking over to Sam, tassels swishing in rhythm with her stride. She spoke with a broad Oklahoma drawl and smiled with her eyes, not just her lips.

"I'm Chiquita," the spider lady said, shoving aside a long strand of hair so black the only other place it could be found was on an Aztec priest. "Everybody calls me Quita." She studied Sam with hard dark eyes that didn't smile any more than her mouth did.

"My name's Della." The third woman had frizzy light brown hair and needed caulk rather than pancake to cover the lines worn into her face.

"I'm Jinx Cavanaugh. Pleased to meet you."

"You might as well take poor Leila's chair. She ain't gonna need it no more," Shelly said, motioning to the seat next to hers.

"I heard on the news she was murdered," Sam said with a worried frown. "You don't think it was anybody from here?" she asked ingenuously. "That Louie guy kinda creeped me out, but nothing like the bartender…" She gave a little shiver.

Shelly and Della laughed. Quita's expression remained sour, ignoring the camaraderie of the others.

"Louie's a cheapskate but he'd never mess with Leila. She brought in too many customers," Della said.

"But Max, he's another ball of wax. I dunno." Shelly turned and checked out her appearance in the mirror as she talked.

"You mean ball of dirt," Della said. "He tried to put the make on her a few times."

Quita finally stopped ignoring them. "Leila knew how to handle him. She got whatever she wanted from any man."

"She was the headliner," Shelly replied without rancor. "Best dancer, flashiest girl working here and we know flash's what it's all about."

"Did Louie give you the eleven o'clock slot?" Quita asked.

"Yeah, that okay with youse?" Sam asked. The last thing she wanted was to make them jealous of her so they'd quit talking freely.

"Just so I keep my 2:00 a.m. gig," Della said. "The slobs are too drunk to watch their wallets then."

Sam figured they were too drunk to notice her sagging flesh, too, but would never say it.

"Leila worked the nine through eleven gigs. Louie moved her around, you know, depending on how the crowd was. She was his biggest draw," Shelly explained.

The hard-looking black-haired woman gave the newcomer a level stare, then shoved back her chair and stood up. "I'm on in five," she said, blowing a kiss at her own reflection in the mirror.

As soon as she left the room, Della and Shelly smiled at Sam. "Don't mind Quita. She don't like nobody," Shelly said.

"How about Leila—did she get on with the rest of the dancers?" Sam was careful to call them dancers, not strippers, a term most disliked.

"Mostly she kept to herself. Quiet, but nice enough," Della replied as she rolled a fishnet stocking up one leg.

"Yeah, she always seemed sad, you know. Maybe that's why she was payin' all that dough for a shrink," Shelly said.

* * *

Matt hung up the phone and leaned back until his swivel chair squealed for mercy. Damned office furniture was made for munchkins. He shifted his weight and considered what he'd just learned from a hacker pal of his who'd supplied him with data not easily—or legally—attainable from any other source. The newsroom was almost deserted, so he'd felt no need for more privacy while calling Artie. What the paralegal Arthur Sellers had found in the terms of Susan Mallory Winchester's will didn't fit with the attempts on her son's life. But somehow it was a piece in a bigger puzzle.

He checked his watch. Sam wasn't answering her cell and wasn't at the condo. He wanted to tell her what he'd learned and let her quick mind pick at it. Her gut intuitions were frequently as good as his. Okay, sometimes they were even better, he conceded.

Matt knew she was at the strip joint but tried not to think of what she was doing there. Since they first met, she'd made it abundantly clear that she'd been in dangerous situations and survived for thirty years before he came along. They had an understanding that neither would interfere in the other's work. The trouble was, when she pulled a stunt like this, he found it nearly impossible to stand idly by. But she promised to shave him bald if he went to the Pink Pussycat. Matt knew his wife never made idle threats.

It was getting late. He tried not to worry or even visualize her up on a stage surrounded by drooling animals while she— no, he had to stop thinking about that! Dammit, he wanted to know she was all right. He started to shove away from his desk to get up, then reconsidered. Sam could take care of herself. If he blew her cover, he'd mess up the case. Sighing, he rolled his chair back and pulled a notepad from a drawer.

Let's think this whole thing through. He began doodling

on the paper to help himself visualize the connections between the major players in Farley Winchester's unfortunate life. There were lots of players, alive and dead. He traced lines between Farley, Upton, his wife, Susan, and Reicht, then drew in Scruggs and Leila Satterwaite with big question marks.

When he'd started digging into the Winchester family, he'd found a few skeletons lurking. The cold case file on Susan's death still questioned if her drug OD had been accidental. But neither the initial investigators nor the recent follow-up had been able to prove foul play. She had been a known drug abuser. An empty bottle of Dom Pérignon sat on the nightstand in her bedroom where her body had been found by a maid. The autopsy showed she'd ingested enough cocaine to drop a Clydesdale.

Mrs. Winchester had not slept with her husband for quite a few years, according to gossip. "A marriage not exactly made in heaven," he muttered, rubbing the bridge of his nose. Susan Mallory had wed Upton Winchester IV for the usual reasons socially prominent people did. "Love had nothing to do with it, like Tina said," he muttered to himself.

His great-aunt had been his role model…after a fashion. Claudia Witherspoon had rocked their proper Boston world by running away with a penniless French musician. But ultimately she returned to the family money—on her terms. He'd rejected the whole enchilada and moved to Florida to get a real job. Not so with Farley's parents. The Winchesters possessed an impeccable pedigree but fading wealth. The Mallorys were very rich, but it was new money and new money didn't get them admitted to the best clubs, even in Miami.

After providing Upton with the requisite heir, Susan had become increasingly unhappy, a recluse under medical supervision. The Winchesters and the Mallorys together agreed to keep her drug and alcohol problems hidden from the media. The night she OD'd had begun with booze. Matt looked at the grainy photograph from the *Herald*'s morgue. A young woman with curly dark hair and a wistful smile. He could see the resemblance between her and her son.

At least she'd fixed her bastard husband in her will. Had she been trying to protect Farley? At best, given her subsequent problems, she'd been an indifferent mother whose only child was raised by a succession of nannies. Matt wondered how Sam would react when he told her that according to the terms of Susan Mallory Winchester's will, all her fortune went to her son.

If he predeceased his father, all the money went to charity. Poor Upton had access to the Mallory millions only as long as Farley stayed alive.

Sam waited until Shelly and Della went onstage to do what they called a "duet." Quita had gone to the bar earlier for a few lap dances before her next gig. That left Sam alone in the dressing room. She opened the drawer at Leila's dressing table. Someone had cleaned it out. According to Pat, Leila had no next of kin they'd been able to dig up as yet. She wondered what had happened to the murdered woman's personal effects. Police custody, of course. She considered what the closemouthed Patowski had and had not told her. He wasn't leveling about this deal.

"What's new? That's Patty," she muttered, moving on to several of the other dancers' drawers, rummaging through to see if anything turned up that might shed light on why someone had beaten and strangled Leila Satterwaite. What the hell did they want from her? The only thing Sam knew for sure was that the killer hadn't been a space alien.

She found lots of the expected stuff—body makeup, hair gel, false eyelashes, even an assortment of feminine hygiene products, but nothing that shed any light on Leila's death. Suddenly, the door banged open and Quita stomped across the floor.

"Hey, bitch, what're you doing with your mitts in my drawers?"

The image of that repelled Sam enough to render her speechless for a minute, but she recovered, holding up a pair of eyelashes in her palm that looked like alien insects mating. "I needed to borrow some eyelashes and you had the best ones. I'm sorry. I'll pay you for 'em if you want."

"Get your own damn kit," Quita snapped, deftly using her clawlike long nails to snatch the hairy creatures from Sam's hand.

"Jinx, you're on next," Shelly said, walking in on the confrontation. She was wearing nothing but a miniscule G-string. Even the tassels were gone and her body was dripping with perspiration. Ignoring the black-haired woman, she looked at Sam and said, "You need help with your costume? Louie'll be back here to check you out. Always does when a new girl starts."

"I'm kinda nervous," Sam admitted, hoping to inspire sympathy.

Shelly smiled, understanding. "This your first time, kid?" she asked, toweling herself dry, then slipping into a shabby blue chenille bathrobe.

"Yeah. I kinda bluffed my way into the job, ya know? All I ever did before was hustle drinks at bars back in Boston, but this pays better and I need rent money."

"C'mon, Quita, give the kid a hand," Shelly said, reaching for a fuchsia-striped caftan and canary-yellow feather boa.

Grudgingly the other woman pulled a sequined G-string

from a hook on the wall and handed it to Sam. "Here. Stick a bunch of the feathers in it and pull 'em out one at a time. Drives those losers crazy."

Shelly gave her a bunch of long electric-green feathers with a wink.

As she pulled off her skirt and briefs, Sam said, "I really don't want Leila's job, you know, after her being murdered and all. Did she have any regular customers who might've done it, you think?" She wriggled into the G-string. Damn, the thing pinched!

"You need a wax job," Quita said critically.

"Nah, a few pubes get the men horny," Shelly said, then turned back to Sam. "Leila had lots of regulars, mostly business types, older guys with enough dough to tip her real good."

"Yeah, but don't forget about that weird kid and his loser pal Elvis," Quita said spitefully. "I told Louie he could get busted for serving a minor, but he never listened, the greedy prick."

Bingo. Scruggs again. That sucker turned up as regular as stickers on cactus. Sam had a funny feeling that Patowski had been stonewalling her about the yokel. And why in hell had the Georgia Highway Patrol let him go? She'd have bet the farm he didn't have a permit for that Glock he'd pulled on them. After she found out what she could here, her next priority would be Elvis P. Scruggs, Florida panhandle man of mystery.

Just then Della came in, sweaty as Shelly. Overhearing Quita, she plopped down on her chair and said, "Farley wasn't weird. Kind of sad, maybe a little spaced-out but he had real nice brown eyes."

Shelly's laugh was a cigarette-roughened rumble. "Spaced-out for sure. What'd you expect since they were all *Space Quest* junkies."

"Leila, too?" Sam asked.

"Yep. Really trippin' on that crap," Shel said.

"What kind of place she from, going for that nutty stuff?" Sam echoed Shelly's disapproval of Spacers, fishing for any background on the dead woman her coworkers could provide.

"Leila only said she'd come from somewhere upstate. Her daddy was a mean drunk. Beat her mom," Della said, shaking her head as she lit a cigarette and took a drag.

"Yep, till one night he got skunked and wrecked his car—with her mama in it. Killed 'em both. Maybe that's why she needed the shrink," Shelly added seriously. "She was pretty straight, ya know. Didn't drink or party."

"Any idea where she went—the shrink, I mean? I—I kinda think I could use some help with a couple of problems…" Sam let her voice trail off as if embarrassed.

Shelly didn't seem to mind as she picked up a jar of glittery goo and opened it. "Let me get your tits glued. Take off that halter so I can work."

If the good sisters at St. Ignacious could see me now! Growing increasingly uncomfortable, Sam unhooked her halter and slid it off.

Della answered her question. "She never mentioned the shrink's name but he had an office somewhere in the Brickell area."

"Say, you got a great rack for not havin' implants," Shelly said as she started to daub pastie glue on Sam's nipples. "Yep, I think she said her doc was in the Seascape Building."

Jackpot! Sam wanted to crow. She had checked the directory at Seascape the day she interviewed Reicht. There were only a handful of psychiatrists and a couple of psychologists listed. She'd bet the farm Leila's shrink was none other than Dr. Reese Reicht. Dammit, the pastie glue tickled! Matt would laugh about that. He was deathly ticklish and she never had been—until this.

"Maybe I'll try seeing a doc, but I don't think I can

afford anybody at the Seascape. How'd she pay for it? She have a man?"

"Nah, I don't think so. None that come 'round this joint anyway," Shelly said. "I don't think you'll wanna twirl the tassels until you get some practice," she added, standing back to inspect her handiwork with paste and glitter. "It takes practice to get the rhythm going just right."

"I can imagine," Sam said, not wanting to at all. Before she could say anything else, Quita more threw than placed the boa around her neck while Shelly stood by with the caftan.

"The trick is," ever-helpful Shel explained, "to take your time, know what I mean? Slide around the pole and pull the silk caftan tight in places." She illustrated, grabbing the gauzy fabric and yanking it over Sam's hips and breasts. "Make the suckers wait for it. They'll throw you more money if you go slow and pick out a decent lookin' guy to concentrate on. You'll get the hang of it, won't she, Quita?"

"She'll never get Leila's job," Quita replied with disdain.

"She made more money than any of us with tips," Della admitted, inhaling smoke.

"Not always. I do okay, too," Quita interjected, preening. Then she picked up Sam's break-neck, spike-heeled strap sandals and shoved them at her. "You got good shoes," she admitted grudgingly. She tapped her toe impatiently until Sam slipped them on.

"Could use a little jazzing up, though," Shel said, smearing more of the nasty paste across the ankle straps and then sprinkling fuchsia glitter on it until the excess became wedged between Sam's toes. It felt as though she'd just stepped in a nettle patch. The G-string pinched in places she really didn't want it to and the pasties were starting to itch like hell.

Great. Here she was in spike heels wearing a see-through gown and trailing a feather boa while every part of her body was in misery. But she had started the other women talking about Leila. She forced herself to focus on what Shel and Della were saying.

"She didn't waste her money on booze or blow it up her nose," Shelly said.

"Guess that doc took most of it," Della replied, stubbing out her cigarette.

Sam pondered the mystery of Leila Satterwaite, a hard-scrabble kid from upstate Florida, just like good ole Elvis. Was there a connection from their past? He was a Spacer so he could get next to a rich kid who needed a friend, but why would Leila do it? The local chapter's honcho was a cop. That smelled funny to her, but she wasn't going to get any more answers here. The key was one Elvis P. Scruggs and his missing seven years.

Now that she'd found out what she could here, Sam wanted to slip out the back door before she was forced to make her stage debut. But how the hell was she going to make a fast, inconspicuous getaway rigged out like this? There was no possibility she was going out on that stage in front of a howling audience of male gorillas in heat.

Loud yells of, "Take it off, baby!" and, "Yeah, sweet ass!" echoed from out front. Sam knew there were no other women performing during the break. The jerk-offs were watching a porn flick on TV monitors!

It was now or never. She started past the women. There was a spare ignition key magnetized beneath her van. All she had to do was make it to the rear door and run like hell.

Just as she reached the dressing room door, Louie appeared directly in front of her, blocking her way like a squat fireplug. And about as movable.

Chapter 18

This is it. I'm fucked. Sam could've taken down Louie, brawny little bastard that he was, if she'd been dressed for action. She was dressed for action all right, just not the kind she was used to handling.

"Not bad," he said, looking her up and down. The caftan was so sheer that the bright lights from the dressing room outlined her every curve for his perusal. "Now, get on stage."

As her mind raced, good ole Shel came up with the solution.

"Hey, Jinx, use your beaded bag. You can swing it instead of tassels. The men'll go wild. Jeez, it's heavy," she said, handing the drawstring bag to Sam.

Yeah, I can use my beaded bag. She shoved her way past Louie turning toward the exit door instead of the stage, almost hoping he'd try to stop her. But he didn't have to. When she yanked on the knob, it didn't budge. Now suddenly they got safety conscious!

"Hey, what the hell you think you're doin'?" he growled. "That's my costume you're wearing and you made a deal to shake your booty out front. Get to it, baby."

The way Sam figured it, she had two choices: she could bludgeon the locked door, which looked pretty solid, or she could use the quarter-filled handbag on Louie. That sounded like a lot more fun.

"Out of my way, scum sucker. I'll mail your haute couture back to you in a plain brown wrapper." She slid past him but he grabbed her feather boa and yanked on it until she thought he'd crushed her windpipe.

"We made a deal," he growled, reeling her in.

"Here's the deal, shorty," Sam replied, pulling the boa loose from her throat, "Either you let me go or I moon crater that cute little cue ball head of yours."

"I got a big crowd tonight and I promised 'em a new act. You're it and you're goin' on if I have to drag you and strip you myself. Come to think of it…" A leering grin made his white teeth gleam in the dim light.

Sam swung the bag and connected with his mouth. So much for the perfect choppers. He fell to his knees, holding his hands over his bleeding lips.

"You fucking bitch! I'll break your neck! I'll yank your tits off and throw 'em at your dying ass," he yelled after her.

She could hear his footsteps behind her as she picked up the caftan and dashed down the hall. There had to be another way out besides running the gauntlet of the horny. When she paused at the side of the stage, scanning the area, looking for an exit, Louie grabbed her again. He raised his fist to punch her. She used one spike heel on his instep, coming down hard.

He squealed and started hopping around on one foot, cursing, furious as a fighting cock being tossed into the ring. His mouth dripped blood, spraying it through busted teeth.

But he came at Sam again. Hobbling, he grabbed a fistful of the caftan. Sam yanked free as it ripped, leaving Louie with only a small ragged piece of the gauzy fabric clutched in his meaty fist. She started to cross to the other side of the stage.

"There's got to be an exit. What the hell about the fire codes?" she muttered midstage seeing no illuminated exit sign in the darkness opposite.

"You're gonna get naked!" Louie shrieked, adding an inventive series of oaths.

Sam knew she was in trouble when the cheap velvet drapes separating the howling audience from the stage began to open. Louie was hopping toward her but abruptly stopped with a big grin when he saw the curtain guy doing his job. The music grew deafeningly loud. So did the roar of male anticipation out front. She could kick off the shoes—if they weren't glued to her feet—and take Louie, but that still left the problem of the locked door behind her.

Decision time, Sam.

She would have to brazen it out and make her way to what she could now see as the only side exit, its dim light flickering from the left side of the room. A horrific vision flashed through her mind as she started to twirl the boa—her Grandma Mary Elizabeth O'Malley looking down from on High and watching her favorite granddaughter bump and grind in front of a bunch of drunks! She quickly suppressed it. *Gram would understand I didn't intend for this to happen.*

At least that's what she told herself as she deftly dodged one big lug trying to grab hold of her ankle. She swatted him playfully with the boa and moved back from the edge of the stage. She had to work her way nearer to the exit before she could make a break for it. The weight of the beaded bag filled with quarters felt reassuring as she twirled it.

Figuring out her strategy, Louie limped to the stairs leading down into the audience, positioning himself beside the exit. If he wanted to play it that way, she'd have to oblige. Sam rolled her hips and flipped the boa again.

"C'mon, baby, take it off!" a guy yelled from the back of the room.

"Yeah, Jinx, you can jinx me any day of the week," another customer seated at the bar cried.

Many of the other yells of encouragement were more explicit, but Sam had heard worse on assignment with vice. She ignored the "cheers" and concentrated on how she could get from point A to point B as fast as possible. The boa could work. So would the caftan. After that, well...

She continued dancing, ignoring the pole at stage center, to the dismay of several males. "In your dreams," she muttered beneath her breath, then realized the pole might be a help in getting rid of the shoes. No way could she make a dash for it in spike strap sandals. And no way could she just kick them off thanks to Shel, who'd glued them to her feet! Her toes felt as if glass shavings scraped between them as she wriggled her way back to the pole.

Sam wrapped herself around it, raising one leg high enough to grab the sandal by its heel and tug it off. The loud music smothered her oath as hunks of skin and what felt like toes came with it. The audience became more appreciative now, seeing her bare leg all the way up to her minithong! *A few pubes get the men horny.* Just what she needed! She used one hand to strategically rearrange the green feathers.

Jeez, I feel like a parrot in molting season. She tossed the shoe to the right side of the crowd and a bunch of guys grabbed for it. Mark McGuire's sixty-second home run ball hadn't created a bigger hubbub. She twirled around the pole and raised the other leg, this time being more coy about the feathers as she removed the second shoe. Ouch, again! Now or never, she tossed it near where a bunch of the losers were cheering.

"Hope I don't slip on the blood gushing from my feet," she muttered to herself, vowing that Louie would bleed even more once she got near him.

When they dived after the glittery spike, she made her dash for the left steps off the stage. She could see the owner motioning for the surly big bartender to come to his assistance. Beautiful. She had to get the hell out of the building before Max got around the bar and made his way through the crowd. When she hit the steps, several men grabbed for her.

She flung the caftan over her head and tented the three nearest ones, then flung the boa around the neck of one particularly persistent fan, pulling him toward her. As he stepped up with a loopy grin, she reached down and yanked his right leg up, jerking on his pants cuff. Almost simultaneously she clipped his left leg out from under him in a version of *Kuchiki-Taoshi,* or "the dead tree drop." He toppled like a redwood, knocking a bunch of other guys down as he fell. She tossed several feathers, one at a time into the crowd, letting the men fight over them as she neared the exit.

Which left Louie.

He didn't look in the mood for a rational discussion. When he reared back to slug her, Sam asked, "Why doncha break these quarters into nickels for me?" She swung the bag low and connected directly between his legs in a judo technique that has no name. Louie's eyes bulged. His mouth worked like a guppy, then his face turned green as the feathers. He had a short trip to the floor. She had a couple more feathers and the boa. The door was a couple of yards away and she could see it was partially cracked open.

I'm golden!

Sam tossed more feathers and used the boa to snap several

guys in the face, backing them off. The last feather went. Then the boa. Her hand closed around the door handle and she started to shove it open when Max's big paw grabbed a hunk of her hair and pulled her back.

"You hurt Ralph, bitch. He paid you to strip. You fuckin' strip!"

"How about you strip?" she yelled, breaking free of his hold by applying pressure on the nerves at the base of his flabby bicep just above his elbow. He yelped in pain and released her. She whirled around to face him, then grabbed the collar of his shirt and ripped it apart. Buttons went flying, revealing a big hairy beer gut as she yanked it down his right arm, immobilizing his uninjured arm.

Sam waited for him to raise his left, ready to lever it for an *Ippon-Seoi-Nage,* the over-the-shoulder throw. But before she could act, a loaded longneck connected with the back of his skull and he collapsed.

"Hey, she's trying to get away!" an angry voice cried out.

"Look what that guy did to Max," from another.

"Hit him from behind. Stinkin' yellow bastard," a third chimed in.

Sam looked up at Matt's furious face, seeing his eyes sweep over her almost naked body. "What the hell are you doing here? I told you I'd shave—"

He cut her off, yelling, "Argue later. Get the hell out now," as he drove the bottom of the longneck into the nose of a dissatisfied customer preparing to launch a roundhouse punch at his kisser.

Suddenly the whole room erupted like a volcano. Every drunken man—and that included most of the patrons—started taking swings at the guy nearest him. Sam had been close to the exit, but during the dustup with Max, she'd been forced away from it. Matt's untimely interference put them squarely in the middle of the melee. She used what she could of her judo training, applying her strong fingers to sensitive pressure points and foot-sweeping the feet out from under guys to drop them onto their butts. Matt applied his loaded beer bottle to good advantage.

Someone killed the music. All Matt could hear was the grunting and swearing of a roomful of drunks. And he and his wife—his naked wife—were right in the thick of the fight. How the hell did the woman manage to get herself into this kind of trouble?

They stood back-to-back, both using every dirty trick they knew, his from Army MP training, hers from police academy martial arts and her judo workouts. Because she was the only woman in the room, she drew every eye in spite of the general brawl. He had to get her out of there, but how?

Then the whining sound of police sirens echoed from down the street. Moments later the cops burst through the front door, yelling for order. The lights came up and batons came down. Hard and often. Finally the crowd subsided into a milling mass. The cops started to herd those still standing to paddy wagons.

"Who appointed you my guardian, Granger?" Sam said as two of Miami Beach's finest escorted them toward the front door.

"If I hadn't been here, that big jack-off would've broken your neck," he growled.

"If you hadn't been here, I would've sent him flying and slipped out the side door. You started a friggin' riot!" she shrieked like a fishwife when a red-faced rookie handed her what looked like a tablecloth.

"If you'll just, er, wrap this around yourself, miss," he said, trying his best not to look at the glittering pasties on her breasts.

"She's not a Miss, she's a Mrs. My wife," Matt said, glaring at the kid.

"Oh, and you think that makes it okay for you to start beaning the customers?" a grizzled sergeant asked, removing the longneck from Matt's hand.

"That guy I hit was assaulting her," he said.

"I could've handled him," Sam interjected. "Look, Sergeant, I'm a P.I. on a job—"

"I can see what kind of 'job' you got, lady," the cop replied, shaking his head. "Show biz. Your limo awaits," he said sarcastically, shoving her into the line of patrons headed toward the bright red flashing lights outside.

"You have the brains of a squirrel, Matthew Granger! No, that's not giving squirrels nearly enough credit. You—"

"Listen, you mouthy little idiot. I kept that pretty little ass of yours from getting turned into pork rinds and gobbled up by those bar stool jockeys," he growled, holding an ice compress to the swelling on the side of his face.

"You know what Vinny Lorussa's gonna charge for getting us out of lockup?" she asked, ignoring his remarks entirely while she paced furiously across their living room floor. "And that's not to mention possible lawsuits! God only knows how many bones you crushed with that longneck!"

Matt snorted. "My compassionate little paramedic, what about your employer, Louie? After the job you did on him with that bag of quarters, he'll never wade in the gene pool again."

"Now there's a real plus for future generations," she snapped. But then the implications of actual lawsuits hit her. "Oh, my God, we'll end up selling Tupperware on the side to pay our legal fees—for the rest of our lives!"

"Money, money, money. That's all you can ever think about. You could've gotten us both killed!" He lay stretched out on the long sectional sofa nursing his injuries.

"Well, since you won't use your trust fund or let Aunt Claudia give us the money she promised me when we got married, somebody's gotta worry about paying the bills."

"Sam," he said with a resigned sigh, "we always pay our bills, every month…that is, when you remember to write the checks and deposit our paychecks in the bank. Now, I'd be happy to take over—"

"Oh, no you don't. I'm not trusting you to handle money. You spread it around like parmesan on pizza to every mooch who ever darkened the *Herald*'s doors."

"A reporter has to grease his sources."

"You don't just grease 'em, Matt, you give them enough to glide from here to Key Largo. And most of the dough doesn't go to sources. It goes to pay off Bennie Lanski's bookie and Chuck Durmont's alimony. You give handouts to every deadbeat at the paper."

"Okay," he said, throwing up his hands. "I couldn't let Bennie's bookie sic leg breakers on him. He's on the wagon. Joined Gamblers Anonymous. I'm a soft touch now and then. You knew that when you married me."

She stopped pacing and looked down at his battered face. Dammit, he looked like he'd been in a three-day board fight and he was the only one without a board. She sat down beside him and took his hand. "I think there were a lot of things I didn't know about you…we did get married kind of suddenly…."

His fingers tightened around her much smaller hand. "Yeah, we did. At first…aw, shit, this is gonna sound dumb."

"Did you think I married you for your money?" she asked, withdrawing her hand. The idea stung. "I know I seem mercenary sometimes—okay, most of the time," she confessed, clenching her hands together now.

A small hint of a smile touched his cut lip, reminding both of them of the fiasco at the strip club. "You know me,

Sammie. I admit I worried about the money—even though I knew it wasn't true, but what really scares me is the way you keep on risking your life. Being shot at, nearly run over, beaten up. That's why I couldn't stay away tonight," he confessed.

She studied his face as if seeing him for the first time. "You'll always be there to back me up—whether I want you to or not." She bent down and kissed him, careful of his split lip. "I kinda have a hang-up or two of my own. You're a prep school kid with all kinds of fancy connections—"

"I took a hike, didn't I? Sam, I hated that life. That's why I don't want us to accept my aunt's money. We'd end up back there in her web."

"That life is pretty scary for a south Boston girl from the wrong side of the tracks. I wouldn't fit in. What if you found someone—here or there—who does? Some woman who went to finishing school and knows how to hold a teacup and doesn't curse and—"

He stopped her by sitting up and cupping her face between his hands so he could kiss her quite soundly. "We may have gotten married without a formal engagement, but I've been through enough with you to know you'll always be there for me…and I'll always be there for you. I'll never want anyone else but you."

Sam drew back when the kiss ended, considering what he'd just said, knowing it was true. "Okay, here's the deal. I promise I'll try not to bring up Aunt Claudia's offer if you try to trust me to do my job. I really am good at it, you know."

Matt grinned. "Damn straight you are. I can't promise I won't come bashing my way in to the rescue, but I'll try not to hover. Good enough?"

"Good enough. And I won't even dope you and shave your head—as a sign of my good faith."

Matt threw back his head and laughed until his split lip cracked open and started bleeding again. Sam reached for the discarded ice bag and placed it carefully over his mouth. "That'll teach you to laugh at me." She stood up and resumed pacing, saying, "I have to get cracking on Farley Winchester's case."

He removed the ice bag and said casually, "Oh, yeah, about the Winchester family..."

She stopped and turned to him expectantly. "What do you know?"

"Guess what I turned up on daddy-o?"

"Roman Numeral?" she asked, excited now.

Matt could practically hear the wheels turning in her mind when he explained the terms of Susan Winchester's will and the nature of their marriage and her death. "So, you can see that the old man definitely has to keep the kid alive, but not necessarily well."

"Especially once Farley turns twenty-one. But keeping him nutty and committing him to some rest home leaves the bastard in control of his dead wife's fortune. All he needs is a shrink unscrupulous enough to do that," Sam said, thrilled by this new twist. "Enter Reicht, who we know isn't exactly on the up-and-up, IRS not withstanding."

"He has to be involved in Leila Satterwaite's death, but why?" Matt asked, musing. "Did your stroll—you should excuse the pun—at the Pink Pussycat shed any light on that?" he asked.

Sam made a face at his rotten joke. "As a matter of fact, Sir Galahad, it did. According to her stripper friends, Leila was seeing a shrink in the Seascape Building."

"That's a big high-rise. There must be quite a few."

"Six. While you were in the shower, I checked the yellow pages. Pretty long odds that Farley'd see her with Reicht in that elevator if she wasn't his patient."

"What's your next move?" he asked, trying to sound casual.

Sam gave him an arch look. "Your head remains unshaven…only because I gave my word," she said with a smirk.

"You just better hope that Louie doesn't have a litigious wife."

Sam smiled beatifically. "Hell, she wouldn't sue me, she'd thank me." Now that she had time to consider the possibilities, she realized there was no way the club owner would dare come after her. "I'll have one of my pals on the Beach PD tell him that I used to be a Miami-Dade cop."

"That ought to work," he conceded. As in the newsroom, there was a camaraderie among police officers. Running a strip club made Ralph Unicker vulnerable to endless hassles if the local authorities decided to go after him.

"While I work some other angles, I could use some help. There's a story in this once I nail Reicht. But you have to stick to my script."

"What's the script?" he asked with a worried frown he couldn't quite conceal.

"I want you to keep digging dirt on Winchester. Find out if there's any connection between him and Reicht. Charm the ever-lovely Ida Kleb and see what you can shake loose on the IRS investigation."

"We still have Elvis Scruggs on the loose. He could be dangerous, Sammie. You won't go after him, will you?"

"Not yet. But I'm gonna give Patowski another grilling," she said, wincing. Bandages encircled seven of her ten toes, thanks to that glitter glue.

"You only use me when you need information," he groused, getting up from the sofa slowly.

"Poor baby, you don't have an unblack-and-blue place on your whole bod, do you?" she said, wrapping her arms around him.

"You could kiss it and make it all well," he suggested.

"It's three in the morning, Granger, and I doubt you're in any shape for more action," she replied, leading him down the hall to their bedroom.

"Wanna bet?"

"I think you oughta join your pal Bennie for his next Gamblers Anonymous meeting."

He started nibbling kisses on the back of her neck, then reached around her and placed one large hand over each of her breasts, caressing them until she sighed and turned to face him.

"Okay, you win," she murmured between kisses.

"Just promise you'll be gentle with me," he said, wincing when his nose bumped her cheek.

"I'll be gentle if you promise not to kiss my toes."

Chapter 19

"You're wasting the taxpayer's time, Mr. Granger. I'd be in violation of every regulation on the books if I revealed confidential information, especially to a newspaper reporter."

Ida Kleb's name should've been Ida Klam, Matt decided. She sat behind a desk as battered and functional as the woman herself. Ida was fiftyish and thickset, with salt-and-pepper hair that looked as if she'd hacked it off just below her ears with a dull machete. Her face was utterly free of makeup and the least trace of humor. So much for the kinder, gentler, new IRS.

God, I'm starting to think like Sam! Matt shuddered and gave Ida his most engaging grin. Normally, women melted like butter in the sun when he did that. Kleb remained frozen as Antarctica. Of course, when she'd shaken hands with him, she commented on his battered face—and squeezed his bruised knuckles in a vice grip. He wasn't exactly at the top of his game after the brawl last night.

He tried again. "Look, Ms. Kleb, my wife was hired by Farley Winchester's father to rescue the boy from a kidnapper. Once she had him in her custody someone tried to kill him—several times. Farley is one of Dr. Reicht's patients. We have evidence that Reese Reicht wants Farley dead. We could cooperate."

"If you know anything about Reicht's involvement in attempted murder, it's your duty as a citizen to tell the police," she said calmly, but the pencil in her stubby fingers started tapping on the edge of the desk.

"What if I could help the IRS with its investigation? This isn't for a story—it's to help keep an innocent kid from getting killed." He waited.

"What would you expect in return?" she finally asked, her face as expressionless as a champion poker player's.

"Whatever you could tell me off the record about Reicht. We both know he's liberal with his prescription pad if the price is right. My bet, that isn't the kind of money a doc could exactly report on his tax forms."

A faint smile curved her thin lips, but there wasn't a trace of amusement in it. "No, it certainly would not be. I will say the sums involved are in excess of what we usually encounter when a physician hands out mind candy."

"Serious money," Matt mused. "He hiding it offshore?"

"Maybe. What do you know about Reicht?" she countered.

He told her about Leila Satterwaite's murder. "Did you know she was a patient of Reicht's?"

"That's a matter for the local police," she said, but the pencil resumed tapping again.

"My wife used to be a Miami-Dade officer. She's working with Sergeant William Patowski on it. Have you found any connection between Reicht and Upton Winchester? I mean, it seems strange that a guy with all Winchester's prestige would hire a quack to treat his only child." This was the jackpot question. Would she answer?

Another sharkish smile. "I should've had you frisked for a tape recorder, Mr. Granger."

"I gave you my word this isn't going to see the light of newsprint until every last guilty person's behind bars. This is strictly off the record."

"Off the record, we occasionally audit prestigious citizens as well as quack doctors."

As Matt was leaving, Ida Kleb said in a voice that doubtless had sent shivers down the spines of many hapless taxpayers, "You will keep me apprised of anything you learn about Dr. Reicht…and Mr. Winchester, won't you, Mr. Granger?" Matt felt like a swimmer too far away from the shoreline.

Sam placed a call first thing that morning to Ethan Frobisher. She requested that he search for info on one Elvis Peter Scruggs, most importantly, those missing seven years of his life.

Then she spent the morning filing an electronic extension with the IRS for their taxes. To get the sour taste of the blood-sucking government agency out of her head, she spent a couple of hours at her dojo doing a hard judo workout, then came home and hit the shower. She was just drying off when she heard the front door open and Matt's footsteps coming down the hall. He turned into her office and started shuffling through the mess of papers on her desk.

"I filed the extension. Now, what's the deal with Ida Kleb?" she asked, pulling a tank top over her damp, curly hair as she walked in behind him.

"One item. Guess who Reicht's accountant is?"

"Roman Numeral. Is he under IRS investigation, too?" Sam asked.

"Dear Ida hedged just enough to make it pretty clear that he's involved in something very naughty right along with the shrink," Matt replied.

"Mmm," she said, leaning back against the sofa where her tax documents remained piled in the same disarray as when she'd first received the call from Upton Winchester IV. "If they're hiding serious money from the govvy, it's probably one of those offshore account scams."

"Seems likely," Matt agreed. "But if the IRS hasn't been able to nail either guy yet, how can we?" The minute he said the words, he could have bitten his tongue off. The gleam in his wife's eyes made her answer clear. "No, you're not going to do a B and E on Winchester's office."

Sam shook her head solemnly. "No, I'm not."

He sighed, pulling her up into his arms. "That's good."

She nuzzled his neck on tiptoe and murmured, "*We* are."

"That's bad. In fact, it's a cosmically dumb idea. It's illegal. It's dangerous. We could get—"

"Get over it, Granger. Either you help me or I go alone." She wrapped her arms around his neck and looked up earnestly into his face. "You owe me after inciting a riot last night at the Pink Pussycat."

"Me start a riot! You were the one—" She kissed him long and thoroughly. When she finished, he stared down at her and knew it was hopeless. "I'm the one who looks like he went ten rounds with Mike Tyson. You owe me."

"Nun-uh. You coming or not?"

Before he could answer, the phone rang. Sam gave him a quick peck on the mouth, then dug through the debris around her desk until she located the phone. "Ballanger Retrievals…oh, hi, Fro. Find anything on our boy Elvis?"

Matt waited, eager to hear about Scruggs, too. After a lengthy and what appeared to be frustrating conversation, she said, "Okay, let me give you a new project. See what you can dig up on connections between Upton Winchester IV...yeah, that Winchester, and Dr. Reese Reicht, M.D., Ph.D. He's a local shrink working out of the Seascape Building. The IRS is investigating both of them...right...yeah, I will. You're a sweetie."

"So?" he asked when she hung up.

"Zip. Oh, the part about Scruggs's abusive childhood in northern Florida checks out with what Patty told me. His old man was a sheriff in Jackson County. He wrecked pop's cruiser on a joyride and spent time in a juvenile detention facility. Mostly teenage pranks that got out of hand. Underage drinking, that kind of stuff. Then got his GED and did a hitch in the army... Interesting that Patty didn't give me that part."

"And?" he prompted, knowing how thorough Frobisher's hacking could be from previous experience.

"Like I said, zip. The guy just drops off the face of the frickin' earth. Reappears after seven years as Farley's newest and best friend."

"More like only friend, poor kid," Matt said.

Sam nodded. "Fro's going to keep after it, but so far he's hit a black hole. Thinks Scruggs must've left the country. Patowski speculated the same thing, but I don't think so."

"Scruggs doesn't strike me as an international man of mystery," Matt said dryly. "What would he be doing abroad?"

Sam shrugged. "Smuggling dope in Mexico? Who knows? But you're right, he seems like a folksy backcountry con artist, not some kind of drug cartel hit man."

"It would connect him to Reicht and Winchester if he was," Matt suggested.

Sam mulled that over. "Naw. If he worked for them, why would Winchester hire me to get the kid away from him?"

"Maybe he worked for Winchester and or Reicht, then double-crossed them and took off with the boy."

"That would work. Which reminds me, I've been dodging calls from Roman Numeral's office for the past two days. He wants to know where his kid is—and where I am. He hasn't heard anything since the Georgia Highway Patrol called to verify the retrieval."

"You can't tell him Farley's in Miami."

"I know, but I could say I'm stuck in Atlanta with Farley all safely tucked in, then ask him if he wants to press charges against Scruggs for GTA. If he's pissed enough at a double cross, he might go for it. He doesn't know Scruggs and the Jag have vanished into the ether."

"Didn't you say Scruggs told you the old man gave them the car?" Matt asked.

"Yeah. Maybe now that he's off the meds, Farley might remember more about that."

Matt shook his head. "I don't think he'd turn his pal El in, even if he did boost the wheels."

"You're probably right. But I am gonna call daddy and see what he wants me to do about Scruggs." She dialed the number and was greeted by the cool dulcet tone of Ms. Chandler's voice. "Yes, this is Sam Ballanger to speak with Mr. Winchester…it pertains to a private matter Mr. Winchester hired me to— Dammit, the bitch put me on hold!"

"Patience, Grasshopper," Matt said with a chuckle. She'd told him all about her initial encounter with the receptionist at Winchester, Grayson & Kent. "You could ask to speak with Ms. Ettinger," he suggested around a mouthful of corn chips he'd snagged from a bag she kept stashed in the top drawer of her desk.

She gave him a raspberry, but when Chandler informed her that Winchester was in New York on business, she was forced to speak with his personal assistant. "Yes, Ms. Ettinger, this is Sam Ballanger…yes, I know I haven't reported in…yes, I have Mr. Winchester's son safely in custody. My van had engine trouble in Atlanta. Elvis Scruggs followed us from St. Louis. He's here with Mr. Winchester's Jag, too. I can call the local police and have him arrest—" There was a long pause as the Wicked Witch of the West went through her drill. "Yeah, well, just thought I'd check. You want I should drive the Jag back to Miami with Farley? I could always pick up my van when it's repaired."

Matt could tell by the grin on her face that she was enjoying herself. When she finally hung up, he said, "I take it Roman Numeral doesn't want you to touch his precious vintage car."

She smirked. "Yeah, and me a professional driver, too. He wants Farley back here immediately. Next flight. When he returns from his trip to New York, he'll arrange to have the car returned—and—"

"He doesn't want the cops to touch Elvis Scruggs."

"You didn't even have to hold the paper up to your forehead, Karnak. I'm impressed," she said, grabbing the bag of chips from him and stuffing the last of them in her mouth.

"It's a good thing your hacker pal Ethan Frobisher set up that untraceable phone connection or they could trace your call and find out you and Farley are already home," he said. "How long can you stall?"

"No flights until tomorrow. Thunderstorms in Atlanta. After that, we're up for grabs as far as Winchester's concerned. He could call the cops and say I kidnapped Farley after I retrieved him from Scruggs."

"If we're right about Winchester's criminal involvement, the last thing he'll do is call the cops," Matt replied. "Does he have any idea where in Atlanta you're supposedly keeping Farley on ice?"

"Nah, I omitted that piece of pertinent info," she admitted. "But the situation means there's all the more reason to head for his office tonight and do a little snooping."

"No, it is not," he said stubbornly.

"Just think of the great story it'll make."

"I swore to Ida Kleb that I wouldn't publish anything until the IRS investigation's finished. She isn't the type to cross."

"So, let's give our friendly local IRS a helping hand. They can't do legally what we can do illegally."

"Yeah, like go straight to jail," he replied glumly.

The Seascape Building, like all the high-rise steel-and-glass wonders glittering on the Miami skyline, had state-of-the-art technology for security. But no one was better at running a con than Sam Ballanger. She'd spent years accumulating phony IDs. She had badges and paperwork to show she was a medical examiner, a registered nurse, an exterminator, a police officer from various jurisdictions, an electrician, plumber, phone company repairperson, even a member of Congress from Northern Florida.

Tonight she was dressed in one of her all-purpose jumpsuits with the logo of Bug-Gone Forever, a local extermination company sewed on it. Getting a jumper to fit a guy Matt's size wasn't easy, but she'd found one, then had him sew on his own patch while she got her "tools of the trade" in order and called Fro for some tech backup.

As they entered the lobby of the deserted building late that night, she flashed her ID and some official-looking paperwork at the front desk rent-a-cop. The guy who looked over her paperwork had a face that had traveled down a lot of roads, most of them not paved. His skin was sun-beaten the color of rusty tin and he had a voice to match. "Looks okay, but I gotta check with the company. Seems funny, bugs in a new joint like this," he said, pulling out his own phone book from under the desk to look up the number for Bug-Gone Forever.

"You got your lunch rooms with fridges and microwaves. Employees get sloppy, leave food out. Did you know a plain brown roach can climb straight up a clean glass surface quick as you walk across that floor?" Sam gestured at the polished marble.

The guard grunted, not particularly wanting to know about the habits of roaches, which in Florida's warm, humid climate grew to the size of well-fed house cats.

Verifying her story was a sensible precaution. Anticipating the guard would do just that, Sam had used the correct number in the forged work order. She had also had Fro cut into the trunk line and switch any call coming from the Seascape exchange to his number. After a few cursory questions, the security guard, whose name tag identified him as Tommy, nodded. "Looks like you got roaches to clean out. Say, they ain't down here, are they?"

"No, just up around the twentieth," Sam replied as she and Matt headed for the bank of elevators across the atrium lobby.

As they walked past a stand of potted palms, he whispered to her, "Good so far, but once we get up there, you're going to trip the alarm breaking into Winchester's front door."

"Oh, ye of little faith," she replied as the glass tube whooshed down and opened for them. "Enjoy the ride and see if you think Farley could've watched Reicht attack Leila from down there." As the elevator started to ascend, she pointed to a cluster of potted flora across the huge atrium lobby.

When they reached the top floor, Matt nodded. "Yep, I think he could if he was wearing his glasses and not too spaced-out. Still, never stand up in court."

"That's why we're here," she said cheerfully. When the elevator door opened, she pushed the fifteenth floor and the tube descended quietly. Tommy couldn't see the elevator leave them off at Winchester's floor from where he was stationed. As soon as it opened, she was the first out. "Let's get to work."

Matt whistled low at the thickly carpeted hallway and smoked glass doors discreetly lettered in gold: Winchester, Grayson & Kent. "Some fancy digs. You sure the cleaning people are done up here?"

"I told you I checked everything out—with a little help from Fro. Yeah, they're done before midnight."

"That security camera's sweeping our way. What if deputy dawg downstairs notices that we don't have the combination to enter the office complex?"

"I need you to give me a boost, quick." Sam darted to the camera as it swiveled in their direction with Matt right behind her. "Now!"

She climbed up his body like a monkey in a banana tree and fixed a small electronic gizmo on the camera. Then she shimmied down. "Keeps the sweep away from door number three," she said with a grin.

"That's the only reason you asked me to tag along—to use as a stepladder," he accused.

Sam shrugged as she walked over to the accounting firm's door. "I might need you for something else. Right now, just keep watch while I do the deed."

"Probably bulletproof," Matt groused as he looked at the heavy lock on the three-inch-thick glass.

"I wasn't planning on shooting my way in," she said, kneeling and removing an electronic sensor of some kind from inside the "Bug-Gone" toolbox.

He watched in equal parts admiration and trepidation

while she worked the gizmo. "What if you trip some kind of alarm system?"

"That's the beauty of having friends who keep me up to speed on the latest technology."

"Frobisher?" he asked.

She chewed on her lip in concentration as she replied, "And Patty."

"Sergeant Patowski's a homicide cop. Why the hell would he do that?"

Sam chuckled as the door glided open. "Not intentionally. But we do talk shop now and then. I eavesdrop whenever we have beers at the local cops' hangouts. You'd be surprised what you can learn that way."

"Only if you are or were a cop yourself," he said, knowing how the police clammed up whenever a reporter nursed a beer in one of their haunts.

Sam walked into the spacious waiting room where she'd first done battle with the sleek Ms. Chandler. "This way," she said in a low voice, heading down the hall. "We'll have the joint to ourselves unless somebody's burning the midnight oil in hopes of making partner."

He glanced at the dark offices. "Now there's a comforting thought."

Sam suddenly stiffened and signaled for him to be quiet. Directly ahead a dim light emanated from beneath the walnut door of Upton Winchester's office. "Looks as if somebody's beat us to the punch," she whispered.

"Or Upton's back from New York early," he muttered.

Sam removed her snub nose from the toolbox and then very carefully turned the knob on the massive door. She could hear the clicking of keys from across the huge room. A figure was hunched over Winchester's computer, scrolling down long columns of figures with annotations beside them.

In the dim light generated by the computer, his silhouette was very distinctive. Cocking the hammer of the .38, she said conversationally, "Hello, Elvis. How's tricks?"

Chapter 20

Scruggs swiveled the chair around and grinned at Sam and Matt, totally ignoring the gun barrel aimed directly at his chest. "Well, now. Ain'tcha the resourceful ones?"

"Oh, I dunno, El. You're pretty resourceful yourself. How the hell did you get in here?" Sam countered.

Matt edged around to the left and studied the monitor. "Looks like our boy's been doing some snooping into Winchester's private files."

"Resourceful and chock-full of surprises, too," Sam said dryly.

Scruggs crossed his arms over his chest and leaned back in the chair. "'Course you folks are just here to check out the view from ole Upton's corner window."

"Find anything interesting?" Matt asked, ignoring the jibe.

Scruggs ignored Matt now. "Ma'am, do you have any idea how much trouble you caused me?" he asked Sam. "How the hell did you get that junker van to run with a busted timing belt?"

"Ace bandages," she replied. "How'd you find us every time we gave you the slip—use the National Reconnaissance Office's spy satellites to search for my van?"

"A few calls to the Tennessee and Georgia highway patrols worked well enough." He scratched his head. "Ace bandages? No shit?"

"And why would state cops help you?" she asked, wondering, not for the first time, how he'd convinced the Georgia Highway Patrol to let him go.

He moved slowly so Sam could see his hands at all times, first inserting a disk into the tower and pressing copy, then reaching inside his pocket for a thin leather wallet.

"I'll take that when you're done," Sam said, eyeing the copy he was making of Winchester's files.

He shook his head. "'Fraid not."

"I'm the one with the gun," she reminded him.

"Yep, you surely are, ma'am. But I'm the one with the badge." At her blink of surprise, he grinned again and tossed her the wallet. "Since you're an ex-cop, I figure you'll recognize the real ticket."

Sam caught it deftly in her left hand and moved closer to the light, examining its contents after she handed the gun to Matt, saying, "Watch him. If he blinks, shoot."

"Don't move, El. I'm considerably more nervous about breaking and entering than my wife is. I might do something rash."

Scruggs shrugged and grinned again. "Well?" he asked Sam, nodding toward the badge.

"I don't friggin' believe it. He's DEA."

"That might account for those missing seven years we

haven't been able to trace," Matt said. "What's the DEA got to do with Upton Winchester?"

"We know he's up to his eyebrows in a scam with Reicht, helping him hide illegal prescription income," Sam added. "So the two of them must be working serious drug connections in addition to being involved in murder."

All traces of illiterate diction were gone as was his good humor when Elvis replied, "You're interfering in a federal investigation and you're in way over your heads. Back off."

"You sound like Ida Kleb," Matt said.

"The formidable Ms. Kleb of the IRS. So you ran her down, too." He tipped his chair forward. "Where's Farley?"

"No way am I turning that boy over to a guy who was feeding him drugs. The kid's not crazy, just doped up to look that way," Sam replied.

"I know that. I was the one trying to get him off the junk Reicht had him pumped full of. That's why I let his old man set me up with the Jag. Winchester has no idea who I am. He thought he could blackmail me into disappearing rather than face GTA once you got Farley back under Reicht's tender care. Upton knows I've been trying to convince his son to toss the pills ever since I befriended him."

"The reason being?" Sam prompted.

"You know too much already. Right now all I can tell you is that I'll see the boy's protected from his father and the bogus shrink."

Sam shook her head. "No dice." Leaning over the desk, she went nose to nose with the big agent. "I have Farley someplace where he's absolutely safe and he's staying put. The only way you're gonna see him again is if you can convince us that you aren't just using him to bust his old man."

"The kid nearly wrecked the car and killed all three of us when he thought you were going to rescue him. He thinks you're really his best friend," Matt said, angry that an innocent boy was caught in the middle of this ugly mess.

"He witnessed Reicht abduct, maybe kill, Leila Satterwaite, who just happened to be another one of the doc's patients," Sam added. "You know anything about her besides her name, rank and serial number in Spacefleet?"

Before Scruggs could reply, the sound of the elevator door pinging down the hall froze all three of them. The agent muttered an oath and ejected the half copied disk from the computer. "You must've tripped some security. Damned amateurs. Come on, let's get the hell out of here," he whispered, turning the computer to rest mode and sliding out of the chair.

Sam grabbed her toolbox and Matt shoved her snub nose into his belt after uncocking it. They quickly followed Elvis to a door on the far wall. Scruggs ushered them inside just as the sound of the heavy office door clicked open. They passed an elegant private washroom and reached an exit sign. Very carefully, the agent opened the door, looking at the video cameras before stepping out into the outer hall. "We're clear if we hurry," he whispered, dashing for the fire stairs about a dozen yards to the left.

Once they were behind the closed door, Scruggs turned to Sam and asked, "You put something on the video camera outside the suite front door to change the sweep pattern?"

"I've used those devices for years. There's no way one should bring security up here this soon," she said defensively. His amateur crack pissed her off.

"Shouldn't have," Scruggs admitted, "but sometimes an extra sharp guard will notice when one of the monitors isn't working exactly right. Come up and check it out."

"Tommy's about as sharp as a plastic spoon and didn't strike me as exactly ambitious."

"Shift changes at 3:00 a.m.," Scruggs informed them.

Sam cursed. "I borrowed that gizmo from a friend. I have to return it."

"Damn straight or Winchester will know somebody was inside his office and have it swept for the listening devices I planted."

He cracked the door and looked at the camera in question. "Hold the door open," he whispered to Matt, then dashed down the hall and made a flying jump that would have done Michael Jordan proud. The instant his hand yanked the small device on the camera free, he whirled around and headed back to the exit.

"Smooth," Sam admitted.

"I could've reached it easier," Matt said. He had a couple of inches on Scruggs but he knew damn well he wouldn't have been able to detach the gizmo as deftly since he had no idea how Sam had attached it.

"You big guys can have a pissing contest later," Sam hissed. "Let's get the hell out of Dodge before that guard comes down the hall."

"Fifteen floors," Matt groused.

"Hey, at least it's down, not up," Sam whispered, leading the way. "Anyway, we have to hit the front desk and sign out, so we'll have to hitch a ride on the 'transponder' in a couple of floors."

"Nobody saw me come in," Scruggs said, not explaining further how he'd gained access.

"Will you two keep your size twenty E clodhoppers quiet? Sound echoes like crazy in stairwells," she said as they neared the next landing. They went down two more levels. "Okay, here's the deal. You want Farley. We want info. Maybe we can work something out. Meet us at the Landing. You know the place?" she asked the agent.

"All-night joint just off Brickell, south side of the river." He nodded. "Catch you there in fifteen." Like the old Elvis, he pointed his index finger at her as if it were a gun and cocked his thumb back. "Don't be late."

As he continued down the stairs, Sam heard him muttering, "Frickin' Ace bandages. Unbelievable."

The Landing had started out as a bait shack before the Brickell district became the home of commercial and high-end residential real estate. It was situated on the Miami River beneath the shadows of freeway traffic and skyscrapers. Surrounding it, hidden behind wooden walls, chunks of concrete lay victim to the wrecking ball. The old gave way to the new. Except for the Landing. "Jerry-built chic" was how one restaurant critic had described the moldy wooden structure which had numerous additions attached to the original in a concentric design totally lacking in aesthetics.

But the fresh seafood was outstanding and the yuppie crowd blended in with stubborn remnants of retired blue-collar night owls who nursed beers while they sat at the battered bar eating heaping plates of fried clams. Sam and Matt spotted Elvis Scruggs at a corner booth in the bar area. The air was blue with smoke despite a large No Smoking sign posted in both English and Spanish.

They greeted the bartender and asked for their usuals. Matt had introduced her to the place when they'd returned from their wedding in Boston. It had long been a retreat of *Herald* newspeople after hours.

If Barney Donovan thought their exterminator jumpsuits looked odd, he didn't comment as he served her Scotch on the rocks and gave Matt a mug of Pacifico draft beer, then asked Scruggs if he wanted another Bud. The agent shook his head and the bartender discreetly disappeared.

Sam took a sip of her Scotch, then said, "We're after the same thing—to put Reese Reicht and Upton Winchester in the slammer. So's Sergeant Patowski. Don't deny you know him. He already tried covering for you. Told me about your juvvie history, but not a peep about the army hitch or joining the DEA after. You want to fill in some blanks for us? Or do I speculate?"

"I guarantee you she won't give up until she has every piece of the puzzle," Matt said cheerfully, blowing the foamy head off his beer.

Scruggs leaned back in the booth and blew out a frustrated breath. "No, from what the sergeant's told me, she won't quit." He looked at Sam. "I went through a rough patch as a kid. Only reason I joined the army was because it was that or jail time. They gave me some tests and told me I qualified for officer's training after finishing my GED." He grinned. "Made it halfway through, then figured I wasn't cut out for spit and polish."

"So you went back to your enlistment."

He nodded. "I was assigned to go undercover, work on a drug ring operated by a bunch of noncoms at my base."

"And you found your niche in life," Sam said, understanding part of what made Scruggs tick. "You'd be a natural for DEA work. You look much younger than you are, country smart, but you can play dumb. You're good, El."

"Consider that a compliment," Matt said.

"Yeah, it is. We gonna cooperate with each other or keep stumbling over each other's feet?" she asked.

"Like to, but I can't afford working with a *Herald* reporter. If this gets out before—"

"I already promised our firstborn to Ida Kleb if I write a line before the investigation's finished. What do I have to do for you, sign in blood?" Matt asked.

Scruggs's shrewd dark eyes studied them for a moment,

then he sat up with his elbows on the scarred wooden table and said, "I guess I'll have to trust you."

She still wasn't sure they could trust him, but they needed his inside info. "We really can help. Or, at least somebody who's involved sure thinks so. They've been trying to kill me ever since the day Winchester phoned me about retrieving Farley from you. Why did you take the kid and skip town?" She waited expectantly.

"Farley, as I'm sure you know, is a real Spacer, has been ever since he was a little boy. He wanted to go to the big con in St. Louis and I needed to get him away from daddy and the shrink."

"What could a drugged-up kid do for your case against either of them?" Matt asked. He felt Sam's foot touch his beneath the table and caught her eye signal. Cops never trusted reporters, least of all him since he broke a big story several months ago exposing an FBI-Miami-Dade PD sting to uncover CIA ties to the Russian mob. He would be wise to let her take the lead, ask the questions. He gave her a look indicating that he understood.

"Farley was really out of it when I nabbed him. Had a couple of drug-related panic attacks that scared the bejesus out of me," she explained to Scruggs.

"I hoped to buy enough time while he was having fun at the con to get him clean." Elvis looked down at the dregs in his bottle of beer, then swallowed the last bit. "I admit, I was using the space conspiracy stuff to get him to open up. You see, Farley's a kind of savant—not an idiot by any means. Kid's smart as hell, just geeky and unhappy."

"He had a rotten childhood. So did you, but you don't strike me as either a geek or a savant," Sam said dryly. That earned her a small tug of a smile. "What does he know?"

"Kid's got a photographic memory. I mean damn near

infinite capacity from what we've learned from his tutors, test results, that kind of thing. A DEA investigation into a Florida drug cartel led the agency to Reicht. Winchester's the money manipulator who hides it for them. That part we got from the IRS. When I was assigned to the case, my job was to infiltrate Winchester's household. Get to his home computer, tap his phones."

"And you found out Farley was playing with daddy's computer data while the old man wasn't around," Sam surmised.

"When he was lucid, the kid could recite back to me twenty-digit bank account numbers in the Caymans, amounts transferred, transaction dates. I made up a game. Told him the money was payment to Klingoff spies and he bought it. Once I convinced him I was a Spacefleet officer, he was ready to send his old man to jail. Far believes Upton Winchester's part of a Pandorian-Klingoff takeover of Earth.

"Of course, the kid wouldn't be a credible witness, but a few pieces of info he gave me checked out when the IRS investigated the money trail. Meanwhile, Winchester got suspicious about his son palling around with an itinerant yardman, even if I did look young enough to pass for twenty. He fired me before I could get enough info to build our case."

"He thought you were, and I quote, 'an illiterate cracker,'" Sam said. "Don't feel bad. He treated me like pond scum, too."

"But he hired you and I lost my inside access to his computers. He threatened Far. Said if the kid ever saw me again, he'd lock him up."

"Let me guess. Far kept sneaking out to meet his good ole buddy El," she said.

"Even before his mother died, Farley and his father didn't get along. The old man had relied on his business associate Reicht to keep a lid on the kid's socially unacceptable behavior for years."

"So after Farley latched on to you, his father had Reicht really hype up the meds," Sam said. "Reicht told me once I brought Farley back, they were going to put him in a rehab facility called Homeside."

"I figured it was either get him away from Reicht quick or the boy might become a vegetable after he'd been locked away a few months," Elvis replied.

Sam nodded agreement. "But Winchester would never let Reicht kill the boy. That would mean he'd be cut off from his dead wife's fortune."

Scruggs grinned in spite of himself. "You have been digging. Or your newshound has." He cast a faintly hostile look at Matt.

Matt put up his hands and said, "I just do what Sammie tells me."

She muffled a snort into her Scotch glass. "We know the terms of Susan's will. Winchester has to keep the kid alive, but incompetent."

"That way he controls the money for the rest of his life," Scruggs said. "Reicht's the one getting the lion's share of the drug money. Winchester's cut isn't nearly as big."

"So Roman Numeral doesn't want his son dead. But Reicht might." Sam looked at Scruggs, who was staring intently at her.

"You care to explain why?" Elvis asked.

"Farley told me he saw Leila Satterwaite 'transponded' away by Pandorians."

"Yes, he told me that, too. So?" Scruggs prompted her.

"What he really saw took place in the Seascape Building. In the elevator, at the top floor. Reicht and Leila were struggling in the glass tube. Then she vanished, never to be seen again until she turned up in the morgue."

Scruggs shook his head, amazed. "I just figured Far had a crush on Leila. We met her at a few local Quest meetings.

But if what you say's true, it would give Reicht a motive to kill Farley. I never could make sense out of what he said about her and the transponder thing," he admitted. "But why would Reicht kill Leila? She was just another Spacer who felt sorry for Farley and was nice to him, far as I know. I was just playing along with his ideas about her alien abduction."

"You had an ulterior motive for befriending the kid. Maybe she did, too," Sam said. "She washed up in Patowski's jurisdiction. It's his case. Let me see what he'll tell me about it. Then I'll dig for the rest."

"Works for me. Now, where have you stashed Farley?" Elvis leaned forward and grinned at Sam. "It's a federal crime to obstruct a DEA investigation. Your friend Patowski won't be able to bail you out if you don't hand him over to me."

"He's safe and under professional care."

"I need to put him under government protection. We have a safe house and a doc all lined up," Scruggs said without a hint of negotiation in his voice.

Sam shook her head, just as stubborn as the agent was. "I've seen how safe 'safe houses' can be around this neck of the woods. This is a seventeen-year-old kid's life you're talking about. Winchester's made you as somebody he didn't trust. That's why he set you up with the Jag and hired me. You admitted it."

"And then Reicht tried to kill you and Farley. Doesn't sound as if you're in any better position to protect the boy. If I sent agents to wherever you've hidden him, there's no way Reicht or Winchester could know to follow them."

"What if he were already in legal custody?" Matt interjected. He could see the two of them had reached a stalemate.

Scruggs narrowed his eyes and looked at Matt. Sam pinched his thigh beneath the table, but he waved her off.

"What do you mean by legal custody?" the agent asked suspiciously.

"Miami-Dade PD custody. You can verify it through Patowski."

"Matt, you know feds of any kind never believe the local cops can slap their own asses using both hands, for crying out loud," Sam said, exasperated. Knowing the police connection, it wouldn't take a sharp operator like Elvis Scruggs long to figure out the Spacefleet link to Montoya.

"The first thing the DEA needs to do is turn that disk over to Ida Kleb and let the IRS crunchers analyze what's on it," Granger said to Scruggs. "You planted bugs in his office, too. Look, you may not need Farley Winchester to break the case wide open. At least give the kid a chance while you work with what you already have."

Elvis muttered an oath. "You can't imagine what it's like to work with Ida Kleb." He actually shuddered.

Matt grinned. "As a matter of fact, I have a damn good idea. Be easier to deal with a poked rattler…to borrow a page from your lexicon."

"For a Boston Yalie, you know your snakes."

"Like I said, I've met the dame. I've also met ex-KGB agents with more charm."

Sam could sense some kind of weird male bonding between Matt and Elvis. Men. Who could ever figure them? Before their uneasy accord broke, she said, "We'll find out why Satterwaite insinuated herself into Farley's life and became Reicht's patient. Somehow it all ties together." She shook the ice in the bottom of her empty glass, tapping her fingers against it. "I have a hunch once we find out why Reicht killed her, you and Patowski can bust up a major drug ring and solve a murder at the same time."

"If I don't make contact with Far, you don't, either. Reicht could get lucky and have one of his goons tail you."

"Fair enough," Sam said. "Just keep in touch about what you find out and we'll do the same. Let's exchange numbers."

"Where does that leave you with collecting your retrieval fee from Winchester if he ends up in jail?" Scruggs asked bluntly.

The DEA agent had done his homework on her, Matt thought with an inward grin he did not show. "Sammie will work something out. She's resourceful that way."

"That's what I'm afraid of," Scruggs said.

"I'll get busy digging on Susan Mallory Winchester. See if there's any way to prove her OD wasn't self-inflicted," Matt said as they left the Brickell District behind.

"I'll check on Roman Numeral's household help. See who else he may have fired recently. He isn't exactly the type to inspire undying loyalty."

The lights from the Miami skyline reflected on the glassy waters of the Intracoastal while Sam steered her battered van over the MacArthur Causeway toward their home in South Beach. Neither the city nor the beach ever slept. Ahead the bright lights from high-rise apartments and condos ringing the Art Deco District beckoned. Since moving in with Matt, she'd gotten used to living close to the stunning view. Her old rental house on NE 110th had a great view, too…if your tastes ran to junker cars, tall weeds and discarded appliances rusting in the yard.

She'd liked her old neighbors, for the most part, and the price had been reasonable. When she first found out what Matt's mortgage on the condo was she'd nearly had a heart attack. Of course, he refused to give up his home and since he was making the payments, she went along with it, grudgingly. But damn, on starry nights like this, the sounds of salsa music and laughter did beat hell out of bikers revving up their engines and wives screeching at their husbands until the cops arrived with flashing lights to quell the domestic disturbances.

The fragrance of lush tropical flowers filled the air and she took a deep breath from her open window. Matt cupped the back of her neck with one big hand and said, "Admit it, you love it here."

"It's pretty cool."

"Safer than that cinder block bastion where you used to hang out," he said.

"That depends," she replied, glancing in her rearview mirror.

"Mmm," he murmured, nuzzling her neck with his lips now. "On what?"

"On whether that's the same tan Mustang that tried to make my van into a sieve back at the Kentucky state line."

Matt looked out his side-view mirror and saw what looked like an identical vehicle approaching them far above the speed limit. Then it pulled into the passing lane and drew even with them. "I think we're in trouble," he said as moonlight glinted off the barrel of the MP5 that suddenly appeared in the passenger window.

Chapter 21

"**D**uck, Sam!" he yelled.

She leaned forward against the steering wheel and slammed down on the souped-up accelerator of the Econoline. It raced ahead of the muscle car just as a burst of automatic weapon fire roared. The rear side panel of the van took the hit. The Econoline swerved on impact, coming perilously close to the causeway guardrail, but Sam quickly corrected course.

"Damn, I just got it back from the shop this morning! Do you know how much our insurance is gonna go up now?"

"Forget the insurance. Just get us the hell away from those bozos who're shooting at us!" Matt grabbed her bag and pulled the snub nose out of it, then started leaning out his window to see if he had a shot at their pursuers.

"Jeez, will you get your head inside before they blow it off! You can't hit them from the right."

She no more than got the words out before another round

of fire thudded into the rear of the van, clipping one tire. A blowout at eighty miles per hour was never good. At that speed on a causeway with nothing to the sides but oncoming traffic and a drop-off into the channel, it was even worse. Sam held on to the wheel and cut it sharply as it kissed the railing, leaving behind a trail of sparks.

Once she was forced to slow, the Mustang pulled into the passing lane again and smashed against the side of the van. "Two can play this game, buddy," she snarled, turning her wheel to slam back at the lighter sports car.

No one knew by looking at the old Econoline that it had been fitted with sheet steel panels and that the engine and drive train had been customized to make it sturdier and faster than an ordinary utility van. Driving on the rim of a tire, however, dangerously slowed it. All she could do was play hard dodgem cars now. She hit the Mustang broadside and knocked it into an approaching car. Horns blared and tires squealed as cars and SUVs swerved to avoid a collision.

"Driver's good," she muttered between clenched teeth as the Mustang held the road. But it bought them a small window of time before the flat tire gave out. "We already missed Palm. Gotta make it to Terminal Island."

"I don't think they'll follow us into the Coast Guard barracks, but that turn's too sharp—"

Matt didn't get any further before Sam slammed on the brakes and cut the wheel hard to the right, peeling downhill onto the narrow blacktop road leading to the Coast Guard station on the island. If not for the flat tire's rim scraping along the concrete, they probably would have rolled making the U-turn. As it was, the van skidded on loose gravel, traveling sideways for nearly a dozen yards before Sam was able to get it under control and limp toward the station's lights.

Their pursuers did not follow.

As they watched the taillights of the Mustang vanish into the traffic swarming toward Miami Beach, he said, "Great driving, Sammie. Wish I could have made their plates."

"No way in the dark. Besides, they'll just ditch the car on a side street or parking deck," she said as she dialed the Beach police. "We might get lucky and have a unit coming up Alton to Fifth."

As she spoke with the dispatcher, Matt checked the rear of the van. Both the left side panel and rear doors were pock-marked with bullet holes. "*Get* lucky? We're already damn lucky to be alive and in one piece," he muttered.

"They'll send a couple of units nearby to look for a tan Mustang but I bet our boys walk before anyone sees them," she said, discouraged. She climbed out of the van and inspected the bent rim and bullet-riddled body of her car. "Uncle Dec's gonna kill me when he sees what I've done to his baby."

"It's your van, Sam," Matt reminded her.

"Yeah, but it was my uncle who did all the heavy lifting when we replaced the engine and transmission." She kicked what was left of the shot-out tire. "And now we have to wait for the Beach cops and fill out a mountain of paperwork."

Just as she said that the bright red-and-blue flashing lights of a police car drew closer. "I'll take you to Jerry's Deli for breakfast when we're done," he said, planting a consoling kiss on her cheek. "You can even order onions with your lox and I won't complain."

Sam continued to stare disconsolately at her van as the cruiser pulled alongside them.

She had a double order of nova lox on a giant poppy-seed bagel with extra cream cheese, tomatoes and onion on the side. They sat outdoors at Jerry's, watching pedestrian traffic warily. They hadn't had the chance to see the gunmen in the

Mustang on either occasion. Any innocent-looking tourist or guy on a bicycle could be one of the shooters. The mustang had been quickly located near Flamingo Park, leading the police to surmise that they'd had an escape vehicle parked nearby intending to switch after disposing of Sam and Matt.

"Never ceases to amaze me how you can put away the chow and stay so slim," Matt said, taking a piece of bacon and popping it into his mouth.

"Getting shot at burns calories like crazy. So does getting run off the road and nearly crashing over a guardrail."

"Now if you could only figure a way to burn off the halitosis from those onions, life would be perfect," he teased, knowing she was still dejected about her van having to be towed in for more expensive repairs. When she didn't respond with her usual sharp comeback, he turned their conversation to the case. "Maybe those bozos left some prints on the Mustang. I bet they have rap sheets longer than a roll of toilet paper."

"Yeah, they're strictly amateur night, trying a dumb stunt like that after they messed up in Kentucky. I bet whoever hired them didn't green-light it."

"If the cops arrest them, they might give up their boss or bosses."

"So far we don't even have a print. And it takes forever to run them through all the databases," she said, polishing off her lox. "We'd better get cracking before Elvis finds Farley—or worse yet, Winchester or Reicht do."

He waved to their waiter and handed him two twenties, saying, "Keep the change."

"What, are you Bill Gates already? That was a twenty-five percent tip, for crying out loud," she hissed as the smiling waiter strolled away. "Ask for change."

"No, yes and no, responding to your remarks in order," he

said, starting to cross the street and head south on Collins Avenue toward their condo.

Sputtering about champagne-taste preppies living on beer incomes, she followed. Right now he had the only set of wheels and she needed them. "While you surf the Net for info on Farley's mother, I'll need your car." She knew his sea-foam-blue Mustang convertible was as much his pride and joy as her refitted Econoline was hers.

"No way, Sammie. You'll end up leaving it in the scrap heap. Besides, it's a convertible, for Pete's sake. You'd be too easy a target."

"So I'll ride with the top up," she argued. "Come on, Matt, you know I have to have a car."

"So, rent one."

"You are certifiable, you know that! Pay those asphalt pirates outrageous rates when we have a perfectly good car sitting at home. I'm not made of money. In fact, this case may cost me a bundle if I can't figure a way to squeeze the money out of Upton Winchester IV before I send him to jail."

Actually, Sam was the certifiable one, in his opinion. "Okay, give your pal Señor Obregon a call. I bet he'd let you have that old Charger for a good price." One of her former neighbors up on NE 110th ran a junker car dealership without benefit of license. She'd rented the incredibly battered old Dodge Charger minus second gear from Raoul Obregon when Matt had first met her.

"I'd still have to get up there to pick it up," she wheedled.

"Use that charm on your buddy Leon, the cabbie. He'll drive you there if you don't haggle about the price too much."

"You're a hard man, Matthew Granger."

"So you've said a time or two." He waggled his eyebrows at her suggestively.

Sam was in no mood for double entendres as she punched

the access code and the condo gate opened. On her way upstairs, she walked past his convertible. The urge to key it was almost irresistible, but she'd had to give her keys to the tow truck driver when he hauled the Econoline away. *I'm just being bitchy because of my van.*

She knew Matt was right. She'd have his pristine car wracked up in nothing flat—and that didn't even take into account any more goons shooting at her. A disturbingly distinct possibility ever since she had accepted this job.

The 1970 Dodge Charger was still missing second gear as Sam babied it through several stoplights en route to the Winchester family manse in a very posh section of Coconut Grove. Winchester's home was newly built with its own private mooring on Biscayne Bay. She recognized a fifty-plus-foot Tiara yacht bobbing gently at its berth. Interestingly, it bore the name Susan M. on the side. She wondered why Roman Numeral hadn't had it changed after his most unlamented wife passed.

"Probably didn't want to piss off his in-laws," she muttered to herself as she walked the flagstone path twisting around poinciana and tulip trees toward the servants' quarters. On her earlier visit she had learned where Dare Rogers, the family chauffeur, lived, along with a small army of other servants. The lawn was as manicured as a golf green and tropical flowers of every hue were perfectly clustered to provide sun and shade color to the lush setting. No weed would ever dare raise its head aboveground.

She grinned, thinking of Raoul Obregon's front yard where the crabgrass was knee-high and the only spring flowers were dandelions. Before driving over, she had called the housekeeper, Mrs. Wachter, disguising her voice with a Southern drawl that would've done Elvis proud. She posed as Dare's cousin Melba from Pensacola, asking if he was at home or out driving his employer around. On her first visit, she had noted his upstate accent and inquired where he was from. That kind of detail often proved useful in her line of work. The old harridan had informed her that Rogers would return from driving "the Mister" to his office in about an hour.

Sam rushed to beat Rogers home so the housekeeper couldn't tell him his "cousin Melba" was arriving for a visit and blow her cover. She was relieved to see the limo pull up the driveway just ahead of her. After he parked the big black monster expertly in the garage, she hailed him as he started to climb the stairs to his quarters above it. The white frame outbuilding was easily the size of four South Beach condos.

"Mr. Rogers, hey! Got a minute?" she yelled, dashing across the grass in what was surely a gross violation of the head gardener's rules. She could see the leer on his florid face as soon as she drew near the bottom of the steps. Dare Rogers wore his thinning hair in a comb-over that didn't shade his scalp enough to keep it from turning pink under the hot Florida sun. The broken veins on his flattened nose indicated that he was fond of booze and had been in his share of bar fights. On the losing end.

"Well, Sam, as I live and breathe. What brings you out here again? You find that boy?"

"No. That's why I need your help again," she said with a big smile. She'd worn a hot pink tank top with a low scoop neck and jean shorts to accentuate her best assets.

"Anythin' to help you find the poor kid. Say, wannna come up an' have a drink?" he asked slyly.

"Don't mind if I do," she said, wondering if she'd have to flatten his nose even more to get out of the joint. She followed him into the upper apartment area. His unit was at the end of the long hall and had a nice view of the marina. A set of deer antlers and a print of dogs playing poker were the sole attempts at interior decoration. The furniture, probably provided by Winchester, was sturdy and functional.

A dark green sofa and wing chair, small oak table and four chairs were unremarkable, but the bookcases filled with porno magazines and Rogers's version of "collectibles" were anything but. She noted several small plastic action figures sold only in "adult" shops. *Are those two toys...aw, sick.*

Sam turned her attention to the living room-kitchenette area's main attraction—a large-screen TV complete with DVD player and a mountain of cassettes scattered around the entertainment center. Driving rich people around all day paid pretty well, she thought as he pulled a bottle of top-drawer Scotch from a kitchen cabinet. When he'd said a drink, she'd been thinking more along the lines of a cold beer. *Jeez, it wasn't even ten in the morning!*

"Whoa, just give me a couple of ice cubes in that, please," she said as he filled the second tall water glass. "I gotta drive back to the Beach and I can't afford another DUI." She'd never had one, but she wanted Rogers to think of her as someone with whom he had something in common. He dropped in several small cubes that looked as if they'd survived the last ice age and handed her the glass.

"Set down, take the load off," he said, sprawling his spare tire across the sofa and patting the cushion beside him.

Sam opted for the chair and took a sip of the Scotch to distract him from the rebuff. "Great stuff. You got good taste, Dare."

"I do okay," he replied, nodding to the entertainment center.

"Yeah, I can tell. Say, you ever see this woman? She's a friend of Farley's and we think maybe she might know where he is."

"You mean he ain't with that Elvis fellow?" he asked as she handed him a photo of Leila Satterwaite.

"Naw, he and Farley split in St. Louis. Musta drunk too much Klingoff blood milk or something," she said with a snicker that he echoed. She watched as he looked at Leila's stripper photo.

He let out a low whistle. "Never seen this one. She's not the kind I'd forget, believe you me. Some kinda hot! She a friend of Mr. W's kid?" he asked, incredulously.

"Yeah. A Spacer like him."

"No kiddin'? Too bad. Anybody who'd watch that crap oughta be locked in a loony bin, you ask me—don't tell Mr. W. I said that," he added quickly. "Farley's a nice kid in a weird sort of way. Real smart," he said earnestly.

"Don't worry. Mr. W. doesn't exactly talk to the hired help, even if I was the type to blab, which I'm not. Between you and me, I think he's a first-class jerk."

That elicited a big grin as Rogers took a long gulp of his Scotch and wiped his mouth with the back of his hand. Sam wondered how he could drink this much and stay straight enough to keep his chauffeur's license. He replied, "Couldn't agree more. He ain't easy to work for. Have to take a lot of crap."

On a hunch, she asked, "Was his wife as big a pain in the ass? I heard she came from a filthy rich family."

He shook his head. "She was too stoned most of the time to give anyone around here much grief." A big lascivious grin spread across his mouth. "She was a lot nicer to some of us than others, if you get my drift."

Sensing a juicy bit of gossip was forthcoming, Sam leaned forward conspiratorially and smiled back. "She had a lover?"

"Big blond type. You know, a muscle-bound pretty boy, Kenny Brio. He was supposed to be a yardman, but the only hedge he ever pruned wasn't green…if you get my drift." He smirked knowingly. "You want a refill?"

"No thanks. Like I said, I gotta drive home and I can't

hold my liquor like you. Sure wish I could," she said in an admiring tone. "This stuff about Mrs. Winchester and Brio, was it just gossip?"

Rogers shook his head. "I caught 'em once in the pool house when I went looking for extra towels. They was so busy goin' at it, they never seen me. Figgered it wasn't none of my business, so I just slipped out. They never knew I was there."

Sam would have bet the price of bodywork on the Econoline that he'd stayed and gotten an eyeful, but she didn't interrupt as he refilled his glass. "I never told Mr. W. He don't know how to treat a woman, anyway. Rather sit lookin' at account ledgers. Man's a fool."

"Yeah, I saw pictures of Susan Winchester. She was a real looker. How'd she treat Farley?"

"Okay, I guess. When she wasn't on drugs. But by the time the kid was in junior high, she was pretty far gone. Mr. W. had her seeing a shrink—that same fellow that Farley goes to now."

"Dr. Reicht?"

"Yep. She seemed to be doin' okay for a while, but then she really went off the deep end. We could hear her yellin' and breakin' stuff all the way from the big house."

"Seeing his mother like that wouldn't have made Farley happy," she said softly.

"No, reckon it didn't. Then Brio up and left. After a little while, she took that OD and that was the end of her."

"Any idea what happened to Brio?" Sam asked.

He shrugged. "One day he was here mowing the grass like nothin' was wrong. Next day, adios. Funny, though…"

"Yeah?" she prompted.

"He left his stuff in his room. You know, like he didn't plan on bein' gone long, but a couple of days later, Mrs. Wachter, the housekeeper, she come up here and packed everything up. Said he'd quit and taken a job in the Tampa Bay area. She was supposed to ship his stuff there. Really pissed her off," he added with a grin.

"She's pretty tight with the boss man," Sam commented. The hatchet-faced harridan fit right in with Ms. Ettinger and the whole hardware-faced crew at Winchester's office. All sharp angles with refrigeration coolant in their veins. Poor Farley never had a chance with a family and people like those around him. "When Susan Winchester died, did Brio show for the funeral or anything? You know, being her lover and all, it just sort of figured that he might at least send flowers or something."

"Never heard nothing from him. Not a peep. Like he dropped off the earth, know what I mean?"

"Kenny Brio." Sam spelled the name for Ethan Frobisher, then gave him everything she knew about Susan Mallory Winchester's lover, which wasn't much. But then Fro didn't need much to trace someone.

After signing off, she poured herself a tall glass of iced tea to sober up from the Scotch she'd been forced to consume to be sociable and keep Rogers talking. The unhappy wife had a torrid affair with a lowly gardener who happened to be a big blond hunk. On a sudden, wild hunch, she called Fro back and gave him another tip.

Chapter 22

Sam walked through the entry of the big Metro-Dade head-quarters building on NW 25th Street late that afternoon and waved at the uniform seated behind the high counter. "Need to talk to Patowski, Max. He said he'd be here."

The tall, thin sergeant had a fringe of silver hair cut regulation short, circling his head like a halo. He gave Sam a wide smile. "Where else he got to go unless he's out bird-dogging?"

She knew her way to the homicide department blindfolded. Pat slumped over the metal desk in his cubicle, puffing on a cigarette as he read from a sheaf of papers on top of the messy pile that was his "filing system." "It's against regs to smoke in the building. A guy could get arrested," she said, slipping into the only chair that wasn't overflowing with folders and other debris.

"So, call a cop," he said, taking the last possible drag on the end of the smoke, then stubbing it out in an overflowing ashtray. Patowski's weathered face was dominated by a perpetually downturned mouth and narrowed eyes that missed nothing. Thinning red hair liberally streaked with gray emphasized his fair complexion. "You look like you want something. I'm fresh out of favors."

"What if I want to do you one?" she asked.

"I'd sooner have the clap, Sam. No, thanks," he said, returning to the report in his hand.

"What if I could link the Satterwaite murder to Upton Winchester?" she asked.

Her old mentor put down the papers and leaned back, his rounded shoulders collapsing with deceptive ease against the worn fabric of the cheap office chair. "I know you didn't get this info legally, don't I?" he asked rhetorically, waiting. "Probably isn't worth squat."

She knew he was interested but refused to show it. "Wrong. It all ties to Winchester's dead wife…whose cold case files you've been riffling through," she said, snatching one of the documents from the top of a pile that she knew contained files he was currently working on.

"You're not a cop anymore, Sam. Give it back," he demanded.

She handed them to him with a tight little smile. "I don't need to read about Susan Mallory Winchester's suspicious death, or her unhappy marriage…or that the shrink treating her at the time she supposedly OD'd was Reese Reicht." That got his attention, although only someone who'd worked with him as long as she had would have recognized the imperceptible stiffening of his hand, the tighter squint of his eyes.

He placed Susan's file out of Sam's reach and leaned back again, waiting. "So, you've been checking up on her brief, unhappy life because you were hired to retrieve her son. By the way, I know Montoya has him."

"You share that with Agent Scruggs of the DEA?"

Patowski snorted. "He said you weren't exactly cooperating with a federal investigation. Neither am I. Talked to Bill Montoya. The kid's safer with him than with the feds." Over the years Patowski had conducted several joint task force investigations with the FBI and DEA, but local law enforcement and feds of any stripe always rubbed each other the wrong way.

"Glad to hear it. The captain has a great family. They're treating Farley better than his own ever did." She waited a beat, then said, "By the way, did Scruggs tell you what Farley told me?" At his blank look, she went on, "Elvis doesn't share, either. Farley witnessed Leila and the good doc struggling in the Seascape Building elevator." She gave him the same details she'd furnished the DEA agent the preceding night, omitting their mutual breaking and entering encounter.

Patowski wasn't surprised that Scruggs had not burned up the phone lines to give him the information. "The Winchester kid's not a credible witness, but it sure would give Reicht reason to want him dead."

"And might just cause some friction between him and his partner Upton, who needs his son alive," she said.

"Okay, I can use that, but how do you connect Leila Satterwaite to Winchester?"

"It say anywhere in that file that Winchester's wife was boffing a yardman at the family manse?"

"The marriage sucked. Wouldn't surprise me if Susan Winchester was boffing the whole landscape company," he said noncommittally. "That wouldn't necessarily give Winchester motive to off her."

"Upton hates scandal. Bad enough she's a drunk and a druggie, but having an affair with a lowly yardman. All the servants knew about it. If she'd really been between the sheets with her shrink, like you were speculating earlier, I don't think Winchester would've found that quite so appalling—if she kept it discreet. At least he's a professional man. But a north Florida cracker?"

"Okay, I get the picture. Maybe you tagged Winchester with a motive," he conceded. "What's the guy's name? I'll haul him in for questioning."

"Only if you hold a séance," she replied. "Kenny Brio's body was ID'd in Jacksonville five years ago, shortly before Susan had her fatal encounter with booze and pills."

"Cause of death?"

"Funny coincidence. My source just located his death records with the Jacksonville M.E. Kenny was drinking, then OD'd, too. He was a real hunk." She handed the portfolio photos that Fro had found on the Net to Patowski. "Big, good-looking, a professional model. Into bodybuilding. Doing booze and pills doesn't quite fit. He was a transient according to the upstate report. Not identified for several days. When he ran his junker car into a shipping canal at midnight, nobody thought it was anything to bother with."

"A blond pretty boy. Bet all the ladies liked him," Pat said, looking at the picture.

"Especially Susan Winchester."

"I'm waiting for the tie-in to Satterwaite," he said.

"See any family resemblance?" she replied, handing him the grainy photo that had run in the *Herald* along with the story of Leila's murder. "I played a hunch and came up with aces."

Patowski started rooting through his desk piles and finally extracted a dog-eared folder filled with photos. "Dammit! I knew the minute you showed me that picture that I'd seen him before, but he was only a skinny kid back then." He handed her the snapshot, a candid obviously taken by another kid or maybe a teacher. It was of a teenage boy and girl on a playground. "We took this from Satterwaite's apartment. No ID on it, but one of her friends said it might be her brother. Wasn't sure. Didn't know his name."

"He changed his name from Satterwaite to Brio when he tried modeling," Sam explained. "Leila was Reicht's patient. Didn't that ring any bells?" she asked suspiciously.

"We questioned the SOB. His alibi sucks but we couldn't sweat him. That's when the IRS stuck their bazoo in, then the DEA." Patowski looked as if he'd just swallowed a palmetto bug. "Both have ongoing investigations into Reicht and Winchester for tax and drug scams," he said.

Pat knew she'd tangled with Scruggs but probably didn't know about Matt's contact with Kleb. She decided to keep it that way for now. Like the rest of law enforcement, he was paranoid as hell about reporters. Grinning, she asked, "How do you like working with Elvis?"

"As far as I'm concerned, he can leave the building any-time," he said. "But I got my orders straight from the top. We lay back, let the alphabet soup bastards work their computers until they nail down the evidence on the offshore accounts and drug connections."

"And they don't want police help with local drug dealers?" Sam suspected the answer.

"Oh, we're supposed to play second fiddle and give up every snitch and source we have from Palm Beach to Key Largo." He coughed and took another drag. "Our narcs gave 'em what they felt like without compromising their own work. But now…" His voice trailed away in a haze of cigarette smoke.

"Now, you have my fresh leads in two murder investigations. You owe me, Patty."

"Whenever you start with that 'Patty' crap, you're after something. And knowing you so well, it always involves the long green."

"Okay, here's the deal," she said, getting down to business.

"I spent a fortune—not to mention nearly getting killed half a dozen times—sneaking into a Spacer con to snatch Farley from Scruggs and return him to Miami. Yeah, I wanna get paid. It's only fair and Roman Numeral can afford it."

"Roman Numeral?" Then he smirked. "The fourth. Go on."

"I work with you on the investigation." She put up her hand when he started to protest. "You know I have sources that'll be useful to you. If I can find out why Reicht killed Leila Satterwaite, and how that's related to her brother's affair with Winchester's wife, you gotta help me collect my legit fees before the alphabet soup guys put both of them away."

"Why not just turn the kid over to daddy now and collect your cash before the government closes in?"

"While I was bringing Farley back I learned that handing him over to daddy's loving care meant Reicht would drug him until the kid was a vegetable. Can't do that. Matt knew Captain Montoya was a Spacer. That's why we took him there. But Scruggs still wants to pick the kid's brains about the offshore accounts. El's one smart hillbilly. He'll figure out where Farley is and try to push the envelope. Can't let him."

Patowski leaned back and studied her. "You're taking a chance on losing a big fee. Not like you, Sam. Kid musta got to you."

"You know why I went into the retrieval business, Pat," Sam said, all traces of humor and bargaining gone.

Patowski sighed. "Your twin cousins died in a mass suicide pact after they ran off to join some nut cult in Pennsylvania. The leader said the group was launching itself onto a higher astral plane or some crap like that."

"Within a year my aunt Betty died of a broken heart and Uncle Joe took a stroll on a Boston freeway in the middle of the night a week after her funeral. Farley's an innocent kid, just like Linda and Rhonda were. And he hasn't even got a family to mourn for him." She waited.

He shoved the pile of folders across his desk. "Here's what we got so far. You keep me posted and I'll let you know what I dig up—and whatever Scruggs and Kleb choose to share." He gave her a hard look. "But none of these documents leave this office and if you so much as breathe a word about our deal, you won't collect a red cent. I'll lift your license quicker than a hurricane lifts a tin roof off a shed."

"It went good with Patty," Sam said to Matt over her cell as she drove the ancient Charger east on I-395, heading to the *Herald* to pick him up. "Yeah, he'll work with me—note I stress me, not you...so... You know he hates reporters, especially you. Matt, you broke the story about the Russian mob... Okay, so it wasn't your fault the boat ran aground after I chased it down the Intracoastal... I saved your ass, sweet thing that it is...."

By the time they'd finished arguing over the case on which they'd met, he strolled out of the glass doors onto the newspaper parking lot. She pulled to a smooth stop and he folded his big frame into the passenger seat.

"How the hell do you manage to shift this wreck without a second gear?" he asked again as she took off as easily as she'd stopped.

"You gotta have a feel for the transmission, Matt. I keep telling you—"

"I know, I know, take a course in mechanics at a vo-tech." He knew he sounded grumpy, but he hated being shown up as a driver by a woman, especially his own wife.

"Uncle Dec might come down for Christmas this year," she said with a gleam in her eye. "He could teach you a lot."

Matt's expression changed to a grin. "You still matchmaking between him and my aunt?" His eccentric great-aunt

Claudia Witherspoon, descended from generations of Boston Brahmins, had taken one of her bizarre fancies to Sam's truckdriver uncle at their wedding. She, too, was supposed to visit them over the holidays.

"You gotta admit, it's fun to watch them together."

"Can't deny that," he said with a chuckle. "They sneaked out of the reception to smoke a couple of her expensive Cuban cigars. She'll give him champagne taste on a beer income."

Sam snorted, turning onto the MacArthur Causeway. "Not a chance. He told me after trying her triangalo that a good Swisher Sweet was still his favorite, but he didn't want to hurt her feelings."

Matt whooped with laughter, then looked over at her. "Where are we headed now? You were rather mysterious when you called me away from my desk."

"Pat got a complete report from the Beach police on the tan Mustang. I know they did a cursory canvas of the neighborhood, but lots of people won't talk to cops. I figure if we give it a try and explain that those two gunsels were trying to kill us and an innocent seventeen-year-old kid, we might have better luck. Pat says it'll be a couple of days before the prints on the car are run through all the databases."

He shrugged. "Right now, they're the only connection to Reicht and Winchester. Why not?"

The area around Flamingo Park was in the heart of the Art Deco District, a showcase of turquoise, fuchsia, chartreuse and lavender stucco buildings sporting rounded corners, flat roofs and porthole windows. The small lots were overgrown with lush multicolored flowering vines and shrubbery, lending an aura of privacy to the condos and apartments. Starting from the place where the car had been found, they first canvassed the park, but no one had been dog-walking in the middle of the night.

After that failed to yield a witness, they divided up the blocks and began ringing doorbells. Matt's ingratiating charm put even the most suspicious blue-haired elderly widow at ease. Small and smiley-faced, Sam employed her Irish charm with equally good results. The problem was that no one had seen the two gunmen leave the Mustang. Just as the sun started to descend over the Miami skyline, Sam gave Matt a buzz on her cell. They decided to call it a day, neither of them having had any luck. The Charger was parked where Jefferson dead-ended at Eleventh.

Sam saw Matt approaching the battered Dodge from across the street. Directly in front of her was a small faded yellow house on the corner. The owner had been away when she'd tried earlier and the single-unit dwelling had a clear view of the street from the second story. Now someone was peering between the slats of the upstairs blinds.

"Oh, what the hell," she muttered, waving to him, indicating that she was going to give it another go. Matt climbed into the car to wait.

The yard was overgrown with mimosa trees and honey-suckle vines. The stucco walls of the low fence surrounding it seemed barely able to support the weight of low-hanging branches growing over them. Sam opened the tall, rusty wrought iron gate which squeaked in protest. She ducked beneath the limbs of the flowering trees and barely put her finger on the buzzer when the heavy wooden door swung open. An elderly woman with sharp dark eyes looked out at her.

"Hi ya, dearie. If you're selling somethin', I gave at the office," she said with a chuckle. She was expensively dressed in designer-logo golf shorts and a matching tee, and her hair was well cut to show off what looked like natural silver-white highlights.

"No, ma'am, I'm not. I was wondering if you were home last night. Around two in the morning a tan Mustang pulled in by the park." She turned to the place where the police report indicated it had been found.

"I heard the cops towed it away this morning while I was at the golf course. We played until around two. That must've been some hullabaloo. Junkers left on the street here all the time, parked illegally, too, and the fuzz don't do a thing about it. What was so special about this one?"

"The two men inside it tried to run me off the causeway. They had a getaway car stashed here to pick them up after that didn't work out," Sam said, watching the old lady's eyes grow round. Her sun-lined face split into an excited grin as she reached out a thin veiny hand and practically snatched Sam through the doorway.

"No kiddin? Why would a couple of bums like them want to hurt a nice girl like you?" she asked, releasing her grip on Sam's wrist and ushering her inside the dark little foyer.

"You saw them?" Sam's heartbeat picked up. At last, a break. "What did they look like?" she asked.

"Say, you ain't a cop, are you?" the older woman asked, suddenly suspicious. "I don't like cops. They roust carneys, shake 'em down."

Even though that didn't exactly track, Sam pulled out her PI license. "My name's Sam Ballanger and I'm trying to keep those guys from killing a teenage boy."

"I raised a couple of teenage boys myself. Lucky for them, they grew out of it. But I was tempted to kill 'em more than once, believe me. Say, where are my manners, Sam? I'm Lola Swift." She went with quick, birdlike movements into a living room filled with bric-a-brac that cluttered every cabinet and table. The walls were decorated with grainy photos of a woman who might have been a young Lola wearing tights and carrying a balance beam as she walked on a tightrope. Others were of a man in a tux and tall top hat, carrying a whip.

"You were a circus performer?" Sam asked.

"Started out with a carney in Sheboygan but I ended up headlining for Ringling back in sixty-three," she said proudly. "Traveled all over the world. After I married Lenny—he was the ringmaster—we settled down here to raise our family. We had some rough patches, but our sons turned out all right. He passed away three years ago, my Lenny, but he lived to see his boys do him proud. Leonard Junior's a doctor and Sonny—his real name's Ralph—he's in real estate. Doing real good."

Wanting to keep the conversation on course, Sam quickly said, "I bet you must've had lots of adventures with the circus, but right now I have a boy whose life is in danger—and so is mine if I can't catch those two guys who left the car here last night. Can you give me a description of them?"

Lola took a seat on a fragile chaise lounge and indicated that Sam should sit on the overstuffed chair near the glass-block window filled with potted plants. The old woman squinted in concentration, then said, "The streetlight's down a ways, so all I could really make out was their silhouettes. One was big, brawny-looking like a wrestler, the other a skinny little weasel. Looked sneaky from what I could tell. The big one was carrying something against his side. Was it heat?"

"An MP5 submachine gun," Sam replied, glancing at the oversize console television. Heat? The old gal must watch a lot of TV. "How did they get away? Did you see another car?"

"It just pulled down the street, slowing right behind the lighter-colored car them men got out of. Like whoever was driving it was expecting them. I couldn't tell what kind, but it was dark blue or black, I think. A big luxury sedan. My Sonny, he has a Lincoln Town Car. It might've been one of them."

"Did you get the license plates?" Sam asked.

Lola shook her head regretfully. "Too dark."

Sam patted the old woman's hand. "You've been a big help." When Lola offered coffee and chocolate chip cookies, Sam reluctantly explained, "My husband's waiting for me and he'll worry if I don't show up soon. Thanks anyway."

"Honey, please don't send any of them cops around. I won't talk to 'em."

Sam raised her hand as if making a Scout's pledge. "Promise, I won't, but I might be back."

"Say, you do that, honey. I always wanted a daughter but all I got's two pain-in-the-ass daughter-in-laws," Lola said with a chuckle.

Sam ducked and dodged her way through the shrubbery, wondering why a woman whose kids had obviously provided her with every other luxury didn't hire a gardener, then decided Lola probably liked the privacy. She pulled the creaky gate open and stepped into the gathering twilight, glancing down the street to where Matt was waiting in the Charger. Her attention was fixed on the car. The sharp prod of a pistol barrel jabbed in her kidney caught her by surprise.

"Don't turn around," a voice almost as squeaky as the gate whispered. "Just walk back to that junker like a good girly."

Chapter 23

It was the skinny little weasel. Sam would have bet Matt's trust fund on it. She glanced toward the Charger and saw another figure in the backseat. The "wrestler" Lola had described. While her mind raced over options, the little guy poking her with the gun said, "I'm gonna put my piece in my coat pocket. Just act nice and natural. Walk over to the car and get in."

What to do now? She knew once she climbed in the old car it would be a one-way ride for her and Matt. "Even you aren't dumb enough to shoot us in the middle of a public place," she said, stalling.

"Keep it up, you smart-ass broad, and see," he hissed, jamming the gun into her back again, hard enough to pitch her forward a step.

Instinctively, she grabbed the gate, which gave out a hideous screech. Sam put all her weight against it, slamming it backward into the weasel. He let out a yelp of pain as one of the rusty iron bars slammed into his nose, making a soggy crunch. Blood spurted. The weasel stumbled against the wall. Sam pulled back the gate and slammed it into him again. This time one of the iron bars made contact with the guy's gun hand inside the pocket of his windbreaker. The pocket exploded and the creep staggered against the wall, sliding to the ground.

He screamed. "I've shot myself in the crotch! Oh, my God! Oh, my wang! You bitch!" He fumbled to withdraw the gun from his pocket but it was caught in the lining. Unable to concentrate because of the pain, he yelled across the street, "Hey, Baldo, shoot her!"

Baldo was busy. When Matt saw Sam emerge from the gate, he shoved the passenger door open and rolled out of the car. A shot zinged at his head, missing by an inch, throwing up concrete chips that lacerated his face. The big muscle-bound guy had a hard time climbing over the front seat of the two-door car.

Matt had enough time to roll beneath the body and scramble to the opposite side of the Charger. He jumped into a crouch and darted behind the trunk, ready to pounce. From across the street he could hear the sound of a shot and then a man bellowing in pain and cursing. He grinned. Only Sam could make somebody that mad.

Sam decided the hysterical weasel was out of the game. At once, she dug her snub nose from her handbag. Matt was behind the Charger, ready to jump an armed man who outweighed him by fifty pounds at least! She couldn't hit the big guy because the car provided him cover. Then she heard the sound of feet running from the house and Lola's voice yelling out, "Here I come, dearie!"

The old lady was carrying a .22 Marlin rifle. She jabbed it into the weasel's already injured groin. "Did I tell you I was a trick shot back in my carney days before I took to the high wire? They called me Little Annie O.," she said to Sam. By this time her victim was doubled up, whimpering.

Sam replied, "If he takes too deep a breath, shoot his dick off—if he hasn't already done it himself."

"Honey, it's a good thing I'm a sharpshooter, to hit that itty-bitty target."

Sam dashed across the street as her husband prepared to tackle the big guy. But the brute paused to look over the roof of the car at the ruckus his partner had created. When Matt moved, Baldo heard him and turned suddenly, gun raised, ready to fire point-blank. Sam tried to aim from twenty feet away but Matt was in her line of fire. Matt's only advantage was speed. He knocked the gun aside, landing a punch to the thug's jaw that would have sent any ordinary man to the pavement, unconscious. The goon was slow, but had the staying power of Rocky Marciano. His head and thick neck vibrated from the blow. Still he raised the gun again, doggedly trying for his shot.

Sam closed in just as his fat finger started to whiten over the trigger. She couldn't shoot him without hitting Matt, but she yelled and fired over their heads as a distraction. That was all Matt needed. Baldo was strong but not bright. He held the gun directly in front of him. Matt knocked it aside with his right hand and the shot went wild. At the same time his left connected with the big goon's throat. The gunman grunted and dropped to the concrete, still holding on to his weapon.

By this time Sam reached them and smashed her gun against the sensitive nerve endings inside his wrist. She then removed the weapon from his paralyzed fingers. "Damn, Granger, I can't leave you alone for even five minutes without you getting in trouble," she said, never so scared in her life as she'd been when Baldo had started to pull that trigger.

"Son of a bitch came up behind me, strolling along like he was a damned tourist. Next thing I know he had that cannon stuck in my ear. By that time I could see the little guy in the rearview mirror, moving along the wall outside the gate of that house you'd gone into." He pulled her into his arms and held her until the sound of loud bleats of pain interspersed with crackly voiced oaths carried across the street.

"I think Lola's abusing her prisoner," Sam said, pulling out of his arms reluctantly. She handed him Baldo's piece. "Hold our boy while I call the cops."

Matt looked at half a dozen people scattered around the park, all talking on cell phones from the cover of trees and shrubs. "I doubt you need to bother."

The first cruiser arrived, lights flashing as Sam was crossing the street. The two uniforms who got out of the vehicle focused on Matt and Baldo. That gave her time to reach Lola. "If you don't want to talk to the cops, this might be a good time to make an exit," she whispered as Lola walked through the gate.

"Thanks, I appreciate it, honey," the old woman replied, quickly closing the rusty wrought iron, which strangely didn't make a sound when she operated it.

"I'm the one who should be thanking you. You saved us, Lola. And that boy we're trying to help."

"You and your husband come visit me soon, okay? Oh, and bring the boy. Maybe he'll like chocolate chip cookies."

"I promise," Sam replied, dragging the weasel from where he'd fallen against the wall. She waited as a second cruiser pulled up to the curb. "Try not to run over the creep. Might mess up his prints," she said with a cheeky grin as she replaced her .38 in her handbag and retrieved her license for the scowling young cop.

She and Matt were going to have a lot of explaining to do, but Patowski could help with it. And now they had the two goons who'd been trying to kill them since she started the trip to St. Louis. Not a bad day's work.

* * *

"Good news and bad news," Sam said, cutting off the phone after a long conversation with Patowski. They were seated in their condo at the breakfast bar, a bottle of Guinness by her side, a tall gin and tonic by his. It was two o'clock in the morning.

He took a drink, then said, "Bad first." He'd already figured out some of the information from listening to her side of the conversation.

"Scruggs and Kleb know Farley's staying with Captain Montoya. I knew Elvis would figure out where the kid was when you mentioned police protection." She slumped dejectedly against the back of the bar stool and took a long pull from the bottle.

"Now that we have those two thugs in custody, maybe it's for the better. Scruggs for damn sure isn't going to hand Farley over to Winchester or his partner in crime. Anyway, in case you forgot, tonight's the big annual chapter party at Montoya's house. Every *Space Quest* junkie in greater Miami will be there in full costume. It'd be decent if they'd wait until Farley gets to participate before they come for him."

"We're talking feds here, Matt. On the scent of a big tax evasion and drug bust. They don't do decent."

"I'll put in a call to Montoya. See if he can get the kid a one-night pass." He picked up the phone and called the captain. After a brief conversation, he hung up with a smile. "Bill already worked out a deal to keep the kid at his place until the case breaks. But he does have to let the feds talk to the boy. It was that or word came down from above that he'd have to let the alphabet soup guys put Farley in some safe house of theirs."

"Better than I would've hoped," she said, not happy.

"Now, the good news you had?" Matt prompted.

"Those two goons are singing like the Mormon Tabernacle Choir. It seems our boy Reicht hired them through his pals in the local drug trade. He had a body for them to dispose of. According to Patty, Leila had been beaten really bad before the shrink killed her."

"He wanted some kind of information out of her, but what?"

Sam shrugged. "They didn't know, but they swear when they got to the deserted office building where he'd stashed her, she was already dead. Place is out in the middle of nowhere but Reicht owns it. Gonna develop it as a strip mall with mob money." She tapped her beer bottle idly, thinking. "I bet this is a triple play—Leila to Brio to Susan Winchester."

"If Kenny was having a fling with Susan, and Susan was being treated by Reicht—"

"The shrink probably used some of the same dandy drug cocktails on her as he did on Farley," Sam said, picking up his train of thought. "Or she just confessed. Either way, Reicht knew about Brio and the threat he potentially posed to Winchester. They'd do anything to get Brio out of Susan's life, but even if they killed him, why would they kill Leila five years later? How would they even know she was Kenny's sister?"

"She went out of her way to make friends with Farley, signed up for head shrinking with the high-priced doc. She wanted access to Winchester and Reicht. Something she did must've tipped them," Matt said.

"Before he died, Kenny might've told his kid sister about Susan, maybe even found out something about Winchester's connection to Reicht's drug scams. I wonder if he stashed some evidence?"

"He could've tried to blackmail Winchester. Reicht would want to get his hands on whatever Brio had shared with Leila and shut her up permanently, just like he did her brother," Sam said. "But after five years, what tipped him to Leila?"

"Maybe she tried to use her brother's evidence for her own blackmail scam," he suggested.

Sam shook her head. "Not the feel I have for her from what the women at the Pink Pussycat told me. I bet she wanted to nail Winchester and Reicht for killing her brother."

"If she had Brio's evidence, it would explain why Reicht tortured her before he killed her. But we may never know if she talked before she died."

"Knowing that snake Reicht, I'd bet she did," Sam said grimly.

"We know he's not averse to using drugs. I wonder why he worked her over," Matt said, rubbing his jaw.

"I bet he likes to inflict pain. Or, maybe she was allergic to the stuff he tried on her. With a bastard like him, who knows?"

"We'll find out," he replied, thinking of what a man who tortured a woman deserved.

"We do know he canceled his appointment with Farley suddenly that afternoon. Leila must have been in his office. Farley saw Reicht take her up in the elevator. It all fits."

"Only if we can prove it." Matt stirred his glass and polished off the drink.

"But the cops have two guys willing to connect the dots to the doc. Besides giving up Reicht, Baldo and Miller—that's the weasel's name—admitted some guy named Gus picked them up after they were supposed to have run us off the causeway last night. They swear they don't know anything else about him. Patty says Gus is one of Rico Salazar's leg breakers."

"Yes, Salazar has a bug ugly goon named Gus Kline. I did a piece on the Cuban drug trade and he's definitely a key player," Matt said. "What's Patowski's next move now that our two canaries have twittered?"

"He wants to haul in Reicht and sweat him, but can't. The DEA and the IRS want the whole enchilada—not just

Reicht, but Winchester and all their friends. Baldo and Miller's arrest is being kept under wraps. They're holding them for twenty-four hours off the record. No one should know they've gone missing."

"Given the track record of those two prizes, I doubt even Reicht would be surprised if they didn't report in," Matt said. "They hoping to locate Gus and his big black car? Work Reicht's mob connection to Salazar from there?"

She pointed her empty beer bottle at him. "Bingo. If the cops arrest two upstanding citizens like Winchester and Reicht, they'll just lawyer up. Apparently, although he didn't know much, Pat thinks your pal Kleb at the IRS has just about nailed down the way Roman Numeral's offshore setup works."

"Scruggs must've put together what he got out of Farley with what he copied from Winchester's computer—probably with IRS help," Matt speculated.

"Probably, but they're going to interrogate the kid some more. And Scruggs didn't share that with us."

"You okay with that?" Matt asked dubiously, thinking of the compassionate way Ida Kleb would question a fragile kid like Farley.

"Hell, no. If Scruggs and Kleb go near the boy, so do I."

"And how do you figure to reach him if the feds and local cops are all watching?" he asked.

Sam grinned at him. Tweety Bird feathers, he always said when she did that. "Oh, didn't I mention that you're going to get your boyhood wish? We have invitations to Montoya's Spacefleet party. We'll need good disguises so nobody recognizes us. I was thinking of a Pandorian for me. Or maybe a Klingoff warrior woman?"

"Miller and Baldo ain't showed, boss. I think they fucked up again," the leg breaker who worked for local drug king pin

Rico Salazar said. "They was supposed to get rid of the woman and the reporter, then call me. That was over six hours ago."

Gus Kline listened as his boss outlined what he was to do, then hung up. He had to drive an old rust bucket sedan with faded paint, not the nifty black Town Car. Mr. Sal said it was too easy to spot when tailing the broad and the reporter. Grumbling curses, Gus shambled out to the parking lot to pick up the junker.

He was six-three with shoulders like a musk ox, an ex prize fighter. Now he had a good job working for Mr. Sal and his friends. Those screw-ups, Miller and Baldo, had blown the assignment. He'd do better.

"If only I didn't have to drive this piece of shit," he muttered, climbing inside the old gray sedan. He switched on the air as soon as he backed it out of the parking space, then pounded the steering wheel. The system was broken. It was going to be a long, hot afternoon.

Somebody would pay for his sweat equity in this deal. If he never saw Baldo and Miller again, he knew where Samantha Ballanger lived….

Hours later, Sam cocked her head so the long bluish-white antennae swayed like sea anemones. "Well, whaddya think?" She looked across the crowded costume shop to where Matt stood in front of a three-sided mirror, smoothing down the waistband of his Spacefleet uniform. A commander's gold and black skintight suit. She let out a low whistle, admiring his buns. The costume left little to the imagination, but hers was already racing in overtime.

He turned and grinned at her. "Somehow, blue and furry just isn't you, Sammie," he said with a chuckle. "Hides all your curves, not to mention that cute little nose." He walked over and pressed a kiss on the costume's snout, nearly poking one of her antennae in his eye. "Ouch! Watch out you don't blind me before the night's over."

"Ha! Watch out for yourself. I'm gonna melt before the night's over."

"This Vulcant head mask won't exactly be cool and comfy, either," he said, holding the pointy-eared latex torture device in one hand. "If only Scruggs and half the local cops didn't know us on sight, it would make getting in to see Farley a lot easier."

"A good thing we have Montoya's handwritten invitation for Mr. and Mrs. Ivan Robertson. El and your pal Ida would never let us set foot in the door if they knew who we were."

"Okay, let's party," he said, tugging on the face mask.

When they drove away from the costume shop, neither saw the nondescript junker that followed at a discreet distance.

"You m-mean Leila's really dead?" Farley asked Matt again. "All those new people who came to question me this morning, claiming to be government agents, they didn't say a thing about her, even when I asked. El told me she was dead, but after finding out about him, I guess I didn't believe him."

After handing their invitations to the cop guarding the door, Sam and Matt had sneaked upstairs to the small, comfortable bedroom that Farley shared with Steve, the Montoya's younger son. The pale blue walls were papered with *Space Quest* designs, and various Spacefleet, Klingoff and other alien ship models hung suspended from the ceiling by invisible wires. Action figures filled a large case on one wall.

Avoiding the DEA agents and cops had not been easy, but Rose, Montoya's mother-in-law, had agreed to help them. She'd quietly shown them the way to Farley's room, then sent him up there to talk with them. They had removed their headgear to make communication easier, then explained why they were here in disguise.

"We know Reicht killed Leila, Farley," Sam said gently. The boy was clear-eyed and breathing normally. No panic attacks. Being with the Montoya family had been good for him. Getting clean from all the dangerous mind-altering drugs hadn't hurt, either. "Now we want to prove it so he'll go to jail."

"Is my f-father part of it?" Farley asked hesitantly.

Sam knew lying wasn't an option. "Yes, he and Dr. Reicht were in it together." She had no intention of telling the poor kid his old man may have been responsible for his mother's death and hoped to God Scruggs wouldn't, either. There was just so much any teenage boy could take.

"El admitted he isn't really Spacefleet, but I guess I already figured that out…once the stuff Dr. Reicht gave me started to wear off. He and the others asked a lot of questions about my father. I have this…this thing with my memory…it always made me feel like I was some kind of freak or something, you know?"

"Your memory's a great gift, Farley. Nothing to be ashamed of," Matt assured him.

"Yes, but sometimes I wonder if it was the only reason El pretended to be my friend," the boy said, miserably.

"He didn't have any choice but to deceive you, Farley. I know that doesn't mean much now, but maybe when this is all over, he'll really be your friend," Sam said. *Elvis P. Scruggs will make up for what he's done if I have to drag him here in a straitjacket!*

"Besides your father's accounting records, what else did El and the others want to know?" Matt asked.

"All about what Dr. Reicht and I talked about when I was in therapy. I—I couldn't remember much. He gave me shots…sometimes I'd b-black out after."

"Did they ask you about Leila?" Sam held her breath. Leila Satterwaite was the key to this whole thing.

"Yes, but I didn't say much. I told them she was my friend, too. Guess I'm pretty dumb. If she was involved with my father and Dr. Reicht, she was pretending. I just said we were in Spacefleet together, that I met her at a couple of chapter meetings, stuff like that."

Sam leaned forward and placed her furry hand over Farley's thin, small fist. Scruggs's deception had hurt the kid and disposed him not to talk about the murdered woman. "But you know more about her, don't you? She must have confided in you if you believed she was your friend—I think she really was, Farley. We know she was spying on Dr. Reicht. That's why he killed her." Supposition, but probably true. "Did she ever tell you she had a brother?"

Farley nodded. "You mean Kenny?"

Sam and Matt exchanged quick glances. This could be a big payoff. "Kenny Brio," she said. "Did she ever say he worked for your father? That he was a gardener back when you were still in junior high?"

"No." Farley looked confused. "She only talked about how he would've been a star model now if he hadn't d-died. She talked a lot about when they were kids and hid out from their dad who was a mean drunk. Kenny protected her. I wish I had a big brother like that," he said wistfully.

"Like Billy?" Matt asked. When he'd talked to Bill Montoya earlier, the captain had indicated he would be interested in legal guardianship.

"He's way cool. So are the captain and Mrs. M. I specially like her mother. She asked me to call her Grandma." His eyes lit up as he talked about the Montoya family.

"Leila and her brother hid from their father. Did she ever

mention a special hiding place she had here in Miami?"
Matt asked.

Farley hesitated a moment, then said, "I never even told
El about it…she made me promise, but if she's really dead…"

Chapter 24

Downstairs the Space Quest celebration was in full swing. Fleet officers of all ranks and aliens of every hue and shape entered after the police inspected their invitations. Revelers filled the rambling house and spilled into the large wooded backyard while a band played on a small stage in the center of the garden.

No one noticed the beat up old sedan parked down the crowded street or the beefy occupant talking on a cell phone as celebrants walked by.

"This is even better than the con in St. Louis," Farley said excitedly to Sam and Matt. "I'm not all woozy from those pills. I can have fun and not worry about Klingoff and Pandorian plots." He was dressed in a spiffy Spacefleet uniform with the junior grade insignia of Ensign Eastly Masher on it. He'd actually gained a few pounds and his coloring looked greatly improved from the bluish pallor of the preceding week when he'd suffered drug-induced anxiety attacks. "Hey, look at the stage. Billy told me the chapter had hired an actor to impersonate a big celeb in a retro hollow deck show. He didn't know who."

"Who would you like to see?" Sam asked as she and Matt exchanged smiles beneath their masks. Farley was getting his life together in spite of the horrific things that had happened in his family.

"I dunno. Maybe Nick Alaska, you know, the gray-haired singer who runs the night club on Dark Space Ten?"

Matt nodded, but Sam didn't have a clue. Just then a murmur went through the crowd as melodramatic theme music vibrated with a clash of cymbals, coming from the band beside the stage. "That I recognize," she said with a big grin. "*Also Sprach Zarathustra.*"

"Huh?" Farley did a double take.

"It's by Richard Strauss, and the intro for a very famous "retro celeb" from the mid-twentieth century."

Before she could say more, the lights onstage came up. A tall lithe figure in a sparkling white jumpsuit and jewel-laden belt leaped from the side curtain. At once the music shifted to a fast, slamming rhythm and the singer began to belt out the opening riff of "Jailhouse Rock."

"Elvis may have left the building but he's still on the premises," Matt said with a chuckle. "He isn't bad."

"Hasn't got the hip swivel right," Sam said critically, watching Scruggs do his impersonation.

Holding the mike in one hand, he slid to his knees at the front of the raised platform where several girls in skimpy Lieutenant O'Hara costumes squealed. One Pandorian, obviously female, ran her antennae up and down his thigh until he pulled away. By this time the crowd was really gyrating and clapping along.

Cries of "Long live the King!" echoed around the yard.

"El told me about his mama naming him for some famous old-time singer, but I thought that guy was fat," Farley said, baffled, as he watched his erstwhile best friend perform.

"Not in his buff days," Sam said with a lascivious gleam in her eye. "Ah, to have lived during the sixties," she sighed.

"Then you'd be the old, fat one now," Matt teased.

In spite of their banter, both of them kept a sharp eye on the crowd since the place was swarming with local cops and DEA agents who would take a very dim view of their being within ten miles of Farley. His revelations about Leila Satterwaite appeared to have been cathartic for the boy. This was Farley's night to have fun.

Billy Montoya was the spitting image of his father—tall, lean, with curly black hair and a ready smile. Although his costume was Klingoff, he'd pulled off the elaborate latex head covering as a concession to the sultry night heat. "Wish I'd come as a Spacefleet Earthman instead of an alien," he said to Farley, who introduced the adults to his new friend.

"How do you like the show?" he asked the three of them. "I was sorta hoping for Nick Alaska but my dad's a big Elvis Presley fan."

"No kidding? I barely heard of him. My family never cared for rock music. Just classical," Farley replied.

"Boring," Billy said and both boys laughed. "You wanna get something cold to drink? They're serving Klingoff blood milk." Seeing Farley's hesitant look, he quickly added, "and regular soft drinks, too. Any kind you want—only they call Coke Pandorian Zinger and Mountain Dew Reemulan Drachma."

Matt and Sam watched the two boys walk away. "Looks like Farley's found a big brother after all. He's going to be okay once the feds nail his father and Reicht," Matt said.

Sam's eyes returned to the stage where El was now crooning "Love Me Tender" and the women in the crowd around the stage were going wild. "Now that he's settled okay, we can check out that storage unit of Leila's."

"If she told Reicht, it'll be empty."

"We have the key Farley gave us. The security in storage places is usually pretty tight and 24-7. I doubt Reicht would send some dumb thug like Miller or Baldo to try bashing in the door with a fire ax. Might get the security guard to call the cops," she argued.

"This is evidence in a crime. The place is full of DEA and IRS agents. We can turn it over to them. Speak of the devil…" His eyes traveled across the crowd to Ida Kleb, the only one in the place not in costume. She was the only one who didn't need one. Ida was wending her way toward them as if she recognized Matt in spite of his Vulcant headgear. She wore an ill-fitting brown suit, sensible shoes and a determined expression on her bulldog face.

"Where does she get her hair cut? A hardware store?" Sam asked.

"Nobody'd let her. It'd take the edge off any ax in the place," he replied before Kleb drew close enough to hear them over the din of the crowd. "Dammit, she's made me."

"Mr. Granger, what are you doing here?" she asked without preliminary.

"What're you doing not in costume?" he countered.

"I *am* in costume. As a human being. A twenty-first-century public servant, who happens to be conducting an investigation in which you're interfering," she replied sharply.

I get the twenty-first-century part, but the human being… Sam let her catty thoughts fade, knowing the old harridan could make their lives pure hell if she turned her attention to Sam's recent tax extension and long ugly history with the IRS. "We just wanted to make sure Farley was happy in the home we found for him," she said ingeniously.

"How did you recognize me with the mask?" Matt asked.

Ida Kleb looked up at him. "Don't be ridiculous. You're half a head taller than any man in a five-mile vicinity, not to mention you have a great ass," she added with a lusty smirk.

Sam, who had been taking a sip from a glass of Diet Coke, nearly snorkeled it up her nose. "Well, Ms. K, that ass happens to belong to me," she said when she caught her breath. Who'd ever have thought the ancient hag was a letch!

Matt coughed in consternation, desperately trying to suppress a laugh. Then he said, "Er, this is my wife, Sam Ballanger, the woman Winchester hired to find Farley. We were just leaving."

"What's the matter? You can't stand Agent Scruggs's gyrating, either?" she asked, looking at the stage where Elvis was now singing "Blue Suede Shoes." And dancing in them. "I remember the King. This is a disgusting parody."

It was apparent that the feeling of shuddering dislike the DEA agent had expressed toward Ida Kleb was mutual. "I imagine working with a guy like Scruggs can be trying," Matt said, grateful the mask hid his expression. "You won't tell him we were here, will you?" he asked in a conspiratorial voice.

"Only if you get out of here right now. I'm sure once this is over, the Internal Revenue Service will have some questions for both of you," she added ominously.

"I tell you, Matt, she was looking at *me* when she said it," Sam said as he drove his convertible west on 836 toward the Rent-A-Space just west of the airport.

"You're being paranoid, Sam. Just like you always are when it comes to the IRS. Of course we'll be called in when they arrest Reicht and Winchester."

"She likes your buns. You're safe. Say, how's your Elvis imitation?" she said with a snort.

"You've heard me sing in the shower. What do you think?"

"You only sing when I'm lathering you up," she shot back, then glanced at the clock on the dash. "Pat's probably waiting. He's a lot closer to the joint than we are."

"I'm surprised you were able to talk him into letting us tag along when he opens that storage space," he said.

"Cops hate the alphabets and besides, this is his murder investigation—and I have the key."

"If Reicht hired someone to pick the lock, you'll both be in for a big disappointment," he cautioned.

"Considering the level of talent Reicht's hired so far, I doubt it. But knowing that Leila gave Farley the key to her 'secret hiding place,' I am glad Montoya's house is crawling with cops, even if some of them are feds."

They pulled into the parking lot of the storage place, where an impatient Sergeant Patowski paced with a cigarette clenched between his sagging lips, puffing away. "Last I checked the calendar it isn't Halloween," he said, looking at their costumes. Although they'd removed the headgear, there was no time to change clothes. "You just spend the day at Disney World?"

"Guess I forgot to mention when I called. Captain Montoya is president of the local *Space Quest* chapter and they're holding their annual 'roll call' tonight. All the alphabet soup's there," she said.

"So are some of Miami-Dade's finest, guarding Farley Winchester. You weren't supposed to be anywhere near the place and you know it."

"If we hadn't been we wouldn't have learned where Leila put all her extra furniture when she had to get a smaller, cheaper apartment. We think it was so she could afford paying Reicht's exorbitant rates," Sam said.

"She told Farley a tale about having her place painted and

needing to move temporarily, so she put her things in storage," Matt explained. "But even the kid thought it was rather odd that she asked him to keep the key for her."

"And not to tell anyone he had it—ever," Sam said.

Patowski reached out his hand, palm up. "Hand it over."

"Only if we get to go with you. Remember, Pat, I didn't have to bring you in on this. I could've given it to Scruggs or Kleb," she said.

Patowski snorted an obscenity. "Fat chance. You wouldn't give CPR to an IRS agent having a heart attack. The key?"

Reluctantly, she fished the key Farley had given her from one of the deep pockets concealed in her furry costume. She had her snub nose concealed in the other pocket.

Patowski walked up to the small air-conditioned booth where the security guard sat and flashed his badge, then showed the elderly man the key. "Official police business. The owner of this unit's been murdered. We need to check what's inside. Where is number seventy-four located?"

"No kiddin'!" The guard's round florid face looked incredulous and his eyes almost protruded from their sockets as he motioned to his right with one pudgy hand. "The seventies are all down thata way."

Across the road, Gus watched Sam and Matt with the cop. He could smell the cop even before he saw the guy's badge flash in the light from the security booth. Although Gus had no idea what was going on, he had a gut feeling that Mr. Sal wasn't going to like this at all. He punched speed dial to ask for instructions.

As they walked down the asphalt, Sam said in a low voice, "Don't look now, but I think we may have company. There's a hardcase in an old gray sedan parked across the road, talking on his cell. I'd almost swear I saw that same car this afternoon, parked outside the captain's place. He hasn't taken his eyes off us since you showed your badge to the security guard, Pat."

They reached a metal sliding door numbered seventy-four and stopped in front of it. Patowski turned, cupping his hand to light another cigarette, glancing across the road. He read off the plate number. Blocked by Matt's body, Sam jotted it down on a slip of paper she pulled from one of the utility pockets in the costume.

"You gonna call for backup?" she asked Pat. The storage place was only minutes from Metro-Dade Headquarters.

"As soon as we get inside where he can't see us," he said, turning to the door and inserting the key. The heavy lock groaned, then tumbled in place. Matt reached down and helped the older man slide the door up so they could enter. The room was filled with the sad remnants of Leila Satterwaite's brief life.

Patowski pulled his cell out as soon as he stood inside the shadowy interior, stepping behind the wall so he couldn't be seen from across the road when Sam flicked on the light switch. "Don't touch anything. You'll screw up the chain of evidence—if there's any here."

Sam grinned. "Remember, I'm not a rookie." She pulled out two pairs of thin latex gloves and handed Matt one. "Got 'em from Josefina Montoya. She buys 'em by the box to color her hair. "You can watch to see we don't compromise your investigation."

Patowski shook his head in resignation, then resumed his call. While he gave the plates and described the sedan, Sam and Matt set to work, shoving around tables, rickety chairs and ceramic lamps with chips at their bases. A stack of boxes stood against the back wall.

"Shit, I think our boy's figured out we made him," Patowski said as the sedan started to drive away. He picked up his cell and called in the direction the car was heading.

"They ought to be able to pick him up no sweat unless he's Harry Houdini."

"Well, well, well, what have we here?" Matt said, pulling out a sheaf of photo paper, glossy eight-by-ten pictures. He riffled through them, handing them to Sam who showed them to Patowski.

"Her brother was creative," Pat said, his eyes narrowing on one incredibly explicit photo of Kenny Brio and Susan Winchester.

"And apparently double-jointed, if you pardon the pun." Matt turned the picture upside down and raised his eyebrows in amazement.

"I don't believe Susan knew he was taking pictures of them. She wasn't the type for that kind of kink. Too afraid of what Upton might do if he ever found out."

"I agree, but since our pal Kenny had a stash of these, I'd bet Upton did find out."

Sam nodded. "Blackmail. Brio knew just how uptight the Winchester clan was and how much money Susan's family had. The only thing he never counted on was her shrink having mob connections."

"I'm calling in the lab techs. Don't touch anything else," Patowski said.

Sam knew it would do no good to argue. As she replaced the photos on top of the old utility bills and other worthless paper they'd gone through, she spied a small book in the open box, slipped sideways next to the photos. Quickly, before he could climb over the chair separating them to stop her, she pulled it out. "It's Leila's diary."

"Put it down, Sam. That's evidence."

"C'mon, Patty. You wouldn't have a case if not for me. Just let me take a peek while we wait. What's the harm?" she wheedled, flipping though the pages.

* * *

Upton Winchester IV looked down at the ludicrous costume he'd been forced to wear. Some hideous sort of space alien creature complete with purple scales and a face mask with a snout! His voice was muffled through the ghastly contraption as he spoke. "You're certain this is wise, Reese? I don't like it."

"Farley's your son and my patient." Reicht replied. "That bizarre police captain has no legal right to keep him. I checked his background. He's the local president of a *Space Quest* chapter. Little wonder Farley ended up with him."

"Then why don't we simply go in and demand our rights— take my son to your psychiatric facility and not humiliate ourselves with these ridiculous costumes?" Upton asked, stiff with fury and humiliation.

"If Farley sees either of us, who knows what accusations he might start throwing around?" the doctor said reasonably. No way was Reicht telling Winchester about the IRS investigation and have the spineless idiot panic—not when the doctor and his friend Rico Salazar almost had everything set up for Winchester to take the fall in their place.

"Montoya may be daft about sci-fi," he continued in the soothing voice he normally reserved for patients, "but he's still a police captain. I bet that grifter Scruggs is still hovering around Farley. I warned you about using that damned woman to locate the boy." Reicht was dressed in full Klingoff regalia. No one, especially Farley, would recognize them until they got their hands on him.

"She brought him back to Miami even if she didn't deliver him to me—if your sources are correct about this whole debacle," Winchester said petulantly. "I still think it would've been best to have had Scruggs arrested for stealing my Jag. Then he'd be out of Farley's life and you could medicate my son without interference."

Reicht gripped the steering wheel of his BMW, sweating profusely in the latex costume. His patience with the patrician prick was wearing very thin. "You hate adverse publicity. How the hell do you think it would've worked out if Scruggs was arrested? You think the media would've ignored your son babbling about alien abductions and being a Space-fleet undercover agent?"

"That boy has been the bane of my existence since he was born. Little wonder, considering the tramp his mother was. I want him locked away and sedated before he ruins what's left of my life."

"Then we have to quietly extract him from Montoya's home," Reicht said as he drove past the crowded street and searched for a parking space on the next block. "I have my syringe prepared. All we have to do is use it on Farley and then take him away. I had an employee canvas the area and find a way for us to slip inside the fence from the neighbors to the back. No one will see us. Once we're in the yard, no one will know a thing until your son's safely in Homeside," Reicht said, forcing a soothing tone into his voice.

He could not help but enjoy Winchester's humiliation in the costume. He'd deliberately chosen the most ugly thing he could find as soon as Gus had called him after tailing the meddlesome Ballanger woman to Montoya's home and casing the neighborhood. All he had to do was take care of the boy. Then his pals in the mob would pin the whole scam on Winchester and he'd be home free.

Inside the Montoya house, everyone was having a great time, including Farley, who watched Elvis break away from a horde of female fans and walk over to him. Using the white towel hanging around his neck to wipe sweat from his face, he said, "The real King had a guy whose only job was to hand him fresh face towels during performances. Some gig, huh?"

he asked conversationally, still trying to make up to the boy for the deception he'd been forced to perpetrate.

"You were pretty cool. At least all the women thought so," Farley replied.

"What'd you think?"

Grudgingly, Farley admitted, "You're a natural actor, El. But then you've been playing a role for a long time."

"I never played being your friend, Far. Remember, I was the one who made you taper off the junk Reicht gave you," Scruggs said quietly.

"But you got what you needed from me to put my father in jail by feeding me the *Space Quest* conspiracy stuff."

Scruggs deflated. "Yeah, that's true. I guess he's still your dad and you have to be loyal—"

"He was never a 'dad' to me. He's never cared about me. Was your story about your dad made up, too?" he asked, his big dark eyes haunted, studying the agent intently.

"I swear, Far, it's the gospel truth. You can look up my record." At Farley's startled expression, he grinned self-consciously. "Yep, I served time in juvvie for stealing the sheriff's cruiser. That wasn't just a tall tale."

"And the sheriff was your own father?" Farley returned the smile.

Just then Captain Montoya and his daughter, Sara, approached. Sara was fifteen and had her mother's delicate features and light brown hair shot with russet streaks. She was absolutely the most perfect girl Farley Winchester had ever seen. He was tongue-tied whenever she said anything to him.

"You like her?" Elvis asked, knowing the answer by the way the kid's tongue was practically lolling out of his mouth.

"Sorta," Farley replied, uncomfortably.

"Let me see what I can do," Scruggs said. After exchanging hellos and accepting compliments on his performance, the agent eased the captain away, talking about the investigation of Reicht, leaving Farley and Sara alone.

"Did you like El's impersonation?" was all Farley could think to say.

"For an old guy, he was pretty good," she said, smiling at him. "You know him, don't you?"

"Yes. He…he's my friend. He helped me get away from Dr. Reicht."

"That's like, really iced. My dad may be a police officer, but I've never even seen a crook. You've had such an exciting life."

"Your life's lots better, believe me. You have a great family and this cool house and yard. Your grandpa's really put in some neat stuff."

"I never thought of that," Sara said, remembering what her dad had told them about Farley's mom being dead and his father in trouble with the authorities. "Hey, want to go check out Grandpa's koi pond?"

"Sure," Farley responded with a big smile, following her across the yard toward the dimly lit back where Giraldo Velasquez had carefully cultivated tall ornamental grasses, lilies and other shrubs and flowers around the pond. Several willows cast the area in shadows.

From a distance, Reicht smiled behind his mask and murmured, "Young love. I couldn't have planned it better if I'd tried."

Winchester said disdainfully, "First crackers and now Cubanos. My son has such good taste. Just like his mother."

Chapter 25

The lab techs arrived at the storage place just as Patowski received a call informing him that two cruisers had run the gray sedan and its mysterious tail to ground. "Guy's name is Gus Kline, a leg-breaker for Rico Salazar," Patowski said to Sam and Matt.

She was still skimming through the diary while Matt responded. "Salazar's one of the biggest drug dealers in the region. If you can link him to Reicht and Winchester, this case will make national headlines, *Lieutenant* Patowski," he said with a grin.

"Yeah and you'll have a shot at a Pulitzer when you write the story—but not until everything's wrapped up or I'll put you so far back in solitary they'll be feeding you with a slingshot."

Matt raised his hands. "Solemn word of honor. Besides, I already promised Ida Kleb I wouldn't break the story until all arrests are made. She's a hell of a lot scarier than you, believe me."

Patowski grunted. "Put that diary back where you found it and get the hell out of here so the techs can work," he said to Sam.

Reluctantly, she replaced the diary, then stripped off the hot gloves. The small brick cubicle had no air-conditioning and the humid Florida night made the room stifling. She and Matt followed Patowski outside. Just then her cell beeped. Sam opened it and heard Grandma Rose's frantic voice on the other end.

"Sara's been hurt and they took Farley!" she said rapidly.

"Who, Rose? Who took him?" Sam asked as calmly as she could.

"No one knows. They wore costumes."

"Is Sara going to be okay?" Sam asked, praying the granddaughter was all right, but knowing Farley was the one in big trouble.

"One of our members is a doctor and he says she's going to be okay. She told us two men in costumes slipped up on them while nobody else was around. One dressed as an Omicron slime creature grabbed her and the other, a Klingoff officer, shoved a needle into Farley's arm. That's all she remembers before the Klingoff hit her on the jaw and everything went black."

By the time Sam had the story from Rose, Patowski was firing angry questions over his cell to Scruggs. Montoya came in on what quickly became a conference call. She and Matt could even hear Ida Kleb's dulcet tones over Pat's cell.

"Shit, they're arguing jurisdictions while Farley's been kidnapped!" Matt said, adding a few of his favorite army oaths.

After doing her best to reassure Farley's new "grandma" that he would be all right, Sam hung up and trotted toward their car with Matt right behind her. Patowski didn't even notice them leave.

"Where are we going?" Matt asked.

"Playing a long shot," she said, climbing into the driver's seat.

"That's my car and you aren't driving it, especially under these circumstances. Move over," he ordered.

Muttering an oath, she did as he asked. "Male chauvinist."

"Nope, driving chauvinist. You go through cars like Evil Knievel went through motorcycles," he said, starting the engine. "Where to?"

"Head north, then pick up I-75 west," she replied.

"Come again? That's Alligator Alley, smack in the middle of the Everglades."

"I saw a map and notation in Leila's diary. Among his other charming hobbies, our friend Reicht liked to shoot gators."

"Strictly illegal. From what you and Patowski have told me about the creep, he'd get off on that," Matt said.

"He has some kind of hunting cabin a ways off the Alley. Leila described the location of the unmarked road after following him there. I didn't see them in her stash, but she took pictures of him and a few of his mobster cronies with their trophies."

"We should call Patowski and tell him this," he said.

"It's a long shot, like I said. Do you want a bunch of DEA hotshots tagging along—oh, and don't forget Seminole and Miccosukee rez authorities? Even Ida Kleb?"

That was the clincher. "Okay, for now," he conceded. "They'll argue jurisdiction while Reicht kills Farley and feeds his body to the gators."

"Or come crashing in and make sure that happens before we can stop it," she said.

"Once we find this place—if we can find it—then we give Patowski a call if we see any lights. Deal?"

"Deal," she agreed. "But that doesn't mean we wait until the cavalry arrives if Farley's life's at stake."

Matt didn't argue that one, just gunned the powerful engine and shot up the I-95 north entrance ramp. Within an hour they were on the flat highway heading through an endless sea of waving saw grass and swamp. The road was pitch-dark except for the narrow beams of their headlights.

"How the hell are we going to find the cutoff?" Matt asked as Sam leaned her head out the side of the open convertible.

"Keep driving. We have another forty miles before we have to slow down and start looking for it. There's a road sign for a boat ramp on the right."

"If they've taken Farley by boat, how the hell are we going to follow to this camp?" he asked.

"It's a public place. Leila hired a guy. Said he had a couple of john boats at his own private dock."

"He'll love being wakened at 2:00 a.m. to take us for a ride. Probably shoot us."

"We could always steal his boat," she suggested.

"Let's try cash first, okay?"

"Cash works," Sam agreed.

"I thought you'd see the logic in that," he replied dryly as they sped through the night.

"There it is!" she called out as a neon green sign appeared on the berm, directing them to a small public docking area used by sightseeing tourists and local fishermen. A large sign, somewhat the worse for wear, advertised Wally's Swamp Tour Boats For Hire. They followed the rutted muddy road until they reached the dock. A tall, dim light cast the rickety wooden structure in eerie shadows as Matt cut the engine of his Mustang. One car was parked on the deserted gravel lot beside the bait shack.

Sam could swear she heard the faint sound of a powerboat fading into the distance. "Get the Colt .45 from the glove compartment. There's an extra clip with it."

He removed the big automatic she'd insisted he carry and checked the action, then dashed after her. She jumped from the car and peered inside a shiny new BMW. "It's Reicht's car," Matt said, shining their flashlight on the vanity plates which read, "SMRTDOC." Sam took one look, then headed onto the dock.

"Wait, Sam! You agreed to call Patowski, remember?" he asked, quickly catching up to her.

"I heard their engine. No time."

"I'm calling," he said, reaching for the cell clipped to his belt. He punched in speed dial for her cop pal as he followed her down the dock. "Shit! No signal."

"No time, either," she replied, jumping into a boat.

"How the hell are we going to get one of these tubs to start?" he asked.

"Never was a yacht type, but I did learn how to run an outboard motor when my dad took us fishing. While I figure this out, you make a dash up to Wally's place and get him to call the local gendarmes," she said, glancing at the small house about thirty yards farther down the road. It remained shrouded in darkness.

"Sam," he said, seizing her by the shoulders, "don't leave without me—swear it." The intensity of his voice penetrated the heavy night air.

She nodded. "I swear, Matt. Give Wally this note." She handed him the sheet of paper she'd been scribbling on while he drove. "This should provide enough info to send in the cavalry."

"Explanations about Reicht's little hideaway for Wally to give the police?" he surmised as he gave her a quick kiss and took off in a ground-eating dash.

"Don't go getting yourself shot!" she called after him, then applied herself to the boat's motor, praying Wally wasn't the sort to shoot first and ask questions later. There was no telling what Reicht would do. He needed info from Farley about Leila. She must've told him the boy had the key to her evidence stash.

"He'll use drugs, maybe even torture," she muttered to herself, remembering the description of Leila Satterwaite's mutilated body.

Sam climbed across the boat seats to the outboard. She had taken the heavy chrome-encased cell flashlight from Matt's car, figuring it would come in handy. Now she laid it on the nearest seat and pointed it toward the engine. After examining the outboard for a moment, she looked over her shoulder toward the house where lights had now come on. She could see Matt's tall figure in the open doorway.

"So far, so good. At least Wally hasn't shot him." She offered up a silent prayer, then returned to fiddling with the engine. After checking the gas tank, she pulled the ignition cord. The big Mariner 90 HP roared to life.

"Jump in," she said as Matt pounded down the dock. As soon as he climbed aboard and hunkered down, she took off. "Is Wally calling the cops?" she asked.

Matt nodded. "I'm not sure if he intends to sic them on us or Reicht, but since I paid his exorbitant rental fee, I imagine help's on the way. He took the note you wrote."

"Now if only we're on the right trail…we just can't be too late to save Farley…."

"Keep the light down," she whispered to Matt as she cut the engine to a slow low growl.

"You sure you know where we're headed? We could get lost in here and never find the kid."

"Shh," she murmured. "Sound carries over the water."

Now he could hear it, too. A loud, powerful engine

suddenly cutting off. The faintest dab of moonlight filtered through a bank of clouds as they inched their way closer. After a few minutes they could make out a small cabin on the edge of the swamp, its dock protruding directly off the front deck. A narrow slough of brackish water cut through the saw grass. Probably where he trolled for gators.

"I'm gonna pull up to the bank far enough down so they won't hear us land. Then we'll sneak up on them. See what's going on, where they have Farley."

Matt nodded. It sounded reasonable and she'd had lots more experience doing this kind of thing than he had, although since meeting his wife, he'd been in more harrowing situations than working a newspaper night beat in Miami's most crime-ridden areas.

After pulling the boat ashore, they picked up what looked to be a very rough path beaten down by Reicht and his fellow "sportsmen." It was a good thing they had at least some freedom to move without walking through the vegetation as their costumes were little protection from the razor-sharp blades of grass. In just a few yards, Matt's sleek uniform, even her furry Pandorian costume, had been reduced to shredded tatters.

As they neared the clearing around the cabin, Sam stopped abruptly. Matt heard it, too. The sound of another approaching boat. "Local cops?" he whispered, dubiously.

"No. Too soon." She began easing closer, light extinguished now as the glow from the cabin enabled them to see. They reached a small window on the opposite side from the slough and crouched down. Sam peeked inside and saw Farley lying on a narrow bed across the room. He appeared drugged but was unbound, his head rolling back and forth as he softly moaned Sara's name.

Reicht was filling a syringe with a clear liquid from a

bottle while Winchester paced nervously. Both men still wore their costumes sans headgear just as Sam and Matt did. While she and Matt listened, the men argued, apparently unaware of the approaching boat.

"We should've taken him straight to Homeside. You know how I despise the swamp." Winchester swatted a mosquito on his cheek and cursed.

"I have to find out what he did with that key Leila gave him. I could scarcely chance a nurse or orderly overhearing when I drug and question him. The evidence she has can put us both in prison for murder."

"You killed her," Winchester quickly retorted.

"But you arranged for me to kill your wife and have Brio killed. If I go down, my dear Upton, so do you. Besides, those photos he took with Susan were really a messy complication, don't you agree?" Reicht spoke with conversational calm. Being so close to ending his association with the wretched accountant gave him patience he hadn't been able to muster earlier.

"All I wanted was for you to get rid of her lover and keep her quiet. You've used that to blackmail me into your illegal schemes ever since," Winchester's protest came out more like a whine.

Reicht shook his head. "Poor, innocent victim, aren't you? We've been partners for seven years, since I started medicating your unhappy wife. If she hadn't slipped that will past you, we could've killed her and the kid and you'd have your money free and clear. Pity." He sounded anything but pitying.

"I hear a boat! Who's coming?" Winchester asked, alarm in his voice.

"Just a couple of friends of mine," Reicht said. "Now, prop that boy up so I can work my magic on him."

"What friends? More of those odious mobsters?" Winchester asked angrily. "You have no right involving any of your thugs."

Outside, Sam and Matt watched two heavily armed men pull their boat alongside Reicht's and tie up to the dock. Light from the open front door poured over them. "The taller one's Rico Salazar's right-hand man. I've seen the other one's mug, too," Matt whispered. "I don't think Reicht intends for father or son to leave here alive."

"Wouldn't take Karnak to figure that one. We need a quick diversion to draw Reicht outside before he can use Farley as a hostage." She looked around them, found a badly rotted two-by-four left over from the construction of the dock and handed it to Matt. "You got a good strong arm. Throw it into the water beneath the dock without them seeing you. Then slip back here and cover me from the window. Watch those sweet buns," she said, giving him a kiss.

He kissed her back, then crept over the muddy earth, crouching low, using brush as cover until he could send the hunk of wood sailing beneath the dock. It landed with a loud splash.

"What the fuck was that?" one of the thugs said to the other. "Hey, Reicht, you got company," he yelled into the house.

Reicht appeared at the door. "What's going on, Tito?"

"Somebody's under the dock—or maybe it's one of them gators you like to take potshots at," the other gunsel said, his piece aimed at the water where the wood had gone in. Unfortunately, being rotted, it was buoyant and floated out.

Before anyone could see what it was in the murky light, Tito's companion yelped, "It's a damned gator!" He started blasting away at it with his Beretta.

Reicht rushed onto the dock and knocked the man's hand away. "Stop firing. The sound will carry across the lake. Last thing we need is for that boat rental hick to come investigating—or worse, call the police." He looked down into the water. "You idiot! You've shot some rotted wood."

"Well, something made a loud splash," the other man said to Reicht.

While they argued, Sam carefully unlatched the screen and climbed through the window while Winchester stood looking out the front door. She almost made it across the wooden floor to him before a loose board groaned softly, causing him to turn. She raised a finger to her lips and pointed her snub nose directly in his face. "Step away from the door. Now!" she hissed over the sounds of the men on the dock yelling at each other.

Something in her tone took the starch out of Upton Winchester IV's spine. He stepped to the side but Reicht caught the motion from the corner of his eye and said, "Someone's inside!"

That was Matt's cue to fire at the men on the dock. Easy targets under the pole light. He hit Tito's companion, knocking him down. The thug cursed, holding his arm as he rolled across the narrow dock and fell off, landing in Reicht's boat. A spray of blood hit the water and dissipated as he thrashed in the small craft. Matt fired again, trying for Reicht, but he was too late. The doctor stood closest to the cabin and moved out of his firing line.

Tito opened up with a burst from a MACH-10, aiming in the direction from which Matt had fired. Matt flattened himself against the side of the cabin and edged toward the window to see how Sam was faring.

She leaped at Winchester, using her snub nose to club him across the kisser. He fell to his knees as gunfire erupted and Reicht burst through the door. The doctor held the syringe in one hand like a weapon, glaring in disbelief at her as he shoved the needle against Farley's throat.

"You are a troublesome bitch," he said. "Now, unless you want me to kill the boy, drop the gun."

"A drug to make him talk won't kill him," she said, stalling.

"It will if I plunge it in his carotid full force. You can't kill me quick enough to stop it. He'll die horribly."

Sam knew he was right. The firing outside continued. She prayed Matt hadn't been hit as she slowly laid down the handgun, all the while watching Reicht and that needle. When she started to straighten up, he kicked the gun away from her. To do that he had to move away from Farley. Suddenly a bloodcurdling shriek filled the still night air, followed by sounds of thrashing in the water.

"Oh, Jesus! It's a gator!" Tito yelled, firing into the water. He tried in vain to save his gunsel as the gator dragged the wounded man overboard by his bloodied arm.

Winchester groaned, still crumpled on the floor across the room. Reicht instructed him calmly. "Take her weapon and hand it to me, Upton."

"He intends to kill you and Farley, Upton. That's why his goons are here."

Winchester looked dazed. "No," he said, struggling to pull himself up against the wall, failing. He crouched on all fours, frozen.

"Think. He can't let Farley live after the kid witnessed him abduct Leila Satterwaite. He can pin everything including the offshore tax and drug scams on you if you're dead," Sam said, poised, ready to move.

"She's lying. If you don't want to go to jail, help me now!" Reicht commanded his accomplice.

Sam had seen the Remington rifle leaning against the wall near Farley and knew Reicht would try for it. When he edged that direction, she sprang, trying desperately to dodge the needle while grabbing the hand holding it. They went down. She knocked his arm aside and the deadly syringe went flying. Then she punched his soft midsection, but a burst of terror-induced adrenaline gave the pudgy man incredible strength.

Reicht grunted as he rolled away from her, seizing the rifle and leveling it with the expertise of a man well used to firearms. Sam clawed for her .38 but before she could grab it or he could aim the rifle, Matt fired a shot through the window, hitting him. Then Tito, having given up on his dead companion, came charging around the side of the cabin, opening up with his MACH-10.

Matt dived around the corner but Tito's fire grazed his right arm before he could reach cover. Sweat beaded his eyes and white-hot agony tore through his bicep. He used his left hand to hold on to the rough logs for balance. Gritting his teeth against the pain as he raised his right arm, he aimed the pistol, waiting for his nemesis to appear.

Inside Sam cocked her snub nose .38 at Reicht, who swiveled the rifle at Farley, cradling it awkwardly because of the jagged flesh wound seeping blood down his side. He slowly pushed himself to a standing position using the wall for support. "Standoff, Ms. Ballanger. You shoot me, I kill the boy. Now I recommend we act like sensible adults."

Sam's gun never wavered. "Get the hell out of here," she said. "Or I kill you."

Reicht started to back toward the door when the gunfire out back resumed. He kept the rifle barrel pointed directly at Farley. He did not see the dazed Winchester on all fours behind him. Now Sam watched as the doctor took another step backward. And toppled over Upton, falling through the door.

Sam's aim quickly moved to Roman Numeral. "I wouldn't try it," she said as he made a feeble attempt to reach the rifle Reicht had dropped.

The doctor rolled to his feet and dashed down the dock in a trail of blood. He leaped into the small john boat and cursed when he couldn't start the engine. He tried again. The boat began to rock, pitching him forward, over the big outboard motor into the black water…into the waiting jaws of the hungry gators who had swarmed toward the blood spoor from the dead thug's remains.

Inside the cabin Sam and Upton heard the screams. So did Matt and Tito out back. Still, the man advanced, his automatic ready to fire. Matt was growing weaker. He had to do something fast or he was meat just like the thug and Reicht. Matt looked around him, searching desperately for something he could throw into the saw grass. Where were those rotted boards when a guy needed one?

Then he heard Sam's voice coming from around the corner. "Matt—don't say a word. I'm coming!"

Tito whirled around, looking for the advancing woman. Using the diversion, Matt moved around the corner of the cabin and fired. The slug went through the drug dealer's left arm and exited under his ribs, knocking him on his right side. He did not move. Matt stumbled toward the body but suddenly everything went black.

Sam saw Tito go down. She raced to him, kicking aside the automatic weapon and making sure the thug was dead. "Matt, if you die on me I'll really be pissed! You don't want to get me that mad, dammit! Where are you?"

She was crying and cursing at the same time as she saw his big body lying on the ground at the corner of the cabin. Then she heard the sounds of a chopper coming across the swamp. Ignoring it, she knelt beside Matt and carefully laid him on his back to examine the extent of his injury, trying desperately to recapture the calm detachment of her paramedic days, and failing miserably.

Sam ripped off pieces of her shredded Pandorian costume and wrapped the thick cloth around Matt's arm to staunch the bleeding. The chopper landed beside the slough and shut down its rotors. A blindingly bright light poured over the pair of them, helping her see what she was doing. After a rush of footstep, a familiar voice came from inside the cabin.

"Just stay where you are, Upton, ole boy. The DEA has a few questions they want to ask you. And when they're through, it gets worse. Then you get to talk with Ida Kleb. You won't like her."

"Scruggs, I could use some help. Radio for a medevac. Matt's been hit," Sam yelled.

"Already on its way. When we heard all the shooting, we figured somebody'd need patching up."

"Is Farley okay?"

"Doped up pretty good, but he'll make it. You know what Reicht gave him?" Scruggs asked her.

"Just a sedative to get him here. The bastard used something a lot nastier on Leila to get her to tell him about Kenny's stash and what she'd been up to."

Matt groaned, listening to their conversation through a haze of pain. "The doc's trouble was that Leila couldn't produce the key. I bet that's why he beat her before he killed her," he muttered thickly.

"Just lie still and be quiet," Sam said, wiping the perspiration from his forehead. "What is it about you and stopping bullets, Granger?"

He ignored the jibe. "Reicht had to get that key from Farley."

"That's what we figured," Scruggs said. "After Reicht snatched Farley from Montoya's, I buttonholed Patowski and he tipped me about the diary in the storage space. We agreed this cabin was a good shot for where the doc would take Winchester and Far to get rid of them for good. Gus Kline didn't know about it, but he admitted he'd been sent by Salazar to follow you to where Farley was hidden, then report it. My gut said go for the cabin. Then Wally Griswald called Patowski with your message."

Scruggs was still dressed in the ridiculous white jewel-encrusted jumpsuit. Sam had to admit he was a dead ringer for the late "King." "Your gut was right but we could've used you a little sooner."

"Yeah, I might even have managed not to inconvenience my wife by getting shot again," Matt said.

"Don't move that arm and start it bleeding again or you'll really inconvenience us both," Sam said. When she'd seen him lying on the ground, her heart had nearly stopped beating.

"Aunt Claudia taught me never to inconvenience a lady. If you're this…nice when I'm shot, maybe I'll have to—"

"Don't even think it, Granger," she said with a shaky laugh, bending down to kiss him.

"Man might have a point. Never saw you go soft and feminine before," Elvis interjected.

"You'd better see to Farley. Who knows what his father might do," Sam said.

The other DEA agents' voices carried from the dock in front as they discussed the feeding frenzy that had ended the lives of Reese Reicht and Tito's companion. Ignoring them, Elvis replied, "I cuffed Winchester to the doorknob, but I'll keep watch on Far till the paramedics get here. Take good care of your man." He went whistling back into the house.

"You heard the agent," Matt whispered, pulling her down for another kiss.

"You're really dealing from the bottom of the deck, using Elvis as an excuse to give me orders," she replied with a loopy grin.

But she kissed him anyway.

"Yes, Auntie, you know I will… Love you, too… Okay," Matt said reluctantly, handing the phone to his wife with a martyred sigh. Sam, who sat on the corner of his hospital bed, took it and walked across the floor, listening as his great-aunt Claudia spoke. Matt didn't like the startled grin that spread across her face as she agreed to something, then hung up.

They were in the Broward General Medical Center where the medevac flight had flown them last night. After stitching his injured arm, the doctor insisted he stay the night because of the blood loss he'd experienced, even though the wound wasn't serious.

"While the doc was working on you, I called Aunt Claudia and told her everything," she said, replacing the phone on the nightstand and resuming her seat beside him on the bed. "Oh, did she mention she's chartering a plane from Boston?"

Matt groaned. "No, but thanks for warning me. What was the rest of your conversation about?"

Before she could reply, Bill Montoya wheeled Farley into the room, accompanied by his daughter Sara. Elvis Scruggs, who had changed into a conservative gray business suit, followed them. One small diamond earring winked discreetly from his right earlobe, a hint of his "alter ego."

"They're letting me go home," Farley said, then glanced shyly at Sara.

Sam could see love in bloom and grinned at the cute kids. "I understand you'll be living permanently with the Montoya clan," she said, looking at the captain.

Bill smiled at her and placed a fatherly hand on Farley's shoulder. "I just wanted to thank you, Sam, for getting the Mallorys to agree to terms."

"Sam's good at negotiations," Matt said dryly.

Bill turned to his daughter. "Sara, why don't we head downstairs and I'll pull the car up to the front entry. I think these folks have business to discuss."

"Thanks again, Sam, Matt. You saved my life. Real Space-fleet officers couldn't have done better," Farley said with a wink.

Sara giggled as Bill pushed his chair from the room. When they were out of earshot, Elvis asked Sam, "How the hell did you get the Mallory family to go along with your plan?"

"Tweety Bird feathers again," Matt said, chuckling as she grinned.

"Farley's only living uncle, Susan's brother, Paul, is an investment banker who travels around the world and has a socialite wife who can't stand kids. The grandparents are too old and frankly, don't care one way or the other about Farley. It wasn't hard to convince the lot of them to give up custody of a boy they'd never bothered to see since his mother's funeral five years ago. But Paul did want Susan's share of the family fortune back. I, er, convinced him that it might be better to place the funds in a trust until Farley turns twenty-five. And let the Montoyas adopt the boy."

"And why would he agree to give up guardianship with all that lovely loot involved?" Scruggs asked, his cynical eyes narrowing on her.

"Paul and his wife are social climbers and the publicity about Upton is already in the headlines," she said, giving Matt a nod since he'd dictated the story from the E.R. before he'd even let the staff attend to his arm. He had scooped even the broadcast media.

"The Mallorys didn't want to be dragged into a court fight over guardianship. Already they have to deal with a brother-in-law who was involved with the mob and money laundering," Matt interjected.

"And I pointed out that my hubby was the guy who wrote the story in the *Herald* and he happens to be very fond of Farley. If they ticked him off and tried to screw over the kid,

Matt would keep Paul and Deidre in the headlines until they looked worse than the mob," Sam said with a big grin.

"Wish I could handle my problems that way," Scruggs said. "At least Kline and those two bozos you took out at the Beach turned on Rico Salazar. We'll nail him, but the DEA's fighting with the IRS to see who gets to indict Winchester first. I've had two meetings with Ida Kleb since last night." He shuddered visibly.

"That why you're looking so spiffy straight?" Sam asked.

"No way I could ever impress that broad. But she did agree to hold off on the tax scam charges until we nail Winchester for funneling drug money to the Caymans for Reicht and Salazar. When all the federal charges are filed against Winchester, Patowski's going after him for conspiracy to commit murder. He asked Reicht to administer that OD to Susan and to arrange Kenny Brio's 'accidental' death in Jacksonville."

"That'll put good old Upton up the creek for a couple of lifetimes," Matt said.

Sam nodded. "Good. Farley will get his rightful estate and Bill Montoya and his family get to provide him with the love he never had before."

"She's leaving one thing out," Matt interjected.

Sam glared at him now. "What, you still think we're made of money? I earned every dime!"

"And I didn't help?" he asked her rhetorically, then turned to Elvis with a big grin. "She wrung her full retrieval fee and expenses out of Paul Mallory, too."

"Sam Ballanger, you are a caution." Elvis started laughing, then stopped abruptly. He looked at Matt and Sam. "You two are quite a pair. Slicker 'n cow slobber," he said, reverting to good ole boy vernacular. "How'd you like to partner with me in a little side venture? I've been wantin' to open a booking agency for Elvis impersonators. All I need is a little capital."

"And I should give you money!" Sam asked incredulously.

Matt laughed until his arm ached from the vibrations. "Sam doesn't lend money—even to me."

Scruggs glanced from Matt to Sam. "Hey, don't look at me like that!" he said as Sam's eyes narrowed dangerously on him. She slipped from the bed and advanced on the agent.

He threw up his hands and started backing through the open door. "All right. Okay. You win. Elvis is leaving the building!"

As they rode home the next day, Matt studied his wife uneasily. "My aunt will be waiting for us at the condo," he said, wondering if she'd share whatever harebrained scheme the two of them had cooked up with him before Claudia lowered the boom on him. *Uh-oh, that Tweety Bird smile again.*

She reached over with one hand and placed it on his thigh, rubbing it suggestively as she drove. "As a matter of fact, I was about to bring up her proposition. Sorta give you a heads up." She snickered at her pun, feeling his response to her caress.

"What proposition? No money to stay married to me," he growled, feeling his ardor cool.

Sam shook her head adamantly. "Of course not. Word of honor." The hand remained in its strategic place.

"Then what did she 'propose'?" he asked, still suspicious.

"Oh, just something that we would eventually consider anyway…if I don't brain you for your bullheadedness first," she replied sweetly.

Ignoring her threat, which she made frequently, he asked, "What, Sam?"

"Aunt Claudia, out of the goodness of her heart—and considering your propensity for placing your life in danger—feels that we should start a family. She's offered me a million-buck college trust fund for our kid as soon as I get pregnant!"

* * * * *

At Silhouette Bombshell, the excitement never quits!
Turn the page for a sneak peek
at one of next month's riveting adventures
RUN FOR THE MONEY
by Stephanie Feagan
Available April 2006
in the Silhouette series section
at your favorite retail outlet.

Chapter 1

"Sorry, but I swear I just heard you say I have another checking account, at a bank in Kansas, with a balance of over two hundred thousand bucks."

"Why didn't you include this on your list of assets?"

"Because it's not an asset. I don't have a bank account in Kansas." I gripped the phone.

The nice lady at the mortgage company was getting less nice by the second. "It's right here, on your report. Whitney Pearl, home address in Midland, Texas. You opened the account two weeks ago."

"I've been in Washington D.C. the past two weeks. How could I open an account in Kansas? *Why* would I open an account in Kansas? I don't even know anybody in Kansas."

"I suggest you get this resolved. Anything not nailed down can be cause for the application to be rejected."

Wondering why I'd been stupid enough to buy a house

while I was on a consulting job over two thousand miles away from home, I told her I'd let her know, then hung up and dialed the Kansas bank. I got Shirley, in new accounts. I explained the situation, then listened while she pecked at the computer.

"Got it right here. Whitney Ann Pearl. Midland, Texas." She asked for my social security number, verified it, then rattled off some other bona fides.

"How was the account opened?"

"Through the Internet." She pecked some more. "Hang on and let me pull the signature card."

I stared out my sixth-floor window of the Mills building and watched the guards atop the White House, one block away. It had become a favorite pastime, ever since I started the engagement with CERF, the Chinese Earthquake Relief Fund. Thus far, I'd resisted buying a set of binoculars. Definitely, that would be crossing the line into Loserville. Still, the tall one who worked the seven to three shift looked mighty fine, even from a block away.

"Got it right here," Shirley said. "Whitney A. Pearl."

"And the balance is over two hundred thousand dollars?"

She pecked some more. "Two hundred thousand, three hundred, ninety-six dollars and fourteen cents. There have been twelve deposits since opening, and four withdrawals."

"Thank you for your help," I said as graciously as possible. After all, it wasn't Shirley's fault. "I wonder if I could speak to someone in bookkeeping?"

"Hold, please."

Eventually, a woman named Courtney picked up. I asked for copies of the deposits, along with information about the withdrawals, and was pleasantly surprised when she said she'd fax me the information. Hmm. Maybe I really would open a bank account in Kansas. My bank in Midland would laugh me off the planet before they'd send me diddly-squat.

Within thirty minutes, I had the copies.

And nearly had a heart attack.

At my desk, I paged through the deposits. Almost four hundred thousand dollars, and every single check came from CERF, the organization that contracted me to act as accounting watchdog, to ensure nobody stuck their fingers in the enormous amount of money the good people of the world donated to help the earthquake victims in China.

Gathering up the copies, I went down the hall to the executive director's office. At his open door, I rapped on the door frame to get his attention. He looked up from some papers on his desk and grinned at me, but after I walked in his office, his grin faded. "Pink? What's wrong?"

Parker Davis could easily be in the movies, he's that good-looking. He'd always get the part of the faithful, handsome, blond-haired, blue-eyed assistant who blindly follows and trusts the sneaky, evil character.

"I just found out that I'm an embezzler." I tossed the papers onto his desk and briefly explained.

Parker flipped through the papers. His handsome face was pale in spite of his golfer's tan. "Oh, my God."

"We have to get to the bottom of this, immediately."

He picked up the phone and punched in three numbers. "Taylor, I need to see you, right away."

Oh man. Things were about to get infinitely more complicated. And aggravating.

Within a minute, Taylor Bunch sailed into Parker's office on a wave of too-strong perfume. She'd put her pale, blond hair up in a snazzy little twist. Maybe I would have liked her, if I didn't dislike her so much. I just don't feel the love with people who are mean, nasty and sneaky.

In my other life, I was a senior manager at a Big Important CPA firm in Dallas. That career, and that life, ended last summer after I blew the whistle on one of our largest clients. Turned out the partners at my firm were all in on the cover-up to hoodwink investors, and that was the end of Big Important.

Taylor Bunch was promoted to senior manager the day I got fired for blowing the whistle. She got my job. Regrettably for Taylor, she only got to crow about it for a few short weeks. After that, she was beating the streets for a job, and just like me and all the other CPAs who'd been in management at Big Important, she couldn't find anyone who trusted her enough to hire her.

I ended up moving home to Midland, Texas, and taking a mercy job as a forensic accountant at my mother's CPA firm. Taylor eventually found a job in the state of Texas's welfare system, churning out financial data for bureaucrats. There she met Parker Davis, and when Parker was tapped to head up the relief fund after the China earthquake, he called Taylor and asked her to step in as treasurer.

He hired me to keep an eye on things, unaware of the animosity between Taylor and me. Maybe I should mention, Taylor blamed her bad luck and misfortune on me.

She stood next to Parker's desk, looking over the copies while he explained what I'd discovered. I can only describe the expression on her semipretty face as joyful.

She looked at me and raised one perfectly sculpted brow. "Why should we believe you didn't do it?"

I ignored her and said to Parker, "I want your authorization to investigate and find out who's behind this."

Taylor said smugly, "Parker didn't get to be where he's at by being stupid. Why would he allow you to look into it when your name's on the account?"

Parker looked from me to Taylor and back to me. "She's

got a point. I'm sure you're not behind this, Pink, but whatever comes to light, it will look mighty weird if you're the one who finds it."

I stepped away from Taylor. "Maybe so, but if you put Taylor in charge of investigating, they'll lock me up and throw away the key. She hates the ground I walk on." It was the first time I'd openly acknowledged the bad blood between us. I've always held to the adage that catfights equal really bad for my career. Under the circumstances, however, I didn't think I had any choice but to speak up.

"Are you saying I'd fail in my responsibility, all because of some personal vendetta?" Taylor sounded righteously offended.

"Gimme a break." I looked straight at her. "After I got promoted, you told everyone you saw me going into the Crescent Hotel with the managing partner, effectively making my success a sexual exclamation point." I folded my arms across my chest and stared her down. "You despise me, which isn't my problem, unless you're the only thing standing between me and prison." Looking back at Parker, I said emphatically, "I am *not* going to prison."

He focused on Taylor. "If you dislike Pink so much, how can you look into this with any kind of objectivity?"

Taylor glared at me as she spoke. "Obviously, someone is stealing from this organization. My concern is for all those unfortunate people in China, who need this money to rebuild their lives. I can be objective because of them, because it's important to stop whoever's doing this."

Parker is one of those people whose only goal in life is to save the world and make certain that truth and justice prevail. And he's incapable of believing the worst in anybody. He practically beamed at Taylor.

I was toast.

Silhouette® BOMBSHELL™

SASSY CPA
WHITNEY "PINK" PEARL
IS BACK IN

RUN FOR THE MONEY

by Stephanie Feagan

Someone was embezzling from the
Chinese Earthquake Relief Fund in Pink's
name—and now she's been framed
for a coworker's murder! To prove her
innocence, Pink followed the money
trail, with Russian mobsters in hot
pursuit...and two romantic pursuers
who really had Pink blushing.

*Available April 2006
wherever books are sold.*

She had the ideal life…
until she had to start all over again.

National bestselling author

VICKI HINZE

Her Perfect Life

Don't miss this breakout novel!

$1.⁰⁰ OFF

your purchase of
Her Perfect Life by Vicki Hinze

5 65373 00076 2 (8100) 0 11209

www.eHarlequin.com

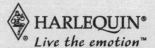 **HARLEQUIN®**
Live the emotion™

©2006 Harlequin Enterprises Ltd

She had the ideal life...
until she had to start all over again.

National bestselling author

VICKI HINZE

Her Perfect Life

Don't miss this breakout novel!

$1.⁰⁰ OFF

your purchase of
Her Perfect Life by Vicki Hinze

5 2 6 0 6 8 3 0

VHCOUPCN

---

www.eHarlequin.com

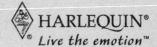

©2006 Harlequin Enterprises Ltd

COMING NEXT MONTH

#85 SURVIVAL INSTINCT by Doranna Durgin
Now living in peace on a Blue Ridge farm, former bad girl
Karin Sommers had escaped her con-game past by assuming
the identity of her deceased sister—until Karin discovered her
new identity came with serious baggage. For her sister had
witnessed a terrible crime, and the perpetrators, fooled by the
sibling switch, were keen on offing Karin to cover their tracks.
Soon she was back on the run…from someone else's past.

#86 FLASHBACK by Justine Davis
Athena Force
The women of Athena Academy looked out for their own. So
when new information surfaced about the decade-old murder of
academy founder Senator Marion Gracelyn, FBI forensic scientist
Alex Forsythe took the case in a heartbeat. With the help of
fellow Athenas and FBI agent Justin Cohen, Alex pursued leads
to the power corridors of Washington, D.C. Was it just a hunch—
or was there a killer hiding out in high office?

#87 RUN FOR THE MONEY by Stephanie Feagan
CPA Whitney "Pink" Pearl felt noble working for the Chinese
Earthquake Relief Fund—until she discovered someone was
embezzling from the charity in her name. She was even framed
for a coworker's murder! Never a quitter, she went on an
intercontinental mission to prove her innocence, with Russian
mobsters in hot pursuit. But it was her romantic pursuers—an
attorney and a U.S. senator—who really had Pink blushing.

#88 MISSING INCORPORATED by Tess Pendergrass
Travel reporter Magdalena "Mad Max" Riley more than earned
her nickname as a moonlighter finding missing persons. So when
her media-mogul client turned up dead and his twelve-year-old
son ran away to uncover why, Mad Max made it her personal
crusade to find the boy before his powerful enemies did. The last
thing she needed was journalist Davis Wolfe to meddle—but was
this sexy cynic the key to saving the child's life?

SBCNM0306